GOING OUT WITH A
B A N G

by

The Ladies' Killing Circle

GOING OUT WITH A

BANG

A Crime and Mystery Collection by the Ladies' Killing Circle

edited by
Joan Boswell
Linda Wiken
Barbara Fradkin

RendezVous
Crime

Cover art: Christopher Chuckry, design by Vasiliki Lenis / Emma Dolan

We acknowledge the support of the Canada Council for the Arts for our publishing program.

We acknowledge the financial support of the Government of Canada through the Book Publishing Industry Development Program (BPIDP) for our publishing activities.

RendezVous Crime
an imprint of Napoleon & Company
Toronto, Ontario, Canada
www.napoleonandcompany.com

Printed in Canada.

12 11 10 09 08   5 4 3 2 1

Library and Archives Canada Cataloguing in Publication

       Going out with a bang : a crime and mystery collection / the Ladies' Killing Circle ; Joan Boswell, editor.

ISBN 978-1-894917-73-5

       1. Detective and mystery stories, Canadian (English).   2. Canadian fiction (English)--Women authors.   3. Canadian fiction (English)--21st century.
I. Boswell, Joan   II. Ladies' Killing Circle
PS8323.D4G63 2008   C813'.0872089287   C2008-905617-5

Table of Contents

Bang the Drum
Loudly for Me

Pat Wilson

When The Creator sent the eagle flying up from the eastern mists and across the great water, Silent Woman, who used to be Lily Underhill, knew that she would be all right.

Lily had no idea how long she'd been on the island. Three, four weeks, maybe more. At first, waiting for help to come, she hadn't bothered to keep track of time. When it became obvious that no one was looking for her, she'd lost several days to despair and fear. From that point on, the days just seemed to run into one another.

Silent Woman didn't like to remember those first days on the island, when Lily Underhill had screamed and cried and torn out her hair. Lily had been weak and would have died on the island, all according to the plan. But Silent Woman had saved her—Silent Woman, pushed away and forgotten, long hidden in the far recesses of Lily Underhill's mind. Silent Woman, who unlike Lily Underhill, could hear the voices of The Ancestors in the still air.

The first time she heard them, Lily thought she was losing her mind.

"You're wet and cold. You need to make a fire, little one. You can do it. Remember how I taught you?"

Lily knew the voice. It was her father's, now long gone,

whether dead or not she didn't know. In her mother's house, no one ever spoke of Robert Francis. When her mother left the little house on the edge of the big lake and took Lily back to the city, Robert Francis didn't follow. Instead, he headed west, then north. The last Lily heard, he lived in Yellowknife, but that was many years ago. He must be dead by now, she thought. And yet, his voice in her ears sounded as young and strong as when he'd spoken to her that day in the woods.

As if a curtain had risen on a darkened stage, Lily was back in her old life, the life that she had long forgotten. She and her father were tramping along a forest path, picking up the catch from the rabbit snares. Although the sun looked bright and warm, the temperature chilled Lily's ears and toes, so Daddy had decided to light a small fire while they ate the lunch that Mummy had packed for them. He'd showed Lily how to gather the birch bark curls, the bits of dried moss, then he'd showed her the magic trick, taking a small prism from his pocket and catching the light of the sun until a small wisp of smoke trailed up into the still air. "I should be able to rub two sticks together," he'd said with a loud laugh, although Lily didn't know why that was funny, "but I'm a modern Indian, so I use this."

In a flash, Silent Woman had realized that Lily Underhill's watch had an intact glass front, just as good as a prism. It seemed like no time at all until Silent Woman sat warming her toes before a blazing fire, chewing a wad of hardened spruce sap to ease the pangs in her stomach. The biting resin flavour tasted familiar, even after so many years. She could hear the Ancestors in Grammy's voice telling her how to pick the tender dandelion greens and where to find leeks, mushrooms and purslane in the scruffy woods of the island. *"Mijjit,"* said Grammy. "Eat, child. The Creator has provided these good things for you."

Silent Woman heard Uncle George's voice reminding her of the mussels that had been around the big lake. Silent Woman now walked to the shore of the island and there found an abundance of mussels clinging to the wet rocks uncovered by the receding tide.

"You must look for stones," said Uncle George. "They are called 'grandfathers'. Look for flat ones."

Just as Uncle George told her, Silent Woman piled the grandfathers on the fire and roasted the mussels on them until the black shells split open and gave up their juicy treasures.

When the skies darkened in the east and a cold wind blew across the gathering waves, the air thickening with the coming storm, Daddy helped Silent Woman build a small shelter. "We will build you an *apsi'kan,*" he told her, "just like the playhouse I built for you in the woods behind our house in Whycocomagh."

As the days passed, soft mornings giving way to long summer evenings, warm rain dropping slow upon the pine boughs, with bright starry nights and flashes of heat lightning out across the waters, Lily Underhill began to fade until she became less than a shadow in the back of Silent Woman's thoughts.

A few times as Silent Woman sat on the beach looking out at the vast expanse of the sea, she would see a boat far out, its masts just visible on the horizon. Then Lily Underhill would stir again, rushing to pile dry boughs on the fire, sending up great billows of smoke into the clear salty air. Nothing ever came of these efforts. He had chosen this spot well, knowing that few boats navigated in these waters, and only the occasional fisherman or kayaker paddled among the myriad of off-shore islands. So far, none had.

Silent Woman snorted in disgust when her memories strayed to that awful day. Foolish Lily Underhill. Weak and foolish, trusting a *kesnoqwat,* a liar, a cheat, a dog. Even now, when she slept, Silent Woman would feel Lily Underhill stir and moan with memories of Kelsey Borden. Despite all he had done to her, Lily's body still yearned for him, betraying the anger that Silent Woman kept stoked hot within her heart.

How could a weakling such as Lily Underhill be so powerful in her world, the owner of a multinational trading company worth many millions of dollars? Silent Woman felt a faint pride in the fact that a brat from Whycocomagh had gone so far, although no one else knew about the brat. They only knew the Lily Underhill of the city, the woman who went to private schools and to university in Boston. They did not know about Robert Francis, the man called Wood Walker by his people, or the little house in Wycocomagh. Lily might have sprung up full grown in the big city house near the park for all anyone knew.

When Lily's mother left Wycocomagh to go back to her family, a battery of lawyers made sure that not one of Robert Francis's people ever saw Lily again.

Silent Woman smiled at these thoughts. The Ancestors were more powerful than any lawyers. They could not be stopped by pieces of paper. They spoke to their children when they wished. The Creator saw to that.

"Hi ya hi di ho." Silent Woman chanted the words under her breath, her hand beating the drum rhythm on the hard ground. Grammy had taught Lily the song so long ago, and now, it waited to be sung again. "Hi ya hi di ho ho ho."

Oh, yes, Lily Underhill, so smart and powerful. "Hi ya hi di ho." Yet, she did not see into the blackness of Kelsey Borden's heart. "Hi ya hi ya hi di ho." Silent Woman's hand beat harder on the earth. "Hi ya hi di ho ho ho. Hi ya hi ya ho." Stupid Lily Underhill. Marrying a man who only wanted

4

what Lily had worked so hard for.

Silent Woman felt a dampness on her hand. Looking down, she saw blood and realized that she had been pounding so hard on the earth that she had broken the skin.

She hated it when Lily's memories surfaced with such power, overshadowing her sense of well-being. Silent Woman tried but couldn't keep the memory words from echoing in her brain.

"C'mon, Lily. You need to slow down. How're we going to make that baby you want if you keep up this pace? Let's take some time off, get away somewhere, just the two of us. How about we take *Wind Catcher* out for a nice cruise along the coast? I know it's early in the season, but the weather is warm enough. We'll turn off the cell phones and forget about the e-mail and be real people for a change. It'll be good for us." His voice felt warm on her ear, and Lily pressed against the length of his body stretched against hers. She had to admit, it sounded enticing. And it wasn't as if she didn't have good, competent people working for her. The company would be fine without her for a week or two. Besides, she was tired. The latest merger had taken a lot out of her. Then there was the baby thing. She and Kelsey had been trying for the last year, but so far nothing had happened. Maybe getting away would be the answer to that, too.

The thought of a week on the boat alone with Kelsey had clinched the deal. She loved sailing with him. He was a good sailor—competent, smart and sea savvy. It had taken him many months to convince Lily, neither a good swimmer nor a strong sailor, to go out on *Wind Catcher* with him, but once she had, Lily had enjoyed every moment on the boat. She smiled at the thought of the starry nights on deck, the soft rocking of the boat on the gentle swells and the musical chink-

chink of the breeze in the rigging overhead. Perfect baby-making ingredients, she thought.

Their favourite passage headed south, along the coast towards Peggy's Cove and Lunenburg. It was a familiar run for them, and Lily liked watching for the leading lights and landmarks along the shore. This time, Kelsey wanted to head in the opposite direction, following the Eastern Shore towards Cape Breton. The weather reports for the coming days didn't look good, but he assured her they wouldn't do any bad-weather sailing.

"There are lots of nice spots we can moor in if need be. We'll just batten down and enjoy ourselves."

They'd made good time up past Musquodoboit Harbour, Owls Head and the long finger of Ship Harbour, an easy run with the wind blowing from the south west. The first night, they'd found a calm mooring in Tangier Harbour, just off of Webb's Point. During the night, the wind had backed to the east, and the next morning they woke to dark and lowering skies, a mean chop on the water and a cold biting wind.

"Let's stay here," she said after they finished their breakfast of hot coffee and rolls. "It's not as if we're on some kind of timetable." Kelsey ignored her and continued to make ready the sails. At ten in the morning, they navigated the choppy waters of the harbour and headed into the wind past the lea of Taylor Head and out to the open ocean.

By noon, the wind blew hard and fresh in the rigging. Kelsey reefed down the main sail and put up a storm jib. Lily could barely see three feet beyond the boat as the waves continued to pile up around them and the spray blew across the cockpit like a wet sheet whipping in the wind.

Lily begged him to stop, to run before the wind into a safe harbour, but he continued to battle each tack, his face set and determined. She began to plead, to cajole, even to demand, but some uncaring demon had taken over her husband. She sat huddled in the corner of the deck, her misery compounded by the growing nausea brought on by the violent pitching of *Wind Catcher.*

At three in the afternoon, Kelsey had turned around, picked Lily up and thrown her overboard.

Silent Woman stirred and shook her head from side to side, faster and faster, as if she could jar the memories loose. I will not think these thoughts. I will not, she muttered under her breath. It was over and done with. *Kaquiq.* Ended. No one cared about Lily Underhill now. No one was looking for her, if indeed, they had ever looked for her. Who knew what stories Kelsey Borden had told? Who knew where he had sent them to search? Not here. Not to this place, thought Silent Woman.

Luck, not skill nor strength, had saved Lily. Her life jacket had kept her afloat long enough to be thrown up on the little beach of the island. Odds were that she should have been battered to death by the storm waves surging against the huge rocks that faced the sea on most of the scattered islands, or else washed out far from land, where she would perish from the prolonged exposure to the cold waters of the North Atlantic. *The Creator saved Lily Underhill,* thought Silent Woman, *so that I might live.*

Time passed slowly on the island. Silent Woman watched *tepgunset,* the moon, make her passage across the sky, three times growing fat, and three times becoming thin. She felt the days grow shorter and the nights cooler. Soon, Mother Earth would settle for her winter slumber, and Silent Woman had much to do. The Ancestors would help her prepare for the long dark days ahead. They would show her how to smoke the mussels, how to make her hut warm and sound for winter, how to bank up sand and moss around the base and stuff the cracks with seaweed. She had driftwood to pile, bark and dried moss to gather, nuts to collect and berries to dry. Soon, the autumn gales would come and after them, the snow. *Yes,* she thought, *there is much to do.*

Silent Woman set about these tasks with grim determination. The Ancestors spoke to her, guiding her, teaching her, helping her. Their voices formed familiar litanies in her head, while Lily Underhill faded out like smoke.

One warm day, Silent Woman sat on the shore looking out to the sea, enjoying the feeling of the autumn sun on her face. A movement on the water at the far point of the island, out past the rock cliffs, caught her eye. It was a lone kayaker paddling through the calm water. Silent Woman's breath caught in her throat as she moved into the shadow of the tall pine tree where she could watch him as he paddled towards the small sandy beach.

The kayak slid onto the beach, and the man clambered out. He walked across the sand to the beaten path to the clearing. Silent Woman trailed him in the shadows. The kayaker stood over Silent Woman's fire pit, then looked towards her hut. Silent Woman held herself still.

"Hello," he called. "Anybody here?"

For the first time in weeks, Silent Woman felt Lily stir. She was trying to call out. Silent Woman clamped down on her jaw, hard.

The man disappeared inside Silent Woman's hut.

Silent Woman shrank back into the darkest shade. A faint trembling began at the back of her neck and continued down her spine to her knees.

The man reappeared, a puzzled look on his face. "Hellooo," he called again. He cupped his hands around his mouth.

"Hellooo. Is there anybody here?"

Silent Woman felt her mouth working. "Please," whispered Lily Underhill. "Please."

Silent Woman moved a step away from the clearing. "Please," begged Lily. Silent Woman pressed her hand against her mouth, stifling any sound. All this time, all this effort—the hut, the food, the piled wood, the good feeling of power and control, the comfort of the Ancestors' voices—and Lily wanted to let it all go. For what? A life filled with stress and anxiety? For money? For Kelsey Borden?

No, thought Silent Woman. I will not let you do this, Lily Underhill. Silent Woman closed her eyes, willing Lily Underhill to go back deep inside where she belonged. But Lily would not go.

"Let me loose," Lily insisted. "Let me loose. You know I can't live here for the winter. You know I won't survive. I will die, and so will you."

Silent Woman let out a long, slow breath. The winter to come had been worrying her brain with thoughts of the black nights, the deep cold of the snow, the island surrounded by shifting sea ice. The Ancestors had lived through such winters, snug in their furs and blankets, warmed before the fire pit, filled with deer meat and bannock. But Silent Woman had no furs, no blankets, no meat or bread. She might survive, but Lily Underhill would not.

For a moment, Silent Woman's determination wavered. Lily stepped out from behind the tree. No! thought Silent Woman. I would rather die here than be lost again.

Silent Woman tried to pull back behind the tree, but Lily Underhill began to speak, her anguished voice filling Silent Woman's head. "Let me go. I promise you, I will not forget you. I will visit the graves of The Ancestors, and there I will burn sweet grass and sing an honour song to them. I will find your people, my people, and I will tell them of you and what you did here. And at the gathering of the people, at the summer pow wow, I will bang a drum for you."

Silent Woman considered Lily's words. She would be remembered. In the heartbeat of the people, her name would be honoured. The drum would speak for her. "Bang the drum loudly for me, Lily Underhill," she whispered.

Lily stepped out of the shadows and stumbled across the clearing towards the man. "I'm here," she croaked.

The author of nine inspirational books, two corporate business books and a best-selling audio program, Pat is also co-author of three humorous books on life in the Maritimes. Her short stories have appeared in several anthologies as well as Storyteller Magazine, *and she has published a mystery novel,* Lucky Strike, *with co-author Kris Wood. Having lived on an island off the Eastern Shore of Nova Scotia and now near the sandy beaches of the Northumberland Strait, Pat writes about what she loves best—the coastal regions of the Maritimes.*

Opera Lover

Joy Hewitt Mann

An opera lover named Moore
Felt the diva was ruining the score.
From where he sat
She was grossly fat
And her range was decidedly poor.

Next time the Fat Lady sang
The opera house thunderously rang.
Moore rigged a bomb
So that she would come
On with a whimper and out with a bang.

For the Sake of Francine

Sandra Beswetherick

Kelly sat in the courtroom quietly composed, eyes forward, hands folded neatly in her lap. She'd committed a crime. She'd commit it again if she had to. She'd accept the consequences as well, if it came to that.

The circumstantial evidence had already been presented. The boot print in the soft ground next to the shell casing, the matching boot. The tire treads and the matching tires. The murder weapon, the hunting rifle with identifiable fingerprints on trigger and stock. The court had heard from the forensic experts and listened now to the testimonies of the witnesses.

"The prosecution calls Mr. William Thomas."

Kelly shifted slightly in her chair and from the corner of her eye watched the older man approach the witness stand. So much depended on Billy T. She was certain only Billy knew she'd done it all for the sake of Francine.

Francine had walked through the door of Gus's diner one Tuesday afternoon in early summer. And Kelly had fallen not simply in lust, but in love. The kind of love where she would do anything to make Francine happy and to keep her from harm. Slender, petite—she was no taller than Kelly's collarbone—dark-eyed, her black hair curling in the damp air. She carried one child, dark like her, in her arms and held the hand of a second child, fair-haired, as she hesitated in the doorway. Her blue station wagon with "je me souviens" plates sat in the lot out front.

Kelly grabbed the highchair on wheels stationed at the far end of the counter and rolled it, one wonky wheel clattering, to the corner booth. She'd told her boss, Gus, a thousand times that they needed more highchairs. That it wouldn't hurt to encourage customers from the new housing development that had sprung up nearby. "Yeah, yeah," Gus always said, but never did anything more about it.

The diner, along with a grocery store of sorts, a hunting-and-fishing emporium and the ever-popular provincial liquor store, occupied a small strip mall that stood at a junction between the expanding civilization of the Fraser Valley and the wilderness of the Cascades. The customers who frequented the diner were mainly loggers, guards from the local forestry camp, hunters and fishing enthusiasts. The type of clientele Gus related to, even though he wasn't at the diner half the time.

Kelly held the highchair steady as Francine lowered the younger child in. *"Merci beaucoup."* Francine's voice was as rich and sweet as maple syrup, pleasing Kelly no end.

"Pas du tout," Kelly immediately responded.

"Vous parlez français!" Francine's eyes shone with both delight and desperation. Which came to Kelly as no surprise. This was British Columbia, after all. A long way from Quebec. Why should anyone in B.C. speak French? The province had more in common with Washington State than Quebec.

Kelly held up her hand, a quarter inch gap separating index finger and thumb. *"Un petit peu."*

Francine's smile faded, and Kelly had to have it back. She swore she would drive all the way to Chilliwack that very evening and borrow every French grammar book and language

13

tape the public library offered. *"Je m'appelle Kelly,"* she said, dredging her memory for any high school French buried there, and surely grinning like a fool. She learned Francine's name and the names of her two children, Nicole, in the highchair, and Daniel.

"Asseyez-vous, s'il vous plaît." Kelly indicated the bench in the booth. *"Pommes frites pour les enfants?"* she asked. *"Un café pour vous?"* She pointed at the coffee maker behind the counter.

Billy T, in the adjacent booth, raised his cup as she swept past. "Can I have a refill, Kelly?" Billy wasn't a permanent fixture but was almost always there. His grey hair stuck out at odd angles, and scrawny wrists and hands showed from his too-short sleeves. His plaid shirt and jeans were faded, like a scarecrow that had done too much duty in the sun.

He could be as silent as a scarecrow, too, when he wanted. "Sure, Billy. No problem."

Billy T had been her father's friend, and he'd lived as long as she could remember in the ramshackle log house perched like an eagle's nest on the bluff overlooking the mall. Long before the mall, of course. Either for want of company or because he couldn't cook, Billy ate breakfast in the diner every morning and the daily special Monday, Wednesday and Friday nights.

"Here you go, Billy." She'd returned with the coffee, but her attention was fixed on the corner booth, on Francine, and her face must have been lit with her *amour*. Billy rapped his empty cup on the table, then raised it eye-level so Kelly would see his cautionary look.

Billy T wasn't the only person in the small community who knew she was gay. As long as she didn't flaunt it—no gay-pride activism, no snuggling with a girlfriend at Al's Bar and Grill, no hitting on customers in the diner—she remained a well-liked, respected community member. After all, her father had been a popular hunting and fishing guide in the area, and, since his death, she'd returned and was taking up guiding herself. She was a single, independent girl who hadn't found the right man yet.

That perception suited Kelly fine. She'd rather keep her snuggling private, and anonymity in Vancouver was only a two-hour drive away.

"C'mon, Billy! She couldn't be more straight. Just being friendly, all right?"

She filled Billy's cup, then continued to the corner booth where she poured the last of the coffee into a cup for Francine. *"Potage?"* she asked, positive "potage" was the French word for soup.

At the blast of a truck horn outside the diner's window, the carafe slipped from her fingers and exploded on contact with the tiled floor. "For the love of—" A truck door slammed and the diner door crashed open. Jay Pierce, his face purple with rage, pushed his way inside.

"Where's the French bastard who parked his damn car in my spot?"

Kelly winced when she realized the station wagon with its Quebec plates was parked in the spot Jay considered his.

"Was it you?" Jay pointed an accusatory finger at Francine. "I want it moved! Or I'll move it, my way!"

When he charged at Francine, arms windmilling, Kelly stepped into his path, her shoes crunching the carafe's remains. "For crying out loud, Jay, she doesn't speak English!"

"That ain't my problem, is it?" Jay roared back.

With Francine's kids whimpering behind her, Kelly stood her ground. Jay wasn't that much taller or huskier. Still, better to face him than turn your back. "It's not like you've got a reserved sign posted out there!"

"I don't need one," Jay snarled. "Everybody knows!"

"Okay! Calm down." Most of the locals did know about Jay's spot and gave it a wide berth. It was the only parking space hidden from the view of Billy T's front porch by the Gus's Diner sign perched on the diner roof.

Kelly turned to Francine. *"Les clefs de votre voiture?"* Kelly could only mime her intention of moving the car. "You sit here, okay?" Kelly breathed a sigh of relief when Francine fished her car keys from her handbag and handed them over.

"Jay, you're coming with me!" No way was she leaving Jay with Francine.

As she fitted the key in the door lock, Jay crept up behind her and whispered in her ear. "Hey, Kelly, let's do it. The back seat looks big enough."

"If I feel your hand on my butt," she warned, "I'm charging you with sexual assault."

Jay had mentioned more than once his desire to have his way with her. Preferably when she was unconscious, she'd discovered one night at Al's Bar. She'd been on her way to the Ladies and happened to glance over her shoulder. Sure enough, Jay had been adding something extra to her unsupervised drink.

Everyone knew Jay hunted and fished out of season, sold bear paws and gall bladders illegally to the Asian community in Vancouver and supplied certain restaurants, also illegally, with salmon caught by local aboriginals. His other crimes included petty theft, uttering death threats and, according to Billy T, attempted murder.

Cursing softly, Kelly slowly backed the station wagon, trying to see around Jay's black, half-ton pick-up that obstructed her view. She then parked the wagon five spaces over, knowing Jay would clip it somehow if it weren't out of harm's way. With a roar of engine and squeal of tires, Jay moved his truck, then leaned across to the passenger window and leered down at her. The jerk.

By the time she got back inside, Billy T had swept up the glass with the broom and set another pot of coffee brewing. *"Voilà!"* she said, returning Francine's keys.

"Hey, you!" Jay had followed her in. He stabbed his finger at his pick-up. "My truck, my spot!" Then he stabbed his finger at Francine. "Remember that, you ignorant Frenchie."

"If you want me to bring you anything, Jay, you'd better sit down and shut up."

Jay smirked, hitched a thumb in a belt loop and sauntered to his customary stool at the end of the counter. He sat down and seemed to notice Billy T for the first time. "Hey, old man, got your cataracts out yet?"

Billy looked at Jay with that poker face he'd perfected, then nudged with his elbow the small pair of binoculars sitting on his table. His way of telling Jay he wouldn't be played the fool the next time

Eighteen months before, late evening, Billy T had witnessed a mugging in the mall's parking lot from his front porch. The attacker had kicked his victim, who was lying prostrate on the ground. At the sound of sirens, the assailant had fled. The jogger had no memory of who'd leapt at him from the shadows. Billy had insisted it was Jay. But Jay's lawyer, who also happened to be Jay's uncle and a recipient, it was rumoured, of Jay's ill-gotten gains, had gotten Jay off, yet again.

"How old are you, Mr. Thomas?" Jay's lawyer had asked. "How good's your eyesight at that distance after dark? Can you describe the attacker's clothing? Did you see his features clearly?" Unfortunately, Billy had sworn an oath and couldn't bring himself to lie. "But it was Jay," he had persisted. "I know how he walks, the way he moves. It was something Jay off-his-nut would do!"

This was the reason Billy carried binoculars with him everywhere and had a second extra-powerful pair sitting by his chair on his porch. He'd even acquired a night scope, Kelly had heard. "Jay's too damn dangerous to be loose on the streets," was Billy's outraged opinion.

Kelly poured Jay a beer to keep him quiet and dropped handfuls of cut potatoes into the deep fryer. She then set a bowl of clam chowder in front of Francine. *"Je le fais,"* she said, pointing at the soup. She ached to touch Francine's hand in reassurance. "Jay's an asshole," she confided, even though Francine couldn't understand. "Once he's had his beer, he'll leave." Normally Friday was the day Jay, half-pissed from drinking at Al's, dropped into the diner to harass her and Billy T. The vehicle with Quebec plates parked in his spot had drawn him in today.

Francine didn't leave until Jay was long gone, and Kelly despaired she would ever see her again. "Come back soon, okay?" Kelly had urged as she'd seen Francine and her children out.

Every day thereafter, Kelly watched for the blue station wagon. She thought she saw it driving past a few times and willed it to turn in. When it didn't, she cursed Jay for spoiling everything. In the meantime, she studied French, poring over the grammar books she borrowed from the library, lugging them to work. She'd even purchased a few kids' toys and colouring books just in case.

Monday of the following week, the third consecutive day of the pouring rain typical of the area, Kelly spotted through the rain-streaked glass a woman in a green raincoat pushing a stroller covered in rain-splattered plastic, a child in a yellow slicker trotting at her heels. Kelly's heart leapt in recognition, and she dashed outside. "Let me help!" She gathered Daniel up, and the four of them tumbled through the diner door, accompanied by Francine's laughter.

"Bienvenue, bienvenue!" Kelly couldn't begin to tell Francine how welcome she was. *"J'ai une surprise!"* Once she'd helped everyone out of their wet clothing, she spread the children's books and toys she'd purchased on the table. Nicole and Daniel shrieked their delight.

Unexpectedly, Francine took Kelly's hand, her touch slamming a jolt of electricity up Kelly's arm.

"Mon amie?" Francine asked. Kelly didn't know whether to laugh or cry. From the ache in Francine's voice, it was obvious she had no other friend.

"Mais oui," Kelly assured her, daring in turn to squeeze Francine's hand.

"My 'usban," Francine whispered, "want me to learn English. I—"

"You want me to help?" Kelly couldn't believe her good fortune. *"Pas de problème, eh? Chaque jour, vous venez ici.* Okay?"

"Merci beaucoup." When Francine smiled, Kelly felt she might weep with joy.

There was a rustling now in the courtroom, of spectators leaning toward their neighbours and whispering. Remarking, perhaps, on Billy T's changed appearance as he stood before the court. His clean-shaven face, his closely cropped hair, the jacket and tie. Kelly took advantage of the disturbance and searched out Francine, who'd returned from Quebec for the trial. At the sight of her, Kelly drew in a deep, heartfelt breath, closed her eyes, and turned away.

Kelly savoured every second she and Francine had spent together, heads bent over grammar books most afternoons. But just as Francine had been making progress, her appearance at the diner became sporadic. When she did come, she was distracted and visibly unhappy. Even Daniel and Nicole were cranky and whiny.

"What's wrong, Francine?" Kelly hoped it had nothing to do with Jay, whom they'd been careful to avoid, their lessons ending Friday well before he appeared.

Francine stared at her reflection in the diner window. Her eyes filled. "I miss my family, my friends, speaking French." Her sob wrenched Kelly's heart. "I miss the sunshine."

"Have you told your husband?"

"Gilles want us to stay. He like his job. It is good money, a good position for him and for his advance. He like the woods too. Now every Friday he fish. He want to learn hunting with his guys at work." She shrugged.

Terrific, Kelly thought, another urban suburban gone native. With the wilderness at your doorstep, it was simple to pack up your camping gear, fishing rod or rifle and head out for the weekend, usually leaving wife and kiddies behind. Although she shouldn't complain too much, she reminded herself, because she intended to make good money from this sort of customer.

"Couldn't you go home for a visit?"

Francine shook her head. "He know I don't come back."

"Go anyway," Kelly insisted, her dislike for Gilles a smouldering ember. "You're unhappy, the kids are unhappy."

"He say his company think bad of him if I leave. How can he be a good manager..." A word they'd had to look up in the French-English dictionary. "...if he cannot manage his own wife? He shouts this at me."

Kelly's dislike burned hotter as she learned more about Gilles. That he denied Francine use of the car, afraid she'd drive home to Quebec, that he constantly phoned, keeping tabs—her

English classes one of the few acceptable excuses for her being out. On the day Francine burst into tears, saying Gilles had threatened her and the kids if she ever mentioned leaving again, Kelly decided something would have to be done.

As if fate had taken a hand, an opportunity presented itself the next afternoon.

Francine and her kids had settled themselves in their customary booth, after greeting Billy with, *"Bonjour,* Monsieur Billy,"* and Kelly had gone to the storeroom for the grammar books. When she returned, the blue wagon was parked outside, and a man sat opposite Francine in the booth. He held Francine's wrist in a tight grip and was berating her in French, demanding to know why she was here and not attending her English classes. Who she was meeting in this place?

"Your wife meets with me, *monsieur.* I've been helping her learn English."

He let go Francine's wrist, and Kelly saw the red mark his hand had made. She saw the alarm in Francine's eyes as she drew as far from her husband as possible in the confines of the booth. Kelly's dislike flared into hatred and fury.

"Who are you, madame?" Gilles looked her up and down. "A qualified teacher or the waitress?" Kelly almost slugged him then and there.

"You must admit, sir, that the lady is making considerable progress with her English." Kelly was surprised when Billy spoke. "What does it matter who's teaching her?"

"Kelly is not only the waitress." Francine raised her eyes to her husband. "She is my friend."

"She's also one damn good fishing guide," Billy interjected. "Her dad was one of the best. Kelly was his right hand when she was growing up. She's been building quite a respectable clientele." The pride in Billy's voice was a second surprise.

When Gilles's condescending smirk was replaced by a flicker of interest, Kelly wondered if she could get at him this way. Take him out fishing and have a few words. "I'm booked the next three weekends, but if —"

The wild screech of tires snapped everyone's attention to the window. Kelly swore under her breath.

Jay threw open the diner door and stormed toward them. "I thought I told that French broad that parking space was mine!"

Gilles turned round and rose to his feet, easily twice Jay's size. "Are you referring to my wife, English?"

Jay had already stopped short. "I want that car out of my spot!" he raged, but well out of Gilles's reach. "Now!"

"Unless that parking spot is reserved for the handicapped, my car stays where it is." He took one step toward Jay. "Understand!" Jay, the weasel he was, backed up. Gilles turned on his heel and returned to the booth, ignoring Jay as if he'd been no more than a pesky mosquito. Kelly might have cheered. Except she wondered if Gilles used his size and temper to intimidate Francine in the same way.

Jay flipped Gilles the bird and hissed, more snake than weasel now. "You'll get yours, Frenchie!"

Kelly saw the sharp expression on Billy's face and knew he had heard Jay's threat. She wondered what Billy T was thinking as his eyes followed Jay to his customary seat.

Jay would remain planted until Gilles left, Kelly was willing to wager. Once Gilles drove off, Jay might follow him for a while in his truck, transferring the rifle he usually carried in the cab to the more visible gun rack in the cab's back window. At the moment, Jay contented himself with glaring at Gilles, trying to burn holes in his back.

Gilles didn't spare Jay a second glance. "You were saying about fishing," he said, returning his attention to her. Avid sports fisherman, Kelly thought. Maybe even obsessed, if catching a darn fish had a higher priority than what had just happened.

"Since you'll be busy over the next few weekends, I wonder if you might recommend..." He flipped his hand back and forth, as though he weren't asking for much. "...a good fishing spot."

"Sure." Perhaps if she got on his good side, it would be that simple. "I'll draw a map."

He took a pen from his pocket, a paper napkin from the dispenser and slid them across the table.

"It's not well known. If you went on a Friday evening, you should have it to yourself." She sketched the route on the napkin and made sure he understood.

"Bien." He nodded, folded the napkin and tucked it into the breast pocket of his business suit. Kelly waited for the *"merci"*, but it never came, and she wondered what Gilles thought he'd gotten away with.

"Come, Francine," he said. "I'll take you and the children home."

"Gilles, I wish to stay."

He pointed through the window at the darkening sky. "It will rain again soon. I don't want you getting wet or the kids with more colds." He helped his children with their coats, folded the stroller, picked it up and gripped Francine's elbow with his free hand. As he drew her toward the door, he spoke to her in French again, his head bent over hers. Kelly understood more French than she spoke and was amazed by how much she now remembered from her high school days.

"You are never to come here again. What were you thinking? Bringing the kids as well, with trash like that sitting at the counter. You will take proper English lessons at the school." He gave Francine a shake. "And the friends you make will be the other wives and women from the company. Not a half-wit waitress." Francine kept her head bowed, saying nothing. But as Gilles let her go to open the door, she looked back at Kelly, eyes brilliant with tears, and mouthed *"adieu"*.

"That bastard!" Billy exclaimed once the door slammed shut. It was the first time Billy had given any indication that he too understood French.

"Hey, Kelly, how about a beer?" Jay made no move to follow Gilles but remained perched on his stool.

Kelly went behind the counter and reached for bottle and glass with a steady hand. The hopelessness in Francine's eyes had extinguished the bright flame of her hatred for Gilles, leaving something dark and sinister in its place.

She set the beer in front of Jay.

He leered up at her. "So Frenchie's going fishing Friday, eh?"

Kelly caught Billy watching Jay, and for a second glimpsed the frustration that seethed behind his cold, hard stare. She poured Jay's beer, intent on the foam rising in the glass. "That's the impression I had," she quietly answered. Not that she would consider entrusting the job to Jay.

*   *   *

The judge rapped her gavel, silencing the court. Billy T raised his right hand and swore that the testimony he was about to give was the truth. Kelly rolled her shoulders, relaxing tensed muscles, and thought of how lucky she'd been. As though fate had indeed played a hand.

One clean shot—bang!—had caught Gilles in the chest, killing him instantly, the force of the blow tumbling him into the river. She'd then been able to drive Jay's truck, with the unconscious Jay inside, back to his isolated shack without incident, and hike home through the bush.

By the time Francine had convinced the Mounties her husband was missing, Kelly was out with her fishing party, and they had to locate her, first, to learn where Gilles had gone. More time was spent in finding and recovering Gilles's body—with Kelly worried criminal evidence would be trampled in the search.

Enough time elapsed between Gilles's disappearance and the homicide investigation that it allowed Jay to wake up, wash up and to piss out of his system the date-rape drugs, purchased in Vancouver, that she'd put in his beer. She'd thought it unlikely that Jay would clean his boots—she'd worn them over two pairs of heavy socks—or wipe down the rifle she'd covered in his prints.

"Now, Mr. Thomas," the prosecutor began, and Kelly looked up. "You've heard that Ms Reid and Mr. Morris carried Mr. Pierce to his truck after he'd passed out in the diner." She'd convinced Gus the drunken Jay, sprawled across the counter, was turning off customers, that if Jay ultimately found the keys she hid in the glove compartment after they'd dumped him in the cab, he would be sober enough to drive home. Should forensic experts find any evidence of her having been in the truck, it was readily explained.

"Did you see this happen?"

"No," Billy T answered. "The diner sign hid the truck." But he did see the truck later when it sat near the parking lot's exit, engine idling. He'd focused his binoculars to see what was up.

It was Jay's truck, he'd written the plate number down. The driver was wearing the plaid shirt he'd seen Jay wearing earlier in the day, the familiar ball cap with F and U emblazoned on the back, the wraparound shades that Jay thought made him look cool.

Kelly had also been lucky no one had seen her climb into Jay's truck the second time. Good thing Jay was a small man. She'd sat on a couple of her grammar books to give her the height, and bulked out his shirt with a padded vest she'd brought to work that morning. She wore work gloves to grip the steering wheel.

"Then it was Jay you saw in the truck?" the prosecutor asked.

Billy T was under oath. "I told you what I saw, and I'm letting the members of the jury draw their own conclusions. I don't want to seem prejudiced."

The prosecutor insisted on a yes or no, and Kelly held her breath. Billy T hadn't looked at her once during the course of the trial. He didn't look at her now. "Who else would it have been, you tell me?" Billy demanded. The judge allowed his response as an affirmative, and Kelly breathed again.

Billy said the truck's driver seemed to be watching traffic on the road, waiting for someone. Kelly had leaned forward over the steering wheel, nestling her head in the fold of her arms, her face half-hidden to the oncoming cars. Everyone driving past assumed it was Jay at the wheel. It was Jay's truck. And everyone on the road that night assumed they saw Kelly walking home from the diner as she did every night. Especially after she'd testified that was the day she was sure Bertie Sanders had offered her a lift.

"As soon as the blue station wagon drove by," Billy said, "Jay's truck pulled out behind it."

The defense lawyer, during the cross examination, asked Billy if he didn't think Jay following the station wagon was more than a little obvious.

Billy answered he'd never known Jay to be too bright. On the other hand, he supposed, Jay had been careless, trusting his lawyer uncle would get him off, as he usually did. This observation, of course, was stricken from the record.

"We find the defendant guilty." The jurors' verdict after four hours of deliberation. That Jay had sworn he didn't remember shooting Gilles, didn't remember a goddamn thing, made no impression. Either the jurors didn't believe Jay, or they refused to accept alcoholic blackout as a legitimate excuse. The judge was a teetotaler, and even the suggestion of Jay driving drunk was enough to raise her ire. "Life imprisonment."

That Billy T showed no reaction to the sentencing, maintaining his poker face, didn't surprise Kelly. As the courtroom emptied, though, she waited for him to raise his eyes to hers. Waited for him to acknowledge everything was square between them, that she'd done what she'd done for Francine's sake and given Billy what he wanted, Jay off the street. Billy left it almost too late, until he would have had to stop and turn round. It was the merest glance, lacking emotion, and Kelly wondered if their relationship would survive.

As for Francine, Kelly found her a changed person, happier, more self-assured and more beautiful than ever. When Kelly said her farewells, Francine pulled her into a tight embrace, kissed her cheek. *"Au revoir, mon amie."* Not *"adieu"* this time, but *"au revoir"*, to see again. Kelly took comfort from that.

Sandra Beswetherick lives near Seeley's Bay, Ontario, with two cats, who come when called, usually, and her husband, who feeds raccoons and chainsaws trees. Her short stories have been published in Australia, Canada, South Africa, Sweden, the UK and the US and have appeared in Ellery Queen's Mystery Magazine, Storyteller, *and the mystery anthologies* When Boomers Go Bad *and* Locked Up. *She has yet to afford a BMW, her husband's aspiration.*

The Robber

Joy Hewitt Mann

The robber was down on his luck,
Bought a cheap gun from a man in a truck,
But when it was loaded,
The gun it exploded.
You get a lot of bang for a buck.

The Thrill of the Chase

Mary Keenan

With a mangled book at his feet, Gilbert Harrington reflected on the number of people who might be, at this moment, considering the slow murder of their employers. Hundreds, perhaps. It would be interesting to know whether the number would increase as the week progressed; it was now just eleven o'clock on Monday morning.

Past experience had taught him the value of flicking a handkerchief out of his pocket before attempting to touch the gnarled mass of paper and leather. He could not bear to resign possession of a signed first edition to the estate's caretaker, even if it was worthy now only of the burning pile. Perhaps he could salvage just part of the signature…

No. What had not been pierced by that cur's sharp teeth had been smeared beyond recognition by a mouthful of drool.

Mr. Harrington dropped what remained of *The Welder's Guide to Lunchbox Design* into the trash can under his desk and sank into the leather banker's chair afforded the keeper of the Culpepper Estate Memorial Library.

He could, of course, give notice. Nobody else would put up with these conditions—the dogs charging around the library, the intrusion of visitors asking to look at the precious books in his care, the subtly amorous attentions of Wilhemina Culpepper…

this alone could drive a man mad. He hesitated between the horror of those attentions becoming more overt and the gratification of legitimately suing for sexual harassment. On the other hand, if he left his job, where would he go?

Mr. Harrington sank more deeply into his unquestionably comfortable chair and considered where he had been: living with Mother and working a few hours a week at a string of public libraries, where his concern for the structural integrity of books was met with no support whatsoever by his fellow librarians. Instead, the fools favoured getting books into the hands of as many people as possible, without making any effort to ensure the books in question would be treated properly. He was certain he had been let go from one position for his policy of "lecturing", as his supervisor called it, young people about not eating anything while holding a book and the importance of washing one's hands before picking one up. This sort of humiliation was repeated over and over until he had read of the opening at the Culpepper Estate, shortly after Mother's death.

It had seemed like a perfect opportunity. He had tired of eating toast at every meal, yet worried about the expense of eating out. He needed the stimulation of some form of employment, and it seemed his particular organizational skills held little value outside the library system. Also, the roof of Mother's house had begun to leak, and he was at a loss what to do about it. The Culpepper's librarian, by contrast, was traditionally given a small but luxurious apartment within Culpepper Manor and invited to enjoy meals prepared by the Culpepper chef. The library itself was well stocked with unusual and beautifully-bound volumes collected by the current owner's father, grandfather and great-grandfather, begun once the latter had retired from the doorknob factory that had made and still fuelled the family fortune.

Best of all, the comparatively remote location of the property and obscure value of the books stored there meant that visitors to the library were few and far between. Admittedly, the town was encroaching on the edges of the Culpepper Estate. Construction equipment was rampant just outside its gates, as builders churned out hideous mansions along the road that led out into open country. Inside the gates, however, the world was still at peace. Mr. Harrington could look forward to long days reading whatever he liked, without any pressure to computerize the card catalogue, thanks to Miss Culpepper's preference for the traditions of the past.

The first signs of trouble, he realized now, appeared during his interview. Miss Culpepper, in her forties but favouring a style of dress that made her appear thirty years older, sat in an armchair with her knobby-kneed legs crossed. As they talked, he was distracted by the irregular swinging of a foot which Mr. Harrington estimated was the length of a fair-sized trout. Her eyes, set deeply into her skull on either side of a nose that dominated not just her face but most of her upper body, sparkled more vividly the longer he talked, and she leaned forward, eventually putting both massive feet on the floor as if to hold herself steady. Her hair, straight and thin and oddly heavy with what Mr. Harrington hoped was merely some product intended to bestow beauty where none naturally occurred, slunk forward toward the tip of her monumental nose. Whenever it obscured her unwavering examination of him, she shoved it back with long fingers marked by knuckles as enormous as beads on a string.

She hired him on the spot. It was not until after he'd moved his favourite books, his suits and his impeccably white shirts into his beautifully appointed, mahogany-lined suite that he encountered Miss Culpepper's odious pets. She worshipped these three tall, thin, hopelessly clumsy dogs—some sort of hound, he suspected, though it was clear they were not purebred. Whatever intelligence they might have possessed at birth had eroded away over the years they had spent lowering themselves to their mistress's expectations. They received no more training than was required to lick their besotted owner's face whenever she demanded a "kissy", and no correction whatsoever. Their names were Becky, Bert and Bertram, Bertram being the sole male of the group and the one most likely to knock down any low-lying book and chew it beyond recognition. Invariably, Miss Culpepper's response to Mr. Harrington's outrage was, "Can't you just buy another copy? I'm sure we can afford it."

To make matters worse, a group of students at the local secondary school had expressed interest in local history, as documented by a group of books that resided only in the Culpepper Memorial Library. Miss Culpepper, whose father had written and self-published the books, was keen to have the "nice young things", as she called them, report on his genius. Mr. Harrington, who had read and been appalled by these volumes, was equally keen to relax his rule about books being used under supervision only. Miss Culpepper, however, overruled him and insisted that all research take place under her roof.

And so, here he was—surrounded by book-chewing dogs and noisy teens and an employer who pestered him constantly as he tried to read.

Mr. Harrington sighed and imagined how different it would all be if Miss Culpepper's cousin, Frederick Culpepper, had been her father's heir, instead of the next in line. Mr. Harrington had met him only once but had been impressed by his quiet demeanor, hatred of all dogs, and aversion to the company of others. It seemed likely that if Mr. Culpepper owned the estate, Mr. Harrington's job would be a good deal more pleasant.

Mr. Harrington's fingers stretched out on the arms of his chair and slowly tightened their grip. Could he…?

*   *   *

Wilhemina Culpepper waded through a seething mass of paws and tails, oblivious to the plaintive and persistent requests for treats as her mind turned over the events of the last few days. Life had been so perfect, and now it was nearly unbearable. What had happened to prompt such a change? And what could be done about it? She simply did not know.

What she did know was that Mr. Harrington, who had always been so deliciously aloof, so adorably out of reach, had suddenly become gracious. Not just friendly, but—yes, it had to be acknowledged—doting.

Miss Culpepper was no stranger to the doting male. In her youth, she had been courted by any number of men who professed to find her charming but were actually, she was almost certain, attracted to the Culpepper family fortune. Her father possessed no doubts of this whatsoever. "There's no harm in it, Willie," he'd say to her over a bowl of steamed cauliflower—Mr. Culpepper was a vegetarian every Tuesday and Friday, and every other Wednesday ate only foods that were white. "Wealthy people have always traded on their money when forming a new alliance. Just be sure you get something worthwhile in return, hmm?"

But she could think of nothing sufficiently worthwhile to justify marrying any of the men who'd come crawling. She much preferred a man who wouldn't speak to her at all. The challenge of winning him over! The romance of never losing hope! Oh dear yes. Much better than flowers from a beaming boy in a too-new suit.

Miss Culpepper had had her share of passions over the years, but no man had excited her imagination the way Gilbert Harrington had, the day he came to be interviewed for the position of Librarian. His suit was decidedly not new, and he most definitely did not beam. If he looked at her at all, it was with an expression of the utmost condescension. So confident, even arrogant! In spite of that appalling resume— it was quite obvious that he did not possess any quality fit for a legitimate librarian, save a love of fine binding—he truly believed himself superior in his field.

He may, for all she knew, have considered himself physically attractive also, something she could not say was the case. He looked something like a penguin with his large belly and short legs. Such a man should realize, surely, the detrimental aspect of perfect posture and instead develop a winning smile or perhaps a knack for telling jokes. Mr. Harrington instead courted the comparison with old-fashioned suits tailored to his form and favoured a still expression on his slightly raised face—a face whose features were overlarge, and whose eyes and lips protruded quite alarmingly—a face that was set, furthermore, over an impossibly small jaw. No, nobody could possibly say that Mr. Harrington was attractive.

What could be said nicely about Mr. Harrington, she did say: he was unique! His faith in himself was admirable, his contempt for others simply adorable. So many women threw their lives away on bad men, thinking what a statement it would be if they could inspire such a man to love. Who then could find fault with Wilhemina Culpepper for longing to find out whether such a man as this could be inspired to love her?

And yet, with so much to gain, and so few other opportunities likely to come his way, he had resisted her gentle hints and discreet invitations for months. Until a few days ago, when he had greeted her with the news that dear Bertram had had another go at the books in the library and suggested that perhaps he could accommodate the dogs with a shelf just for them? Lacking the wit to close her open mouth, she'd had to raise a hand to her quivering lips. But it hadn't ended there. The very next morning he'd asked whether there was anything he could do to help prepare Culpepper Manor for its annual fête. He, who despised social occasions and had openly scoffed at the tradition her grandfather had borrowed from English gentry—the tradition her own father had maintained to such great effect in the community. He had expressed concern for her health when she shuddered in response. And then—oh, horrible!—he asked her whether she had allowed herself to catch a cold, walking the dogs so early each morning.

At least he stopped short of offering to walk them himself.

But the worst was yet to come. This morning, unprompted, he had remembered her birthday with a friendly greeting and an impeccably wrapped gift. It was a stole, which he told her he hoped she would wear on those early morning walks and— she could barely bring herself to acknowledge the fact—he had remembered her allergy to all things woollen. He had selected a garment fashioned from synthetic mohair.

Something had to be done. But what? She was under no illusions about the library her forebears had amassed. She had had it valued on taking over the estate and learned that her father's works were of the most significant interest. Judging by the tone of the report she'd received, this did not represent high praise. She had herself always questioned the merit of the books chosen to grace those lovely mahogany shelves and strongly suspected that more than a few had been selected for their size, or the colour of their binding, not to mention their affordability. It was not rare for her to catch her father in the act of snatching a volume out of the leavings from the local church rummage sale.

Still, the library had been a source of family pride for generations, and its maintenance was fully guaranteed through the generosity of the estate. The librarians to whom her father and grandfather and great-grandfather had offered the position held it as a sacred trust; none had ever been fired. She could not even imagine how to go about telling Mr. Harrington to leave. Had she not heard that in these modern times there was some legal requirement to give proper notice? She did not know what might constitute "proper", but feared it would involve additional weeks spent enduring the attentions of a fish-headed penguin-man. Surely no one could expect her to live under such conditions.

Perhaps she could take a trip…but then what would become of her precious pups? So few hotels of quality were enlightened enough to welcome dogs of their size, and it would be impossible to leave them behind.

It would be much better, really, if Mr. Harrington could be persuaded to leave. Not that anything was likely to woo him or his prodigious appetite from his career and accommodation at Culpepper Manor.

Miss Culpepper stopped her pacing, her hands reaching out from habit to the heads of her ravenous dogs, as she considered the possibilities of Mr. Harrington's appetite…

*　　*　　*

Mr. Harrington looked into his reflection and saw a man who was torn between satisfaction and fury. Damn her! And damn that shop! And damn all mushrooms, while he was at it. One hand crept instinctively to his belly and caressed it, as if to further worship the delectable soup that lay comfortably within.

His plan had failed. Miss Culpepper had not worn his birthday tribute long enough to break out in the painful hives that would send her into a bath softened with baking soda, from whence her librarian could dispatch her by drowning. Drowning would have been so simple, and it appeared that hives were the only justification for the trouble it would take for her to bathe. She had, it was true, slipped the shawl around her shoulders, but not before noting with pleased surprise that it was woven from artificial mohair. Artificial! The most important word on the label! The one thing he ought to have noticed! It was not as though the price could have given it away. The damned rag had cost a fortune, if a slightly smaller one than that required by the ones on the next table. Those had been absolutely unacceptable. He supposed, now, that they were the real thing. His nostrils flared, and he gripped the sides of the marble sink in his private ensuite bath.

And now, not only did he still have to endure the companionship of dogs, children, and Miss Culpepper—she had grown even more determined to please him. Oh yes, there was no mistaking it. It was not just the way she had been haunting his steps, looking nervously desperate when he turned and saw her. It was much worse than that.

Today, she had cooked for him. Told the chef to take the day off and made his lunch with her own beady hands. Not just any dish, but a dish he favoured above all others: mushroom soup. And not just any mushroom soup, either. She had, on one of those infernal morning walks through the woods at the back of the estate, discovered a cache of false morels, whose flavour, in his opinion, surpassed that of all fungi. True, false morels could sometimes be poisonous. But properly cooked in a well-ventilated room, the poison within them could be driven off to leave the most marvellous treat for one's taste buds. He smacked his large lips at the memory, before pursing them again in revulsion at Miss Culpepper's audacity.

He had to think of another way to dispose of the woman— a more straightforward way, if possible. He glared at his reflection and thought hard.

* * *

Miss Culpepper was decidedly put out. She had had a perfectly brilliant idea to dispense with the problem of Mr. Harrington. Early on, it seemed as though it would go without a hitch. Even though he'd caught her preparing what was meant to be his last meal during a highly irregular visit to the kitchen for what he termed a mid-afternoon snack, and even though he had, to her great surprise, immediately recognized that she had harvested possibly poisonous false morels rather than the true version, he had not shown the slightest hesitation to consume the fruit of her efforts. All that work, and the man was still perfectly healthy. As he ate, he had informed her—with pleasure, if not with the awareness that a cleverer man might have employed— that the downfall of her plan was the technique she had employed in preparing the dish. Had she served the dreadful things raw in a salad, he would not now be here annoying her with inane suggestions regarding the fête.

Frustrated, Wilhemina kicked open the door of the garden shed. In the next instant, three things happened. She reached down to rub her sore foot, a cement pot sailed from the top of the door through the air where her head had been a moment previously, and a wonderful idea unfolded inside her precise, focused mind.

Mr. Harrington, crouched on the ground near the switches for the Culpepper Estate's garden railroad, felt a heat spread across his cheeks not prompted by the soaring temperatures of this July afternoon.

First, Miss Culpepper had refused to retain an appropriate position under the cement pot he had propped up over the door of her beloved retreat, the shed where he knew she enjoyed collecting spiders for her disgusting dogs to chase and crush. Next, she had taken him up on his offer to assist with the hateful fête, an offer he had extended only to retain her blind trust.

And now, after granting him time to repair the garden railway for the fête, a task that would normally be a mixed pleasure to him—he loved trains, but hated sharing them, particularly with the rambunctious children for whose entertainment the railway had been maintained—he found that she had already resolved the one problem whose solution had eluded him for months.

She had fixed the short in the branch line.

Mr. Harrington rose to his feet, and glared up at the front of the house where Miss Culpepper sat on her bedroom's balcony, gently swaying back and forth on the old swing that hung there. Noticing that her eyes were trained upon him, he forced a smile and waved, and while executing the motion shifted his own gaze to the wooden support structure for the balcony on which she so often took the early morning air. His smile became genuine. Mr. Harrington had a new idea, and this time, it was one that could not possibly fail.

* * *

"Waving at me, and with such familiarity! The nerve!" At dusk of the day her cleverest plan yet had become a spectacular failure, Wilhemina Culpepper was still livid. She sat at the mirror of her dressing table and brushed her heavy hair with fierce strokes, having read in her youth that this technique would evenly distribute the natural oils in which she took such pride.

She had been very much looking forward to watching Mr. Harrington electrocute himself during branch line repairs, after she had tangled some of the wires and placed others nearer the water of the creek than strictly advisable. She had not done this without referring to her own father's work on electricity and felt particularly wounded on that account, as though her late parent had let her down in her hour of need.

There seemed so few options remaining to her. She could not shoot the man. Indeed, she did not possess a gun, all firearms having been removed from the house after that unfortunate incident between her father and the milk delivery man. There was a ceremonial sword hanging on the wall of Father's study, but she suspected that using it would make a terrible mess. It also lacked something of the finesse she would require if she were to catch Mr. Harrington by surprise. Her dear dogs were too kind to do the job for her. Even if they were not, she suspected that the city to which she paid taxes might have something to say that neither she nor they would enjoy hearing about dogs who killed a human.

There was no objection when they killed other things, of course. And sometimes those other things were dangerous in themselves…

Miss Culpepper put her hairbrush down and moved to the wardrobe where she kept her most precious items. It seemed that a call to Mr. Harrington's room was in order.

*　　*　　*

"If this does not work," Mr. Harrington muttered as he dragged his heavy form up an alarmingly rotten ladder outside the house in the dead of night, "I might have to give notice after all. The way she stared at me tonight when she asked me to pick up supplies for the fête in the morning—she seems more infatuated with me now than ever before. It is without question enough to make a grown man scream in terror."

In fact, he had been more inclined to scream at the sight of his employer, her hair slick with a fresh layer of whatever salad dressing she saw fit to pour over it, than he had at the leggy spider crossing his starkly white bedspread half an hour previously. If only Miss Culpepper were so easy to kill.

And so she might be after all, Mr. Harrington told himself, squeezing a pair of pliers around a rusty bolt.

*　　*　　*

Miss Culpepper looked desolate as she stepped onto her balcony the next morning, a heavily bound copy of *War and Peace* in her hand. The innocent looking, yet highly venomous spider she had tossed into Mr. Harrington's bedroom seemed not to have done him any harm.

"Perhaps it was hurt in the landing," she reflected. "Or perhaps it didn't care to bite such a poor specimen."

She watched the man's car pull out of the driveway and pass slowly in front of the house. He was watching her again, his expression hungry, as though he could not bear to be out of her presence for half the time it would take to pick up paper plates and party streamers. She tossed her book onto the porch swing and sank, with her weight on her elbows, onto the balcony railing. Even the sound of wood snapping could not distract her from her despair, though the enormous crash as her book, the swing, and the floorboards immediately beneath it dropped down to the main floor porch did strike her as unusual.

Glancing at the carnage, she made a mental note to call a carpenter, and possibly an exterminator. Then she looked back over the railing to lock eyes with her librarian, who had stopped his car halfway into the road and was staring intently at her upright figure. He didn't even notice the cement truck barrelling out of her neighbour's construction site.

*   *   *

What an attractive man the funeral director is, Miss Culpepper thought admiringly, as she signed the contract for Mr. Harrington's burial arrangements. So intent on his work, so warmly impersonal, so completely unaware of me as anything but a grieving source of income. I must invite him for dinner some time.

She always had loved the thrill of the chase.

Mary Keenan is a writer and editor whose short stories have appeared in Storyteller *magazine, The Ladies' Killing Circle anthology* Fit To Die, *Crime Writers of Canada's holiday collection* Blood on the Holly *and the first* KnitL *anthology, published by Three Rivers Press. When she is not writing, she is updating her procrastination diary at* www.marykeenan.com.

Cobwebs

Lorie Lee Steiner

Brookfield is a lovely place, downright charming if you go in for that "old folks come with wheels" environment. I do not. I would prefer to use the same pair of legs the good lord gave me, though lately I'm afraid the bones have exceeded their best before date. Spongy is the best way to describe them, like walking on stilts made of angel food cake. The skin down there, too, has changed, become curiously patterned with cobwebs the colour of ink stains. Sometimes at night, when it's dark, and still, and that confounded tingling starts, I take comfort in the thought that it's only the Daddy Long Legs from the corner above my bed, come down to weave blue silk across my shins. It's better than being alone.

My stepsister put me here. Danella. She's younger by fourteen months, big as a house, and dumb as a post. Her only claim to fame was a lucky ticket on the Irish Sweepstakes back in the seventies. She and that rat-faced husband of hers lived high on the hog for a while after she won, but when the money ran out, he did too, and poor Danella ended up crying the blues on my doorstep. I always was a sucker for a sob story, so I let her in. Thirty-two years ago this week, and damned if she's not still there in Holly Cottage, drinking tea from my Royal Albert and rocking on the front porch like she owns the place. (Must make a note to change the will.)

I was perfectly content hobbling around my pretty little stone house—in spite of Danella's presence. Sure, the going was getting slow, but I had Shorty, my orange Tabby, to keep me company and, besides, once you hit eighty, there's no rush. Then one day I came home from the fruit market and, out of the blue, everything changed.

Danella was on the front porch, shoe-horned into her cushy rocking chair, when the bus dropped me off. She watched me struggling up the walk with a basket of fresh peaches in one hand and my cane in the other and didn't lift a pudgy finger. When I finally did reach the veranda, I found her blubbering into my favourite handkerchief; the lacy turquoise one with daisies and buttercups embroidered on the corners.

"Somebody die?" I asked her. It's a perfectly valid question at our age. Her Plumpness ignored it and started in on me instead.

"Oh, Hilda, just look at you, dear, hardly able to make it up the sidewalk. It pains me to even watch. You're going to need a wheelchair before long, I'm afraid. And I hope you're not expecting me to push you. I'm not a strong woman, you know."

No, you're not, I thought. You're fat and lazy, and you stink to high heaven. I held my tongue and focused on a big-bellied yellow spider hugging the fretwork above her, willing it to drop down and stick its fangs into that smug face. No such luck. The creature didn't so much as twitch when Danella leaned forward and dropped her little bombshell.

"And just how do you think you're going to do the stairs, Hildy? Your bed's up there, and so is the bathroom. I can't possibly pick you up if you fall. I think it's time we talked about other arrangements for you."

My hand was white-knuckling the cane. I wanted to crack it right across her empty skull. Other arrangements, my arse! The nerve of that cow!

I remember gritting my dentures and saying something sweet like, "Oh, Nellie, aren't you just chock full of sunshine today. Now don't get yourself all in a tizzy over me. I can take care of myself."

Then I plunked the peach basket down just out of her reach and went into the house for a piddle—getting angry really makes me have to go. I think I was about halfway up the front staircase when the old gams gave out, and I tumbled like Jill, all the way down the hill, to Jackson Memorial Hospital. My memory's a little foggy on the details. I might have been knocked out. Anyway, they stitched me up, gave me a bed for a couple of days to heal the ribs, then I was shipped out here to Brookfield.

Danella must have given them one doozie of a story—poor distraught caregiver "just can't do any more." Boohoo. She certainly couldn't do any less. I haven't seen her once since I moved in. But then visitors are a rare commodity here. The hunchbacks and drool tend to make them uncomfortable—though I can't for the life of me figure out why. Dementia is only a state of mind, after all, it's not like it's catching.

Mrs. Corey, my flatmate next door here, has it—the Old Timers. She sits in front of the telly, day in and day out, reciting her special recipe for dandelion wine. And Freddie Jenkins, over there by the window (Jinx they call him), he's still back in the thirties running bootleg with his wire-haired terrier Joe. I'm not sure what the deal is with Henrietta, across the hall, but you don't want to be near her on "poop Tuesday".

This is my room—213. I don't understand why they stuck me in a home with all the fruitcakes. Primrose Manor is a much nicer place—I hear they have double beds, and baby kitchens, and big comfy LaZBoys that lift you straight up and out of the chair when you push a button. All I have is a metal toilet and sink, and this skinny bed with the straps on the sides. I told them they don't need to use them, but I think they're afraid I'll fall out, what with my legs being so bad.

Well, I'll be damned, would you look at that? Right here under my pillow. I've been looking all over for this hanky—it's my favourite, you know. I spent hours stitching these buttercups and daisies. Huh, they still didn't get the stains out, even after I told them how. I hate to complain, but the laundry service here really isn't up to snuff.

That's all right, though. I won't be staying much longer. Danella's back at the house with the workmen right now, getting Holly Cottage ready for my homecoming. She's so good to me. That's why she hasn't been for a visit, I bet she found my drawings in the hidey hole, and she's going to surprise me. I have everything all planned out. The front parlour is going to be my bedroom—with a huge bay window and a fireplace. And the pantry off the kitchen will be my bathroom—painted pink. And I'll have a ramp from the side veranda right to the rose garden, so I can get around just fine in the wheelchair and I won't need the blasted cane any more...where is that thing anyway?

"NURSE! Where is my cane? Somebody's taken it. YOU! What are you doing with my walking stick? GIVE IT BACK, IT'S MINE. In your hand, it is NOT a hat, that's my cane. I'll have you arrested, if you don't...

NO! Please, nurse, I don't want to go to bed. Don't want any more blue pills...please..."

*　　*　　*

He's coming down the wall now, Daddy Long Legs, even in the dark I can see him. He's coming to spin cobwebs around my cane and put it back together. It's broken, you see, it cracked in half that day on the porch when I split her head open. BANG! She put me here you know, Danella. It's all her fault. And she hasn't even come to see me…not once…

Lorie Lee Steiner finds writing in the vintage atmosphere of an 1860s heritage cottage an inspiration. Her entertaining stories have appeared in The Country Connection Magazine, Our Canada, *and* Learning Through History, *and she is now hard at work on her first whodunit novel. A member of Crime Writers of Canada, she credits a childhood obsession with the writings of Dame Agatha Christie for her love of all things mysterious.*

By the Book

Joy Hewitt Mann

Sing a song of sixpence
A socket full of wood.
Try to mug an old lady
And she will get you good.
When my cane splintered
It went into your brain.
Oh wasn't it a dainty switch
To make me Killer Kane?

Courting Frank

Susan C. Gates

I'd been "fallen away from the Church" until a recent brush with my mortality forced a re-examination of my faith—and many other aspects of my life. I've never hauled myself from bed for church on a glorious summer Sunday. But that day, I had a post-church brunch date—with a man. Lately my social life had been as dry as a hag's hands, so I was excited about this third date.

Frank Manette was handsome in a subtle way. His mid-life dark looks weren't flashy, but the fresh shave, a pressed shirt and khakis reflected his reserved demeanor. I was attracted to his lack of bravura and aggressiveness—unlike most men from my past.

He waited for me out front of St. Timothy's. "Good morning, Bernadette." Frank said as we climbed the stone steps. "A great day to be alive, isn't it?"

"You're right! Want to skip church and stake out a primo patio for brunch?"

Surprise registered on his face before he laughed. "What a kidder."

I never kidded about food! Thankfully, my growling stomach quieted as Frank placed a warm hand on mine and smiled down at me.

In the after-service coffee line, I was startled by a deep voice.

"A friend of Frank's, are you?"

Hot coffee sloshed from my mug, landing first on my skirt then on my sandals. At thirty-seven, I should know myself better—white wasn't a smart fashion choice for me.

Swallowing my curses, I looked up to see a brawny man with a deep tan—someone who lacked respect for my personal space.

I set my mug down on a nearby table, wiped my right hand with a serviette, then offered it. "That's right. I'm Bernadette. And you?"

"George Bowman." His grip was strong.

"How do you know Frank?"

"Met him when he first arrived at St. Timothy's a few years back. You look familiar. Have we met?"

"Perhaps you've read my byline. I cover the police and court beats for the newspaper."

"Huh," he said, blasting me with hot breath from his snort. "I'm a cop, so maybe that's it."

I sensed how intimidating this guy must be on the street. I widened the distance between us. "I don't recall seeing you around."

"They have me riding a desk now—till I take retirement." Bowman shifted his weight. "What's the last name?"

"Doolan."

"A Mick?" Hands on his hips, practically groping for the butt of his absent gun.

"Officer Bowman, how are you?" The Reverend Penny Perrin wore a lavender print dress. While shaking his hand, Penny grabbed his forearm with her left hand. For a whiff of a woman, she'd managed to exert her authority over the cop. I was impressed. "How wonderful to make Bernadette feel welcome. I suppose you know many of the same people."

"So far, just Frank Manette." Bowman crossed his thick arms over his chest.

Frank caught my attention from across the room. Using two fingers, he made a walking motion and nodded toward the door.

"Ah, yes. Justice, punishment and redemption. Common threads for you two." The minister smiled. "Sorry to interrupt, but I must steal George. Something only he can help with," Penny said, taking Bowman by the crook of his arm.

A woman in a taupe power suit, two lanky teenagers hovering at her elbows, had cornered Frank. Armed with a fresh cup of coffee and pretending the brown blotch on my skirt was perfectly normal, I joined them.

"Bernadette!" Frank beamed at me. "Meet Gillian and her kids."

I smiled at this woman who vibrated tense energy and said, "I can't get over how many young people are part of this parish."

"It's the music," she said, her gaze glued to Frank. "The choir, the band, the plays. A busy teen is a happy teen, I say."

Her son hid behind long bangs. His younger sister rolled her kohl-lined eyes, swung out her shiny blonde hair and cracked a large bubblegum balloon.

Gillian yanked the insolent girl by her arm, forced her to attention then yanked up the zipper on her pink cardigan to cover a maturing bosom.

"Didn't you tell me you wanted to learn the guitar? You've been on my case day and night! 'All the cool kids get lessons!'" Other conversations in the room paused at the shrill.

Whoa. Gillian needed to recalculate her lithium dosage. She turned back to Frank.

"I know your schedule's full, but I'll make it worthwhile.

Charge the top rate, and I'll bring them to you. Even if you would just take my daughter for now."

Should I say something to help Frank out? Something more constructive than planting my Shanghai-heel into this woman's Pilates-toned butt?

Ruth Kuhn stepped into our little circle. I knew Ruth as a retired parole officer, famous for her no-nonsense, commanding style with the worst offenders.

"Gillian?" Ruth's tone caused the over-wrought woman to back away from her ledge of parenthood hell. My sympathy, however, lay with the teens. "Is there a problem here?" Ruth turned an imperious stare from Gillian to Frank.

"No problem, Ruth." Frank sidled in behind me. "Gillian's disappointed that I can't take on new students."

Frank's damp palm cupped my elbow. Eew! Honestly, Gillian's unrelenting insistence made me uncomfortable, too.

"Good heavens, isn't that the truth?" Ruth said. "We keep Frank pretty busy around here, Gillian. Surely a woman of your position will be able to find another music teacher for Kirsten, someone who's good with teens."

I'd started to think of Ruth as our deliverance from Gillian, but what did this old battleaxe know, anyhow? "I think Frank's very good with kids," I said.

"I've promised Bernadette brunch." Frank steered me toward the exit. "Must be a man of my word, right Ruth?"

"I'll be in touch." Ruth's parting remark was drowned out by my rolling stomach. Talk of brunch had triggered an overwhelming craving for eggs Benedict.

Never stand between a Doolan woman and her next meal.

*　　*　　*

After a successful brunch, I'd asked Frank to join me for Sunday dinner at my friend Marianne's. Uncharacteristically rash of me, but presentable men in my age bracket were as rare as original programming on Saturday night television.

When Frank was settled with a beer and chatting comfortably with other dinner guests on the patio, I excused myself.

"I'm going to give Marianne a hand," I whispered.

"Can I help? I peel a mean potato."

"No—relax, enjoy."

I headed to the kitchen. And was promptly whacked on the shoulder.

"Mother of God," I hollered, wrenching a plastic tray from Marianne's grip. "Have you flipped your lid?"

Don't you remember?" She laughed. "After your scum-bag fiancée hit the road, you said, 'If I ever decide to date again, smack me upside the head'."

"We're just friends," I huffed.

"Hello?" Marianne pinched my arm. "You never bring 'just a friend' to Sunday night supper. Where'd you meet him?"

"At church," I mumbled.

"What?" A gurgle bubbled in her throat. She made the sign of the cross. "Your mother must be over the moon—back in the Pope's graces and seeing a good Catholic boy!"

"Chill!" I wandered over to the fridge and pulled out a beer. "It's the Anglican church where that hospital chaplain was reassigned. She'd been so kind to me, I thought I'd give it a try." I popped the cap and chugged beer.

Marianne washed some plump tomatoes. "And?"

"And nothing. I met Frank at Coffee Hour."

"What's he do? Ever married? Kids? Does he dance? Where's he been all these years?" She turned to face me, her upturned hands dripping juice.

"He works with the John Howard Society helping convicts reintegrate into society. He's had relationships before, but never married. Almost made it down the aisle once, but her parents broke them up. No kids. Don't know if he dances. He completed a master's degree at Queen's."

Marianne's pubescent step-daughter, Chloë, shot through the patio doors, grabbed a guitar from the floor, whistled back around and slid the door closed with a window-rattling smack.

"Hmm, I see he's good with delinquents." Marianne pointed out the window. "The ever-charming Chloë deigned to talk to him. She hasn't spoken to me since we picked her up from her mom's Friday."

I watched Frank inspect the instrument Chloë had slipped over her shoulder. He listened to her strum a chord, then directed her to tune some strings.

"He seems comfortable with kids. Said he'd like to have a few himself. Doesn't think late thirties is too old."

"Whoa! Aren't you getting ahead of yourself?" She wrapped me in a bear hug. "I'd hate to see you hurt again."

"It's bound to happen." I pulled away from her embrace.

Marianne stacked plates. "You a crime reporter, him a con-lover—how's that going to work? He is cute, though. Is he a good lay?"

"Marianne!" I roared, throwing a package of paper napkins at her.

I was loath to admit our physical contact had been minimal. Was I even ready for intimacy? I needn't have worried. After dinner, Frank dropped me off at the entrance to my apartment building with an awkward hug and a shy smile.

Yup, the weekend was over.

*　　*　　*

Crime reporters receive their fair share of anonymous tips. So discovering a 'blind' e-mail Monday morning sent my adrenalin pumping. I opened a message with the subject line "You Should Know", and read:

Your new boyfriend's nothing but trouble. Frank Manette's a ticking bomb. Get away.

Coffee spewed from my mouth. I blinked, wiping furiously at the screen, trying to reread the message.

If they hadn't used Frank's full name, I'd have written this off as a crank letter. Even my mother didn't know I was dating.

What the devil did it mean? Had Frank told an old girlfriend he was seeing me? It was pretty easy to get my work e-mail address. Was a spurned ex trying to break us up?

Nobody manipulates Bernadette Doolan.

When life throws me fastballs, I call Marianne.

"Why don't you just ask him?" Marianne said, ever the pragmatist.

"Are you crazy? You never ask an interviewee a single question until you've done your research and mapped out an attack."

"Well, what do you know about Frank? Have you checked him out?"

"I met the man at church, for God's sake."

"So?"

"No," I finally admitted. I started typing furiously into my browser.

"Well, you'd better find out," Marianne said. "The last thing you need is another jerk in your life. Oh, and my beleaguered husband plans to take his wretched girl-child to Frank for guitar lessons. It's all Chloë talked about. So let me know, okay?"

Within seconds, I was able to confirm Frank's address and phone number. A resident of a run-down apartment in the Canal district for the past three years. No previous listing in the city.

A few minutes later, I'd found no mention of him on the John Howard Society website. Calling them would be a waste of time—damn privacy laws. His name appeared on St. Timothy's website as an assistant music director and founder of the folk choir. The local Craigslist advertised his guitar lessons. Couldn't find him listed as a recent Queen's graduate or in their alumnae newsletter. What had he studied? Damned, if I knew.

It was pretty obvious who had done most—all right, all—of the talking so far in our courtship. Frank was a good listener, he hung on every word and took what I said to heart—very appealing, indeed.

Enough guessing. I called and invited him to dinner.

*   *   *

Late afternoon delivered the full force of an Ottawa Valley thunderstorm. I drove downtown with my headlights on, wipers on max. He'd suggested the Elgin Street Diner. Thwarted in my search for a legal parking spot, I whipped out my press pass, popped it on the dash and ran. My curls had sprung into a frenzy with the day's high humidity, so the short dousing provided a welcome antidote.

Having scored a booth, Frank waved in greeting. His soaked windbreaker suggested he'd walked. Droplets clung to his eyelashes in a tantalizing fashion.

Smarten up, girl! Keep your wits about you. A windbreaker? Only grandpas wore them.

While we waited for our food to arrive, I tried some gentle probing questions about former girlfriends.

"Really, Bernadette, I haven't dated in quite a while. While I was in Kingston, I had more important things on my mind." A warm, reassuring smile and a pat on my hand. "There hasn't been anyone serious for a long time. This," he pointed between us, "is quite new for me. Honest."

Harumph. When an interview subject says "Honest", my antenna goes up. "What did you study at Queen's?"

"Well, mostly sociology at the undergrad level. Then criminal psychology and offender treatment for my Master's. Did you study journalism at Carleton?"

"Yeah, but that was more than a few years ago." Oops, look how he'd changed the subject back to me. "So your education prepared you to work for the John Howard Society?"

I'd lost his attention. Frank was staring over my shoulder to the far side of the diner.

"Earth to Frank."

"Oh, sorry. Thought I recognized someone."

The arrival of two humungous plates brought our thoughts back to the table. I waited until Frank forked in clumps of poutine and laid waste to half his burger—which didn't take long. I took a copy of the e-mail from my purse and slid it across the table upside down so he could read it.

A look of bewilderment crossed his face. I waited for his explanation.

He started choking, his face reddened then paled. I pushed a glass of water his way. He knocked it over, clutching for his throat. Frank gasped for air.

Before I could slide off my bench to get to him, a man was at Frank's side.

The rescuer grabbed him around the neck with one arm and used his other to haul my date out of the booth by his belt.

"Hey! Back off, that's not the way you do the Heimlich!" Frank's face was turning a dusky shade of blue.

I grabbed Frank just below his diaphragm, knit my fists together and heaved toward his spine with all my might. A glob of cheese curds flew out of his mouth and onto the chest of...George Bowman.

Bowman flicked the offending food back in Frank's direction. "Quite the gentleman, huh?" A smirk cut across his weather-beaten face.

The diner's manager was all over us like a grease on a griddle, anxious to avoid a lawsuit. Frank didn't feel much like eating any more. My appetite had dampened, too, but I asked for my shake to go.

"I see George around the neighbourhood a lot," Frank said, as I helped him into the passenger seat of my car. "Do you think he lives nearby?"

"He strikes me as a suburban guy. But the police station is just down the street. Remind me to ask Bowman where he learned his emergency services training."

A cell phone trilled, and before I could find mine, Frank was speaking.

"Hello?" He sounded surprised and curious. "Yes. Okay. All right. Sure, Ruth."

"Ruth? Ruth, who?" It's difficult to put your hands on your hips for emphasis when both were required on the steering wheel.

"Ruth Kuhn," Frank said.

Frank didn't seem the least bit clued into my curiosity. I elbowed him. Confusion met my chilly stare. "From St. Timothy's, remember? Could you drop me off there instead of home?"

I bit my tongue, gunned the engine, made an illegal U-turn and headed north on Elgin. He wasn't well enough to finish a dinner date with me, but he was well enough to run when Ruth called? How did she have his cell phone number, when I didn't?

"What's up?" I tried to keep my tone below a whine. After all, we had nothing exclusive and single, straight, church-going men were a rarity in Ottawa.

"She wants to talk to me," Frank mumbled, "about a client."

"I thought she was retired."

"It's a volunteer thing."

No time for further questions, we'd arrived at the church. Frank planted a peck on my cheek, smiled, said thanks and was gone.

I turned the fan to defrost—either the humidity was climbing again or steam was coming from a mysterious source inside my car. I'd garnered very few answers and several new questions. Ruffles potato chips and a box of chocolates called me home. Junk food therapy and my Internet connection might help calm me.

*   *   *

Tuesday morning dawned hot and humid. My sugar levels still revved on high, and my ankles had puffed up like marshmallows. You'd think Frito Lay could do something about that.

All I'd learned from Google was that Ruth Kuhn co-ordinated St. Timothy's Circles of Support Program, whatever they were. I could use one of those myself—one for cranky reporters who had to sit through brain-drillingly-boring legal motions on butt-numbing court benches.

By lunch, I was going crazy. Who could I trust to be straight with me?

I reached Penny Perrin at her home office.

"Lovely to hear from you." The Reverend's happy voice always unearthed her faint British accent. "How are things?"

"I'm fine. Could you tell me about the Circles of Support?"

"I thought you would know about them in the course of your work."

I assured her I didn't, reminding her I'd been off the job for several months. Her answer stunned me.

"Bernadette?" Penny's worry crackled over the line.

My stomach lurched. Finally, my tongue moved. "St. Timothy's supports pedophiles?"

"Not just pedophiles, other sex offenders, too. Goodness, Bernadette, I thought you knew. Hasn't Frank discussed this with you?" The minister's words tumbled in a rush of explanation. "It's a Corrections Canada initiative—one Ruth championed in the years before her retirement. She's poured her heart and soul into setting up the pilot project here with us."

"How can the Church be involved with this?" I couldn't wrap my head around the concept.

"What's the alternative? These guys have a high recidivism rate, and they usually complete their full sentences without benefit of any kind of day parole or re-entry programs. The Circle volunteers meet with them weekly, helping them reintegrate into society and holding them to account so they don't re-offend."

"I get that. But why the Church? Haven't there been church officials who have served time for molestation? What about their victims?" Acid cut a nasty swath through my gut. "What about sin and evil?"

"You're right, of course. Even more reason to exercise some responsibility for prevention, don't you think? And Bernadette—you're forgetting—forgiveness plays an even greater role in Christian faith. A more difficult act, indeed."

Penny Perrin was a force. I changed tack. "So Frank's helping with these Circles because of his job with the John Howard Society?"

I heard an intake of air. "Frank is indeed involved with one of the Circles. He told you he's employed with the JHS?"

"He said he works with JHS. So he must be a volunteer?"

My stomach was doing back flips.

"Ask Frank." I heard pencil-drumming on a desktop. "If you don't get satisfactory answers, call me back. I have other calls to make right now. We'll be in touch." And she was gone.

*   *   *

When court adjourned for the day, I fired up my laptop, only to find another blind e-mail message. My reflux flipped to "Broil".

It's The Circle, fool! Check court records from the early 90s for Francesco Amali. Tick. Tock.

Who was this nosy Parker? Sounded less like a scorned girlfriend, more like that charming George Bowman. It had to be someone who knew about court proceedings as well as the Circles of Support. Ruth Kuhn sprang to mind. Perhaps privacy issues prevented Penny from telling me directly?

I called our IT security guy to see if he could trace the origins of the message. "Sure, give me a week," was his uproarious reply.

With a few keystrokes, I signed into the online database of Federal Criminal Court proceedings and typed in the suggested name. "No online record," was the response, along with a docket reference number for the paper file. The newspaper was down to one in-house librarian, but she was a crackerjack. She promised to locate the fifteen-year-old material and e-mail me the scanned pages pronto.

Now what?

I called Frank.

"Sorry I can't take your call right now, I'm either out or with a student." Beep.

Doolan women don't sit on the sidelines.

I tried newspaper reports for the years 1990-96, finding several from the *Toronto Star*.

November 19, 1991: "Folk singer, 24, arrested. Francesco Amali of Mississauga was charged with sexual interference and statutory rape of three female students, aged 12 to 15. Parents threaten to sue parish priest and school board for recommending Amali."

March 28, 1993: "Forensic psychiatrist testifies Amali is psycho-socially stunted, particularly when it comes to engaging in romantic relationships with women his own age. 'He sees himself as a peer of these girls, thus, unable to comprehend the gravity of his situation.' The doctor also testified Amali was not developmentally delayed in his mental capacity nor would he label him a violent offender."

October 12, 1993: "Amali found guilty, sentenced to twelve years. Families outraged sentence amounts to only four years for each victim."

Marianne called while I was waiting for Amali's photo to download.

"So, what's the scoop? What did you learn about Frank? I assume it wasn't anything horrific, or you would have called me back. Step-brat's mother couldn't handle the whining. She's taken Chloë for her first lesson."

"She's what?" My eyes were glued to the monitor as the press photo appeared, strip by pixelated strip. "Where's she taking Chloë? When?"

"To Frank's apartment. For guitar lessons! Right now. Are you listening to me?"

I squinted at the grainy image. Dreamy Mediterranean eyes, sharper features, about ten pounds lighter, more hair—but I knew this man. Bile shot up my throat.

"Holy Mary, Mother of God. Marianne, I gotta go."

*   *   *

I careened over speed bumps and honked every glacial motorist out of the passing lane. Pressure built inside my banging skull.

I scouted for parking spots half a block from Frank's apartment building. Nothing. All the spots in front were full, and someone had even abandoned a gold-coloured sedan in the driveway.

I didn't have time for this! I wheeled into the mouth of the lane and angled onto the patch of front lawn. Racing into the foyer, I rang Frank's buzzer. No answer. I pounded the glass door and rang all the buzzers.

Someone tapped my shoulder.

"Problem, Doolan?" Frank Bowman towered over me.

The shock of seeing the cop had me stuttering. "I...don't know. I'm not sure..." What if Frank hadn't harmed Chloë? Would Bowman jump to conclusions and arrest him anyhow?

"Bernadette?" Chloë stood at the opened lobby door, her thin face ashen with anxiety. "Did my step-mom send you? Something's wrong upstairs. We don't know what's happening."

Behind her, I saw the girl from St. Timothy's sobbing into a cell phone.

"Anyone hurt?" Bowman brushed past me and cast a glance between the girls and up the stairs, where I spotted a trail of blood.

Chloë shivered, but shook her head, "No, we're okay, but

two other people showed up. The first one threw us out of Frank's. There was a big scene or something. Only one has come back down."

"Christ," Bowman hissed, drawing his service revolver.

He took the stairs two at a time, turning to yell at me, "Stay," as I began to follow.

"Manette," Bowman hollered when he reached the landing. "Police! Get down on the floor, I'm coming in."

I heard the door to Frank's apartment bang open, wood cracking from the blow.

No gunfire, no yelling, no sounds of a scuffle. I crept up the stairs. An eerie calm greeted me at the gaping entrance to Frank's apartment.

I called out, "George? Frank?" I inched my way into a short hall.

Frank's sparsely furnished apartment was a shambles. A guitar amplifier had a yawning hole, electrical cords had been yanked from audio equipment, posters ripped from the walls. All that remained of an acoustic guitar was its jagged neck and splinters of wood. A shiny teal Stratocaster seemed intact but was smeared with a bloody glob.

At the far side of the room, Penny Perrin sat on the floor, cradling Frank's battered head. Her denim skirt was soaked through with blood, as were the sleeves of her pale blue sweater. Only her white collar had escaped the carnage.

"Penny?"

"He's dead," she said, meeting my gaze. "God bless his mortal soul."

Bowman emerged from a back hall, holstering his gun. He scowled at me. "Get the hell out of my crime scene, Doolan."

He reached down, lifted the Reverend Perrin up by her arm pits and hustled us both out of the apartment to the landing.

Bowman spoke into his radio, "What's the ETA on my back-up? Send a bus, pronto. And the coroner." He barred further entry into the unit.

It was only then that I wondered about Bowman. Had he kept Frank under surveillance all this time, as an off-duty project? I ventured a guess my IT guys would trace the warning e-mails to the police station.

"Penny, what happened in there?" I peered into her large green eyes, but I was pretty sure she hadn't heard me. I shook her arm. "Penny!"

She looked at me and whispered, "He said, 'I thought it would be okay, as long as they came together'."

Her face crumpled when Bowman placed her under arrest, handcuffs snapped over her wrists. One of the responding officers immediately stepped in to separate me from Penny, but not before I heard her mumble, "Bernadette, find Ruth."

* * *

Banished to the lobby, I watched as paramedics, the police forensic collection team and others arrived to attend to the dead. Two officers took statements from the teens.

A female officer escorted Penny Perrin down the stairs and into a waiting police car.

"It wasn't the minister," I heard the other teenager say. "You've got the wrong woman."

Penny's mention of Ruth now made sense. After receiving my phone call, Penny must have called her. As the force behind St. Timothy's Circles of Support, Ruth probably raced over to confront Frank, only to find the girls in his apartment.

Where was she now? I felt ashamed that I'd believed, even for a second, that the minister could harm Frank. I needed to find

Ruth. I slipped, unnoticed, out the rear door to the parking lot.

Proceeding up the laneway to the street, I realized two things. My car was hemmed in by emergency services vehicles. And the gold sedan blocking the lane when I'd arrived was gone.

Could that have been Ruth's vehicle? Where would she have gone?

St. Timothy's was five blocks north of Frank's. Blending into the gathered gawkers, I turned and race-walked to the church.

How had I been so wrong about Frank? He was a shy, gentle man, but he'd also sexually abused adolescents. Blood pounded behind my ears. He was a convicted pedophile living under a different name. Had dating me been part of his treatment? It was because of me that Chloë had been put in harm's way. I ran, gasping, the final block.

A gold Buick was in the small lot, next to a secondary entrance. The church door stood open. Tip-toeing down the darkened hall, I heard a low wail that swung between a loud keening and an injured, wild animal mewing.

Every so often, I made out human words.

"He promised me!"

Passing the Sacristy, it dawned on me that I might be in some danger, but the only object in there that might serve to protect me was the heavy chalice. My Roman Catholic upbringing quickly ruled out that idea. I turned on my cell phone before proceeding to the side entrance of the Chancel.

Ruth Kuhn lay at the altar steps, clutching a crucifix. Her hands and face were streaked with blood.

She cried out, "He betrayed us both, Lord." Ruth rolled from side to side, wailing, "You wanted me to give the pervert a chance. He's destroyed my life's work."

Using both hands, Ruth struck her forehead repeatedly with the large altar cross.

The self-flagellation continued unabated, despite my attempts to intervene. It didn't take a psychiatrist to realize Ruth was in the throes of an emotional breakdown. I called 911.

*   *   *

It took two muscle-bound paramedics and the responding police officer to wrestle Ruth onto a stretcher, where restraints were applied and the crucifix wrenched from her grasp. She's under heavy medication at a forensic psychiatry unit. If she doesn't improve, there will be no justice for Francesco Amali who, by all accounts, had lived a clean life until he'd caved in to the pressure of two mothers desperate to appease their teenaged daughters.

Going out had become way too dangerous for my tastes. Crime reporting was losing its lustre too. And I wasn't at all clear how I felt about my place at St. Timothy's.

Another bomb had gone off in my life. Junk food therapy, retail therapy, even desperate trips to the gym—none of my regular rituals brought me peace.

Time to find a new bomb shelter.

Susan Gates is a reformed banker and a recovering civil servant. An Anglican, Susan lives, writes and, remarkably, still dates in Ottawa. Her work has appeared in the two previous LKC anthologies. She serves on the executive of Capital Crime Writers. Appreciation is extended to the members of her critiquing group, CrimeStarters, and to Carleton University professor Craig Bennell for sparking this story's "what if" question.

Listening In

Liz Palmer

Let us enjoy this blessed silence while we may, Ori." Matthew ran his hand over the soft fur, heard the deep throated purr, and smiled. The perfect companion, quiet, independent and a great listener.

The cat sprawled limply across his knees. "She doesn't like you, my friend. A dirty black beast she called you when she chased you from your own kitchen. And why does she shout at me? Do you think she's under the impression that all people of my age are deaf?

"Senile too, you say. That would account for the way she treats me." He sighed. "I feel most uneasy. She has far too much influence over young Tim. Whatever possessed him to fall for an overbearing, managing Englishwoman?

"Ouch. Be careful." He rubbed his leg where Ori's claws had dug in as he jumped off. "My skin isn't as tough as it used to be. Yes, yes, I'm coming." He pushed himself up and limped towards the French doors, through which the afternoon sun shone on the dust motes that rose from the faded Persian rug.

"Professor, Professor, we're back."

"Ori, your ears are sharper than mine." Matthew opened the door. "Make your escape. I wish I could move as quickly." The cat slipped out and disappeared into the bushes.

Alison, bride of Matthew's only nephew, Tim, swept into the study. "There you are."

No knocking on doors for her, thought Matthew, caught halfway back to his chair. With her fair hair and blue eyes, Tim called her his English rose. He had yet to feel her thorns.

"Oh, heavens. Just look at you, covered in cat fur. And, are those crumbs? What have you been eating?" Alison bustled towards him. He knew she would try to brush the crumbs off, and Matthew found himself backing away like a wayward child. He stopped when he felt the bookcase behind him, gathered his dignity and fended her off.

"Bread and cheese. I know you left soup for me, but I've been enjoying bread and cheese for most of my life without ill effect." He didn't tell her the lentil and bean soups she insisted he eat had given him stomach pains and a nasty case of the runs. "Tim will tell you I'm an old stick-in-the-mud." He looked over to the door, relieved to see the grinning face of his nephew watching him. "Isn't that right, Tim?"

"It's no good, Uncle Matthew, if Alison decides on something, there's no changing her mind, and she's decided to take care of you."

The doting smile Tim bestowed upon his wife sickened Matthew. The sooner they were out of his house, the better. "Did you have any luck with the house hunting today?"

Tim came into the study. "Yep, I think we did. It's the old stone one in Portsmouth Village. It needs a lot of work, but it looks sound, has the requisite number and size of rooms and is in a great location. You liked it, didn't you, honey?"

Both men turned to Alison. She frowned. "Well, I think it has potential. But we would have to look into a lot of things before committing ourselves. Tim, darling, come and help me in the kitchen. I'll bring you a cup of ginger tea after we've had lunch, Professor. That should help you digest the cheese."

"I don't need help…" Matthew began, but Alison had whirled from the room, dragging Tim behind her. Matthew limped to the French doors as quickly as he could. Outside he made his way through the shrubs, pushed aside the tangled honeysuckle and lowered himself onto the bench which stood, almost hidden, beneath the straggling vine. He'd learned a lot whilst resting on this bench.

"…and it really worries me." Alison's clear English voice carried through the window.

"But he's lived here by himself for as long as I can remember. He bought it when he and his wife first moved to Kingston," Tim said.

"His wife? You never told me he'd been married."

"It was before my time. He was already married when Gran and Grandpa emigrated from the UK. Mom's younger, and she came with them, but Matthew came much later, and his wife hated it here. Mom said she suffered from an inferiority complex because she grew up in foster homes and left school at sixteen. She felt out of place in a university town and kept nagging Matthew to go back. When he wouldn't, she left him." Matthew could picture Tim shaking his head as he told the tale. "Hope you're not going to do the same to me, darling Alison."

"As if I would, you silly. But where did she go?"

"Back to England, and he never remarried. I spent a lot of school holidays with him when Mom and Dad were abroad, and he is really quite competent."

The clatter of plates had Matthew straining to hear Alison's response.

"…should say is 'he *was* competent'. He's eighty-three now. A big difference from when you were a schoolboy. Do you really think he takes care of himself? The place was filthy when we arrived. His clothes…well, I wouldn't want you looking like that when you get to his age. He doesn't seem to have any social life, and he talks to that disgusting animal as if it were human. And what sort of a name is 'Ori', anyway?"

"Short for Orion. Hunter in the sky. Matthew is totally absorbed in astronomy. He took it up when he retired from teaching. He must have every book there is on the subject."

"Books! There's enough dust in that study to give a person allergies, and the floor, well it's positively lethal. The things he has strewn around, piles of books, an old iron boot scraper, even an umbrella. It's a huge room and would make a gorgeous sitting room, but he won't let me move anything."

"The umbrella's there because he likes to go out into his courtyard when it's raining. He says it's to remind him of why he left England." Tim laughed. "And he hasn't tripped over anything yet."

"Yet. But I keep picturing him falling over the brolly, banging his head on the iron thing and lying there all night. It haunts me. And we'd feel so guilty. Oh, Tim darling, not so much butter, it's really bad for you."

Matthew willed Tim to tell her he'd eat as much butter as he wanted, but Tim said nothing and Alison ranted on.

"And what about the courtyard? There's another hazard. The paving stones are uneven, and it's full of tangled bushes. It could be lovely. Take the view from the kitchen window here, for instance. We could have a neat row of hollyhocks growing along the wall over there instead of that untidy bluebeard."

Matthew looked across at the blue flowers glowing against the grey stone. True, they were unruly, but the butterflies didn't care.

"Properly landscaped, this area would make a perfect sun trap. but he won't even let me walk in there. Mind you, I have had a little look "

"How did you get in?"

Alison giggled. "I'm not completely decrepit, darling, and this is a large window. I'll show you. He can't see from the study."

Oh, Lord. Matthew looked around for somewhere to hide.

"No, you don't, Alison. Remember, we're just guests."

"But if he saw it already done, I know he would be pleased and…well I've been thinking, Tim, wouldn't it be better for him if we stayed here and looked after him?"

There. She'd said it. Matthew had known all along that Alison coveted his house. It was why she'd turned her nose up at all the places they'd looked at. Not while he lived. He'd suffered enough years with Janet without having his final years ruined by another difficult female. The kettle began its high pitched whistle, and he missed part of Tim's reply.

"…his house."

"Not legally. You told me he'd signed it over to you to avoid inheritance taxes."

"But with a binding agreement that it was to be his home for as long as he was alive."

"He'd have a much better chance of surviving longer if we stayed and cared for him. Think about it. Oh, look. That filthy cat's been on the counter again."

Matthew wended his way back to the study, stepping carefully over the cracked paving stones. He had to get them to leave before Tim started his new job, or he'd be alone with Alison all day. But with Tim utterly infatuated, she had the upper hand. He might employ some of her tactics. A word dropped here and there. Cause Tim to think a bit. He sank into his chair seconds before the door swung open and Alison appeared with the tea. Tim hovered in the doorway, an anxious frown on his face.

"Why, thank you, my dear." Matthew smiled at her, ready with his first shot. "Now I'm going to make a request, and I don't want you to be offended."

"Well, of course, I wouldn't be." She looked at him, head on one side.

"When my door is closed, would you mind knocking before bursting in? I do enjoy an afternoon siesta." He watched the colour rise on her face. "And while it is kind of you to bring me a cup of tea in the morning, seven a.m. is too early. I spend a good deal of the night with my telescope, and I'm sure you'll agree that it's important for the elderly to get enough sleep." Matthew sipped his tea and watched Alison's face. Her lips tightened. He thought she'd like nothing more than to flounce from the room, but she restrained herself and fired back.

"You should have said something before." The sweetness of her voice belied the look in her eyes. "I wouldn't upset you for the world, would I, Tim?"

"Of course you wouldn't." Tim walked over and put his arm around her waist. "Now, Uncle Matthew, you must tell us if we're interfering."

"I'm sure you mean well, but we all have our own little ways. That's why children leave home when they grow up." He yawned and rubbed his eyes.

Tim looked down at Alison. "We must be off. We've lots of things to discuss." He patted Matthew on the shoulder. "Don't forget to tell us if we're crossing the boundaries."

"Will do, my boy. Thank you for the tea, Alison. I am enjoying it."

"But," he muttered, to himself, as soon as the door closed behind them, "the ivy will enjoy it more." He poured the bitter brew into the plant pot and limped over to the roll-top desk. Taking a key from his pocket, he unlocked the desk.

How ridiculous to have to lock things up in his own house. However, he had no intention of letting Alison know he took the occasional drink. She would not approve. He took out the bottle of Glenlivet and measured two tots into a glass. "Ginger tea," he snorted.

He sat by the desk, looking out into the courtyard. It was the reason they'd bought the house in the first place. This secret square around which the house was built. The windows of the kitchen and his bedroom opened on to it, but it was only really accessible from this room. And Alison was right. He had neglected it for too long. The buddleia had gone mad, with fronds of white flowers sagging over a stunted hydrangea. He should have pruned it in the spring, well, each spring, he thought, breathing in the fumes of the scotch, relishing the warmth as it slid down his throat. The bush had grown leggy and weak, and the hydrangeas ought to have been removed years ago. They'd never done well here. He liked the lilac, but if you didn't keep on top of it, it pushed suckers up everywhere. That was part of the problem with the paving stones; lilac roots.

A cramp in his gut interrupted his thoughts. It was time to head for the bathroom again. After the third trip to the bathroom that afternoon, an astonishing thought crept into Matthew's mind.

Was Alison poisoning him?

He'd not had any digestive problems before they moved in three months ago. In fact, he had been fine until Alison insisted on doing the cooking. So far, he'd put his problems down to the change in diet, but could it be more sinister? And if so, what could he do about it?

He grappled with the problem until dinnertime. That was another bone of contention. Matthew normally sat down to eat between eight and nine in the evening, but Alison thought eating late gave one nightmares and served dinner at six.

Perhaps, mused Matthew, sitting down at the head of the table, he could use the early hour as an excuse not to join them.

The dining room fronted King Street, with a view across the park to Lake Ontario. "Lots of wind surfers out this evening." He watched the bright triangles skimming the waves. "I'd like to have tried that. Have you ever done it, Tim?"

"Not yet. But I mean to have a go as soon as we're settled."

"Oh, do you think you should, darling?" Alison came in with two plates. "It looks awfully dangerous." She put a plate down before each of the men and returned to the kitchen for her own.

Matthew stared at his dinner. Mashed potatoes, ground meat and peas. He glanced over at Tim's. Pork chop, roast potatoes and Brussels sprouts. "Tim, does Alison not realize I have my own teeth? I'm fed up with eating mush." He pushed back his chair. "I'm going to call for an Indian take-out."

"What's the matter?" Alison stood in the doorway, her plate in her hand, a bewildered expression on her face.

"Nothing's the matter, honey. Sit down, Uncle Matthew." Tim removed Matthew's plate and replaced it with his own. "We're switching dinners."

"But that's much too rich for your uncle, Tim. I have been trained, remember? I worked in the geriatric department for a year." Alison turned to Matthew. "You're not going to do yourself any good eating this. At your age, you need a bland diet and one that's easily digested. That's why I take the trouble to do yours specially."

Matthew cut into the chop. "I'd rather you didn't, thank you. This will do me nicely."

Alison frowned. "Luckily, I've done extra chops." She went

out with the "special" dinner and came back with a chop for Tim. Matthew felt he ought to get a sample of the meal she'd made for him. He wondered how one went about having things tested for poison.

He declined the jello and took his coffee to the study. Time to make a plan. The first move must be to retrieve part of the dinner Alison had prepared for him. He could do that after they retired for the night, then he would take it to the Faculty Club and talk to some old colleagues. But more urgently, how could he avoid eating things that might be contaminated?

Ori scratched at the glass doors, and Matthew heaved himself out of the chair to let the cat in. A waft of perfume from the buddleia invaded the room as Matthew opened the door, and he stood there for a moment, taking in the softly scented evening air. "Life is too good not to fight for, Ori," Matthew said and went over to the table for his coffee. He swallowed a mouthful before he could stop himself. It tasted awful. But she couldn't have poisoned it, because he'd watched her pouring the three cups from the same pot. But what in God's name was it?

He stomped out to the kitchen and found Tim, bent over the sink scrubbing the grill pan. "Where's Alison?"

"She's gone upstairs to watch *Coronation Street*. She hates to miss an episode. What's up?"

Matthew held out his cup. "What in tarnation is this muck she calls coffee?"

Tim threw back his head and laughed. "Chicory. Awful, isn't it? But Alison is into healthy eating. She's done a lot of research into it, and it's been proven, caffeine is bad for you."

"I'm eighty-three, Tim. I plan to enjoy my last few years of life. I can't get around as much as I used to, but I still get a great deal of pleasure from food and drink. I think it's time to start making my own meals again." He could see Tim was about to protest and went on quickly. "No, I mean it. Eating at the hours you do doesn't suit my constitution, nor does the diet you follow. Tell Alison not to cater for me any more."

Back in the study he chuckled. "That went rather well, Ori, I…" he stopped. The cat was retching violently. With a final heave it deposited a pile of ground meat on the carpet and fled into the garden.

"Tim." Matthew shouted, "Tim."

Tim rushed into the study. "What is it?"

"She fed it to Ori." Matthew noticed his hand shaking as he pointed at the heap on the rug. "She's trying to poison him."

"Now, now. Come and sit down," Tim soothed. "Ori will be fine. He probably ate it too fast." He steered Matthew into his chair, patting him gently. "You rest there for a minute while I clear this up."

Matthew huddled in the chair, his breath coming in short gasps. It had been meant for him. It wouldn't have killed him, but it would likely have made him really sick. Given her more ammunition for persuading Tim they should stay. He passed a hand over his eyes. But what of Ori? Where had he fled to? He eased forward in the chair ready to get up and look for the cat, but before he'd got his knees under him Ori stalked in from the courtyard. He followed his normal pattern, sliding his body against the door frame, caressing the bookcase then jumping onto the desk, where he always paused for a second to see if there was anything worth eating or if there was something he could knock onto the floor.

Relief welled up in Matthew as he watched the cat stop to lick a paw before springing across to the back of the sofa. There was nothing the matter with him. He'd rid himself of the poison. So, too, had Alison, since Tim had apparently flushed the evidence down the toilet.

"See. I told you he'd be okay." Tim thrust a mug of tea into Matthew's hand. "Drink this and don't argue."

Much later that night Matthew sat, with his telescope, at the front of the house. Instead of concentrating on the night sky, he was listening to the conversation being held on the balcony above him.

"That's how it starts."

"What?"

"Alzheimer's, dementia, whatever you like to call it. One of the symptoms is paranoia."

"And you think Uncle Matthew is paranoid?"

"Well, Tim, I wouldn't know what else to call it. He told you I'd poisoned the cat. He knows I fed it his mince, therefore he must think I'm trying to poison him. That's why he wants to make his own meals and doesn't want me to bring him tea."

"I don't know, Ally…"

"Don't call me 'Ally', it sounds so common."

"Sorry, honey. But I'm not convinced that his mind is going. He's real fond of that old cat, and you've made it clear you detest it. I think in the panic of the moment he accused you."

Matthew silently cheered for Tim. Stand up to her, boy. He heard a disbelieving snort come from Alison.

"That's what you think, Alison, but remember I grew up with him, and he isn't that different now. He's independent, likes to do his own thing, and we've kind of taken over and changed his life. That's tough at any age."

"You may be right, darling, but I still think we should hold off making an offer on the house for a few days while we observe him. I have had rather more experience than you with geriatric patients."

"If we don't put one in, we may lose it. It's a good house in a great location and a few minutes bike ride from here. I say we go ahead. I'm sure Sara next door will keep an eye on him. She used to pop in every day before we came, and I can check on him all the time, too."

"Well, he's your uncle. And if you're comfortable leaving him, that's up to you. Personally it would be on my conscience all the time. Brrr, that's a cool breeze."

"You're shivering, sweetheart. Why didn't you say you were cold? Hey, I know how to warm you up."

Oh, Tim, how long before you realize you can never warm her? For Matthew, the discovery had taken too long. His enthusiasm and joy in teaching English literature had absorbed him in the early years of marriage. He'd expected support from his wife while he forged a career for himself. He'd received nothing but antipathy and continual whining. He had not neglected her, he'd been working for their future, but she refused to see it that way. Life without Janet had been much easier.

He abandoned the stars and retired to his room. Tim must be encouraged to stand firm.

In the morning, Matthew waited until he heard Alison turn on the bath water. She would, he knew, spend at least thirty minutes in the tub. He puttered into the kitchen, where he found Tim clearing the breakfast things.

"Ah, Tim. I owe you an apology. I was distraught yesterday, said some stupid things."

"Hey, that's okay. We all say things we don't mean when we're upset." Tim smiled, and his grey eyes twinkled. "What say we make some 'real' coffee while Alison takes her bath?"

They took it into the study. "So she won't smell it," explained Tim. "She's got a thing about it. Ah, there's Ori, looking just fine." He walked over to stroke the cat. "Don't gulp your food down in future, eh. You scared Uncle Matthew."

"I must admit I am rather on edge these days. I'm not used to living with other people. When you asked me if you could come and stay, I hadn't envisaged it being such a prolonged visit." He sipped the coffee, relishing the richness of fresh ground Java beans.

"Me neither. But Alison has something in mind, and it's hard to get her to compromise."

"Some people are like that. They get a mindset, and it's as though they're driving down a highway with a sound barrier on each side. You cannot get through to them. It can be an asset, that kind of ability to focus, but it can be rather difficult at times."

Tim leaned against the door, staring into the courtyard. "Yes. I hadn't really thought about it, but I guess Alison does focus on things. Right now it's your health she's worried about."

"I leave that to the doctor, he is the expert. Has me in twice a year now for a check-up, and the last time he told me he hoped he'd have hearing and eyesight as good as mine when he was my age. The only parts I have problems with are these." Matthew patted his knees. "I can live with that. But if I couldn't read..."

"What are you into now?" Tim came over and picked up the book beside Matthew. *The Big Bang: A History of the Universe.* A bit lowbrow for you, isn't it?"

"I know it's written for the masses, but he has an interesting perspective on some matters. You might enjoy it." He stopped. "Listen. Is that the bath water draining? Perhaps you'd better sneak these cups back into the kitchen before Alison comes down. She certainly has fixed ideas about eating and drinking."

Tim laughed. "That's for sure." He collected the cups and headed for the door. Matthew fancied he had more of a spring in his step than when he'd come in.

The morning coffee became a ritual, and Matthew felt he

was making headway. Despite Alison's protests, Tim put in an offer for the house on Yonge Street, and for the last few days Matthew's bowels had behaved themselves.

On Thursday morning, Tim came in waving a letter. "They've accepted the offer. I must tell Alison."

"I'd like to see her face, Ori," Matthew began, but Ori had followed Tim out, probably heading for the kitchen, and Matthew settled down to read.

Well into an absorbing discourse on black holes, he was startled by shrieks coming from the kitchen. Looking up, he saw Ori come flying through the door, jaws clamped on a large piece of red salmon, with Alison not far behind. Matthew grinned as Ori neared the French doors.

But then Alison snatched the Astronomical Society paperweight from his desk and threw it at the cat. Ori howled, staggered and fell. "Got you," she yelled.

Without thinking, Matthew hurled his book at her. It hit her hard on the back. She arched backwards, her arms going up, tripped over the umbrella and fell with a crash.

"Ori." Matthew pulled himself to his feet, his knees shaking. He shuffled past Alison, who lay so still and on to the silky black body lying by the door. "You nearly made it," he whispered, bending down to touch the soft fur. "You'll be okay, my friend." He creaked upright again. He needed the vet. What was the number? His head felt strange, as though he wasn't really there. He reeled. Have to sit down, he thought and stumbled over to his chair.

"What's going on?" Tim stood in the doorway. "Oh my God. Alison."

Matthew sat in a daze, unaware of the activity exploding around him. He knew he had to do something, something important, but he couldn't remember what.

He heard the grandfather clock in the hall strike and began to count. Eleven. Someone touched his shoulder. "Drink this, Matthew." Sara from next door put a mug into his hand. A young policewoman pulled up a chair and looked closely at him. "The doctor's coming to see you in a minute. Can you tell me what happened?"

"She tried to kill him." To Matthew his voice sounded far away, thin and shaky. He gulped a mouthful of hot, sweet tea.

"Who tried to kill who?"

"Ori. Alison hit him with the paperweight." A tear escaped. He felt it rolling down his face. "That's what I have to do, call the vet. I must call the vet. Look, over there, he's lying…" he pointed towards the French doors. "Where is he? He was there. Who's taken him. Where's Tim?"

"Hey, Matthew, calm down." Sara rested a hand on his shoulder. "No one's touched Ori, he must have got up again. And Tim's gone to the hospital with Alison."

"Is she badly hurt?"

Sara nodded. "I'm sorry. She hit her head on that iron thing near the door."

"Good," said Matthew.

"I don't think you really mean that, my dear." Sara bent down and looked into his eyes. "Would you like me to go and look in the courtyard for Ori, while you tell the constable what happened?"

"Please." Matthew hardly dared hope, but maybe…he stared around his room. It seemed to be full of people. He focused on a policeman standing by the French doors talking with a young man. The policeman had the paperweight in his hand.

"That's what she threw at him," Matthew said, pointing.

"Take your time and tell me from the beginning." The constable had a notebook in her hand.

Before Matthew could speak, Sara appeared at the door, her face a greyish green. She looked at the policeman. "You'd better come." Her voice wobbled.

"What's happened?" He asked.

"It's Ori, isn't it?" Matthew's heart felt tight.

Sara shook her head. "He's okay, just limping. He was hiding in a hole someone's dug. Where the blue flowers were. I got him out then I saw something shiny. I pulled it up. It was a ring." Her voice rose. "And a bone fell out of it. A finger bone. I think I'm going to be sick." She ran from the room.

Within seconds, the room had emptied.

The idea of planting bluebeard on Janet's grave had always tickled Matthew. He heaved himself to his feet. He'd like to finish the chapter on black holes if he had time.

Ori limped into the room, ears back, fur dishevelled. He stalked over to the chair and began to groom himself. Matthew smiled. He picked up the book he'd thrown at Alison and settled down next to Ori. He smoothed the crumpled title page.

"The Big Bang".

"Not a bad title for a murder story, eh, Ori?" he said, reaching over to stroke the cat's head.

Liz Palmer's commute between the Gatineau Hills and the Rideau Lakes gives her ample time to dream up plots, and she loves the challenge of a themed short story. She has been published in almost all of the LKC anthologies and in Locked Up*, a collection of mysteries set on the Rideau Canal.*

The Porsche

Joan Boswell

P erry's in trouble." Marsha's voice quivered.

"Mom, tell me something new. Perry's always in trouble," Harriet replied, holding the phone with one hand and sorting invoices for her accounting clients with the other.

"No, he's not. He's a saint. An absolute saint."

Well, maybe—if the criteria for sainthood required them to live very weird lives. But more like a nut, a fruitcake, a flake. He might be her brother, but she didn't have any illusions about him. What man with two first-class university degrees took what amounted to a vow of poverty and lived in the slums with his social work clients? Maybe a Catholic aiming to be canonized, but her brother called himself a Buddhist, and she didn't think they had saints.

"So, what's happened now?" Harriet asked, although she really didn't want to know.

"Well, he was in the back of the van handing out sandwiches to the homeless, and the driver, stupid man, drove forward unexpectedly, and Perry fell out. He put out his arms so he wouldn't land on his face and broke both wrists and sprained several fingers. He says he'll be fine, but how will he manage with both arms in casts? I've been imagining how I'd cope if I couldn't use my hands and arms. It's impossible."

"What about Summer? Isn't she looking after him? Isn't that what partners do?"

Summer had to be as crazy as Perry if she chose to live with him in a building that Marsha said was a tenement. Harriet had never visited, but she'd seen enough TV shows to figure out what it must be like. Maybe Summer loved him. Love wasn't on Harriet's radar, but on TV people did strange things and said love made them do it, so that might be the explanation.

"Summer is in England at a World AIDS conference."

Harriet guessed where this was going. Time for fast thinking, for the quick double shuffle. Her mother might expect Harriet to leap in and help her brother, but there was no way, no way at all. Mom had always wanted her to be the supportive big sister. She'd refused when she was young, and she wasn't about to start.

When Harriet didn't say anything, Marsha continued. "You know I'd help, but I'm not strong enough to go to him. And with only my bed and the living room love seat, there isn't anywhere he could sleep if he came here. Besides, the nurses drop in at odd hours, and they'd disturb him."

Not strong enough? An understatement. Her mother's metastasized cancer left her barely able to care for herself.

"I'm on morphine, and it's working well. By next week, when it really kicks in, I could help Perry, but that doesn't do him any good right now."

"I suppose not." Morphine was a last ditch medication. "Does Perry know about the morphine?"

"Of course. He visits almost every day. I still expect to recover, but last week, when I knew Perry would be here, I had my lawyer come in. I signed a living will giving Perry power of attorney for health and finances. And, just in case it's necessary, I've put my name on the waiting list for Brook

House, the palliative care hospice."

Oops—this could be bad news. Why had her mother only given Perry the right to make decisions? Shouldn't Harriet have had an equal voice? And why hadn't they told her? She didn't care about health decisions, but what if Perry could cut her out of the will? Maybe this meant her mother had already done that. Time to say the right thing.

"I'm glad you're being so positive. I'm sure you'll get better."

"We'll see. Right now it's Perry we should be talking about. He could stay with you for a few days, couldn't he?"

Not a chance. She invited no one into her condo, but she had to offer an alternative. "That wouldn't work, but I could check in on him at night and make sure he's ready for bed." She thought how much she didn't want to deal with the unpleasant physical tasks this might involve. "Surely his friends in the building are helping."

"You're right, they are—they love Perry and Summer. However, many have their own problems." Marsha's voice brightened. "But there's Russell. How could I have forgotten Russell? Have you met him?"

"I've never been to Perry's place or met his friends." And Harriet would like to keep it that way, but didn't think this was the time to say so.

"Russell is one of Perry's success stories. He lives across the hall. Perry arranged for him to rent the apartment. Russell now has a job and is doing well."

Harriet saw that Marsha expected her to show some interest. She didn't give a fig what Russell did, had done or would do, but she'd go along. "How nice of Perry to help."

"Poor Russell. What he went through in prison. That's what happens when you're chief financial officer of a big company and embezzle to pay for your drug habit."

"And now he's okay?" Harriet asked. Fat chance. A man who sank that low wasn't likely to rise again.

"More than okay. Perry brought him to see me. He's a terrific, positive man. He really has it together. I'm so glad Perry was able to help. Russell's right there across the hall, but he works evenings. I'd feel better if I knew you were keeping an eye on Perry."

"And how does Perry feel? Does he want me to help?" She seriously doubted that he did.

"You know Perry. He says he'll be fine. He dropped in earlier this afternoon. A friend drove him over. Did I tell you that he or Summer or both of them come every day to see me?"

Harriet had managed one quick visit and two short phone calls in three weeks.

Uh-oh. She sometimes wished she were better at navigating her way through life. This was serious. If she wanted to be sure to get her share of her inheritance, she'd better make an effort and turn up more often.

Maybe she should offer to drive Perry places. She shuddered. That definitely wasn't an option. No one ever rode in her vintage Mercedes, her chariot, her pride and joy. Not one speck of dirt or dust marred the interior. Every week she drove it to the car wash and watched while they hand-polished it. Her car. She sighed.

Beautifully engineered cars were works of art. Her gaze turned to the bookcases filled with neatly filed back issues of her favourite car magazines.

"He says he'll cope," Marsha said. "Of course, he's well connected to social services, and he'll get help from them."

"Mom, you could use your money to pay people to come in and make sure he has everything he needs."

"I could, but it's much better if it's a family member."

Her mother's money was an issue with Harriet, who'd once told Marsha that leaving money to Perry was useless; that he wouldn't hang on to it, wouldn't invest it to provide for his old age or buy a house or do any of the sensible things ordinary people did. Her mother's eyes had been cold, and she'd said that what Perry did was his business. Her mother had closed the door on the subject before Harriet could tell her how prudent she planned to be.

She knew she should feel guilty recalling this conversation, but even thinking about inheriting money made her heart pound. She envisaged paying off her condo's mortgage and maybe, just maybe, buying a silver Porsche Turbo Cabriolet. Beautifully engineered, rear-mounted engine, good stability, smooth handling and above all-fast. Perfect. Owning a Porsche was her dream.

"I'll drop by later this afternoon for a visit with you then go to Perry's this evening," Harriet promised.

*   *   *

Harriet used her key to let herself into her mother's light-filled apartment. She called hello.

"I'll be right out. I was napping. Will you make us a cup of herbal tea? I love 'Calm'. Read the promo on the box, it's very funny," Marsha instructed from her bedroom.

Harriet did as she was told and snorted to herself when she read it. Typical hype written to endear the Tazo company to the kind of people who drank herbal tea. Maybe she didn't think it was funny because she wasn't one of them. Wasn't one of any group, if it came to that. And happy to be a loner, to run her own life to suit herself. She rummaged through the cupboard and found a tin containing three lonely digestive biscuits.

Harriet hoped she didn't look as shocked as she felt when she saw her mother. In three weeks, Marsha had lost even more weight and had that large-eyed look that went with cancer-induced starvation.

After taking slow steps across the room, Marsha lowered herself carefully into her recliner. She caught her breath before she pulled a quilt over her knees.

"Summer made it for me. Isn't it lovely?" she said, smoothing the subtly- patterned quilt with almost transparent fingers.

Harriet agreed that it was and thought that if she wanted to stay in her mother's good graces and in her will, she'd better make an effort. She picked up the plate with the three cookies. "Next time I come, I'll bring you lime shortbreads from the bakery you like on Yonge Street," she offered.

"Lovely," Marsha said. She looked at Harriet then closed her eyes briefly as if the sight of her daughter was too much for her to deal with.

As Harriet considered whether this would be a good time to talk about the will again, the doorbell rang and she heard a key in the lock. A cheery-looking middle-aged woman bustled in talking as she entered.

Her mother scrunched her lips into a rueful grimace. "Darling, this is Carol, the V.O.N nurse—it's time for my shot. I'm going to have to send you on your way, but I'm so glad you came."

Maybe that was true, but to Harriet it seemed Marsha looked even happier to see her go. That was nothing new. When they were children, her mother had always preferred Perry.

"After you see Perry, phone and tell me how you think he's doing. It doesn't matter what time it is, because I don't sleep much."

Harriet stood, bent forward, kissed the air next to her mother's cheek and tried not to inhale the pervasive smell of ill health. She drove home breathing shallowly and showered immediately. Clean again, she microwaved a dinner and watched two back to back episodes of *Law and Order.* At eight thirty, she drove to Perry's. She'd considered going by bus to protect her car from neighbourhood vandals, but the thought of people standing close to her on the bus upset her even more than the fear that her car might be damaged.

A developer, anxious for profits, had divided what had been a Parkdale mansion into a warren of apartments. Harriet pushed open the front door and stepped into the tiny vestibule. Cheap plywood doors and artificial partitions left the downstairs hall cramped. Fifteen apartment bells. The unmusical sounds of too many people living too close to one another and the unpleasant smell of cheap cooking assaulted her. The only light came from a dirt-encrusted transom over the front door.

There was no light at all in the stairwell. She longed to fling open the door and bolt for home. But a promise was a promise. Gingerly, she fumbled her way up three flights of steep stairs, glad she had sanitizer in her purse. At the top, she rapped on the south side door.

"Door's open. Come in," Perry called.

Harriet entered a different world. To begin with, there was light, lots of light, and it reflected off pink-tinted, cream-painted walls where mirrors made the space seem bigger than it was. She stared around. She imagined most of the disparate furniture had come from Goodwill. All exposed wood was painted. Most pieces were white, but a navy blue Windsor chair and poppy red desk added zip. Brightly hued quilts, vibrant posters and a multitude of books created a warm, welcoming space.

"Nice apartment," she said. "But shouldn't you lock the doors?"

Perry shook his head and looked down at his arms, both in casts and in slings. "I'm almost helpless, and my neighbours are wonderful, so why would I lock the door?"

As well as Russell, reformed addict and thief, she could just imagine his neighbours—the flotsam and jetsam of the criminal and mental health systems.

"What can I do for you?" Harriet said.

"I'm sure you don't want to do anything. Actually," Perry smiled and looked down at his tartan pajama bottoms. "I'm relieved, if you can stand the pun, and you will be too to know that I can take an arm out of its sling and manage to do the bathroom thing for myself, if I have enough pain killers."

Her apprehension must have been obvious.

Perry nodded toward the door behind her. "Russell, he lives across the hall, did brilliant things to make my life easier. He wrapped my toothbrush, my pen and some cutlery in wads of duct tape." He nodded at his right hand. "See how my fingers are? I can't close them to get a grip, but Russell has made it possible for me to use the few utensils that are important. I'll give them a try tomorrow."

Russell's ingenuity impressed Harriet. She'd steeled herself to do who knew what and was relieved that she wouldn't have to touch Perry. She'd never liked physical contact.

"Russell's coming over in a few minutes. How about you make us all a cup of tea. And if you'd give me two painkillers, that would help."

In the kitchen, tiny but clean, Harriet turned on the gas, boiled water and made tea. Perry managed to clutch a rough ceramic mug with both hands. Harriet did have to put the pills in his mouth, but she managed this minimal contact with what she thought was grace.

"Perry, don't you feel guilty that you can afford a better

apartment, yet you're taking one that someone who really needs it could be renting?" she asked.

Her brother considered her. "Summer and I talked about that. But twenty-two, get that, at least twenty-two and sometimes more people live in the building, and we act as the superintendents. When the toilets break or the heat isn't on, or there isn't enough heat, we mount an assault on the owner." He grinned. "And it must be working. Our lovely slum landlord has offered us much better accommodation in one of his tonier buildings. I think we cost him a lot of money because we're connected in the community and threaten to make big trouble for him if he doesn't fix things."

"He could start with the hall lights," Harriet grumbled.

"That isn't the landlord. Tenants pinch them. You won't believe how many we've replaced." He smiled. "We consider that as our contribution to the house. We can afford it—others can't. By the way they're in the cupboard next to the door. Will you replace the bulbs? There's one outlet on the wall next to our door and another on the north wall of the second floor landing. You'll see it when you get the first one in."

Harriet's tea was still too hot to drink. She opened the cupboard and wasn't surprised to find a stock of energy efficient lights. Bulbs in hand, she opened the door, stepped out and shrieked as she crashed into someone. The light spilling from Perry's apartment shone on a tall, thin man.

He disentangled himself and stepped back. "Sorry, I scared you. I'm Russell, and you must be the renowned Harriet." He reached for the bulbs. "I'll do that."

What had he meant by renowned? She and Perry had minimum contact with one another—what had Perry said about her? She hadn't liked his tone.

When he returned, she and Russell sized one another up.

She'd expected the kind of ex-con she saw in TV programs, a tattooed wonder with long greasy hair and shifty eyes; but Russell looked every inch the professional businessman he had once been.

"I showed my sister what you'd done to help me cope. I'm really grateful," Perry said.

"Considering that I owe my life to you, it wasn't much. I only wish I could do more," Russell said.

"That sounds very dramatic," Harriet said and knew her voice reflected her distaste for excessive emotion.

"And not true. You would have done fine without me," Perry offered.

"No. I wouldn't." Russell placed his cup on the table. "Harriet, you may think that I'm exaggerating, but let me tell you exactly how it was."

Harriet nodded, although she didn't care.

"First, you have to know that a crack addiction is terrible. I lost my family, my job—everything I held dear because of it. When I came out of prison and couldn't find work, I figured I might as well start using again. But the night I decided my situation was hopeless, I stopped at the truck where Perry was giving out sandwiches."

"I looked at you, saw your desperation, saw that you were about to do something drastic," Perry said.

"'Wait until I finish, and we'll talk', you said. I did, and you offered to help me find a job and an apartment." He smiled at Harriet. "Perry *did* save my life, and I'll owe him forever."

"If you owed me anything, and I don't think you do, you more than repaid it with the help you've given me." Perry turned to Harriet. "You visited Mom today, didn't you?"

"Damn shame about your mother," Russell said. "Perry told me about her very generous financial contributions to the food banks and the homeless shelters. You must be proud to have such a community-minded mother."

Alarm flooded through Harriet. Had her mother given everything away?

"Perry, Mom said she showed you her will. Has everything gone to charity, or has she left something for us?" She really wanted to ask how much there was for her but knew that asking would be unwise.

"The vultures are circling," Russell said.

Perry coughed, "Russell, don't be unkind. Harriet, I'm sure she wouldn't mind me telling you that she's left $150,000 for you and $300,000 to Summer and me. The rest goes to designated charities."

Shit. Why would he get twice as much? This wasn't fair. A Porsche Cabriolet cost at least $190,000. She tried to control her dismay but suspected she hadn't done it well.

Perry frowned. "Summer's pregnant, and Mom wanted to be sure we had a nest egg for the baby."

Russell was watching her. "You look disappointed," he said. "Not enough for something you want?"

The observation was too close for comfort. Harriet forced a smile from her reserve of practiced expressions. "Let's talk about something else."

Perry grinned. "You're right. It's macabre."

Russell finished his tea and excused himself, explaining that he worked a late night shift at the nearby 7-Eleven.

Harriet assured him she'd make sure Perry was okay for the night before she left. Later, she called her mother, reported that Perry was doing well and promised to drop in every evening until Summer returned.

She lay awake that night, thinking of the future and what she'd do with the money. Eventually she must have dozed off.

When the alarm buzzed, she thought it was the phone and, expecting to hear bad news, groped to reach it. Realizing her mistake, she smacked the off button and lay for some time staring at the ceiling.

Next evening, when she entered the front hall, the pitch-black stairwell again confronted her. Probably it took a bulb a day to keep it lit. She carefully felt her way up the three flights of uncarpeted stairs. When she answered Perry's invitation to enter, she found Russell there as well. He stood leaning in the kitchen doorway with his arms crossed over his chest and his head cocked to one side. He stared at her steadily until she began to feel uneasy.

"Great move you made," he said. "Could have blown us all to hell."

"What?"

"Don't what me. I wasn't born yesterday. I'm sure you know you left the gas on and the door locked. Good thing I have a key, or we all would have done a little sky surfing."

"My god. How could that have happened?" She knew she looked surprised. It was one of the expressions she'd practiced in the mirror when someone had told her she never registered any emotion. She shook her head and frowned. "Something must have distracted me after I made tea. I can't think what it would have been. After we'd drunk it and had a chat, I helped Perry into bed, turned off the lights and left. I suppose I pushed in the door knob's lock, because I automatically lock doors." She turned to Perry. "I'm so sorry and glad that Russell arrived in time."

Perry said nothing. He considered her for several minutes before he spoke. "Forget it. It was an accident. Could have happened to anyone. Russell is a suspicious guy, but with the life he's lived, that isn't a surprise." He looked over at his friend. "Stay awhile and get to know my sister. She isn't the villain you're making her out to be."

Russell's gaze fixed on her. "I'm sure she isn't," he said, and it was apparent he meant exactly the opposite. "Thanks, but I have things to do."

Harriet talked about car emissions, a topic that interested her. Perry, who didn't own a car, said nothing. Eventually, when she couldn't think of anything else to say, she washed the mugs, tidied the kitchen, helped Perry into bed, collected her purse and turned off the lights. She closed the door behind her and stepped into the engulfing blackness. She wondered why Russell hadn't replaced the bulb and where the draft was coming from.

Two hands on her back propelled her into space. As she crashed down the stairs, she thought of the gleaming silver Porsche. She knew as she gathered momentum, hit the floor and felt her neck snap that there would be no Porsche.

Joan Boswell won the $10,000 Toronto Star's short story contest in 2005. A member of the Ladies Killing Circle she co-edited Fit to Die, Bone Dance *and* When Boomers Go Bad. *Her first mystery,* Cut Off His Tale, *was published in 2005, and her second,* Cut to the Quick, *in the spring of 2007.*

Eve Gets Even

Joy Hewitt Mann

"She didn't mean a thing to me,"
He tried to tell his wife
As she approached him wrathfully,
Preceded by a knife.

He wished he'd been more careful,
He wished he'd been more hep…
He wished he had eyes in the back of his head
As he slipped on that first step.

"He meant all the world to me,"
Sobbed his grieving wife
While she ate the perfect apple
She was peeling with her knife.

The Dog on Balmy Beach

Madeleine Harris-Callway

"My life is over," Ora said to the sky, the sand and the implacable blue lake.

Melanie, content on the hard wooden bench, ran her swollen, misshapen fingers through her guide dog's golden fur. As always, she didn't acknowledge Ora's heartfelt declaration.

Sometimes I wonder why we're still friends, Ora thought. *Nothing's changed since our teacher put us at the same reading table in Grade One. After fifty-five years, can't she sense that I'm desperate to talk to someone? Especially today.*

Melanie leaned down, touching Basil's nose with her own. "You want pet mode, don't you, boy?" His feathery tail thumped on the boardwalk. She fumbled with the metal clasps of the dog's harness while he struggled to be free.

"That is a really bad idea," Ora said.

"Basil needs to run off his spring friskies." Melanie's mouth curved in a mischievous smile. "He already got away from me once this morning."

A nightmare image flashed into Ora's mind of the big golden retriever plunging in front of the Queen streetcar, dragging Melanie with him. She made a grab for Basil's harness, but he slipped free, bounding onto the wide stretch of silver beach before them. "Relax for once. He'll be fine."

Melanie turned her broad face to the pale morning sun and folded her hands over her worn beige parka. "And you'll find another job. You're a survivor."

No, I won't, Ora wanted to scream. Melanie floated through life oblivious to its malicious blows, even to the multiple sclerosis that had stolen her sight. But then she'd never really had to worry about anything. Her disability pension covered her modest needs. And her friends always leaped forward to care for her whenever she had a crisis.

No one does that for me, Ora thought, pulling her red cashmere coat tighter against the biting wind. *I can't get up again, not this time.*

"Come on, they'd be crazy not to hire you," Melanie said. "You're so organized."

Oh, yes, I'm very organized, Ora thought. She felt in her pocket to make sure the bottle of pills was still there. She'd set everything out on the dining room table back at her condo: her list of instructions, cash to cover the costs, her best black dress…

"Aren't you curious to know how I got Basil back?" Melanie asked, startling Ora back to reality.

The dog had reached the water's edge. He ran back and forth full of energy.

"All right, I'm listening," Ora said. Basil remained immune to entreaties, toys and food whenever she tried them.

"A nice young man helped me. He startled me in the first place—that was the problem. He came rushing out of those bushes up by the reservoir. I tripped, dropped Basil's harness, and off he went."

"You shouldn't walk on the beach when nobody's around," Ora said. These days, only dark human motives occurred to her.

"Oh, come on. Anyway, I figured Basil would head for the

lake just to be a bugger. I kind of staggered off the boardwalk, so the man said sorry, he hadn't seen I was blind, and he'd fetch Basil. 'Hope you like swimming," I told him. And he said: 'Your dog won't go in. The water's too cold." So I said: 'Forget that. Basil thinks he's part polar bear.'"

Ora watched Melanie's polar bear leap at a seagull and miss. "So Basil rewarded him with a soak."

"Not exactly," Melanie chuckled. "When the guy brought Basil back, he asked me why nobody was on the boardwalk today. Obviously he wasn't a Beacher, or he'd know that only dog walkers are nutty enough to brave the lake on a cold spring day like this one."

"And that didn't make you feel scared?"

"Honestly, I don't know how you can go through life being so paranoid."

A loud noise burst through the pale quiet.

"What was that?" Ora sprang up. She looked up and down the boardwalk, but spotted no one. "That sounded like a gunshot."

"Relax, it's just kids with firecrackers."

But it's not Victoria Day yet, Ora thought. She gazed at the shoreline. Basil had dwindled to a tiny yellow dot amidst the silvery driftwood and white specks of gulls. Time to drag him back, if she could manage to catch him. She studied her impractical black business pumps. How to navigate the sand in these?

"Look out!" an arrogant voice shouted next to her ear.

A hard blow to her shoulder sent her staggering. A man on roller blades shot past. She had a brief glimpse of a straggling grey ponytail and knotted veins in muscular calves.

"Bastard," she managed, brushing off her coat. Seething, she watched him stride away over the rough boards, heading east toward the reservoir.

"I'll bet that was Tyrone, the old hippy," Melanie said from the bench. "Grey hair? Frisbee?"

"Yes," Ora bit out. She resumed her seat next to her friend and tugged her coat even tighter.

"He blades here every morning, hoping to find young boys."

"How do you know that?"

"The other dog walkers told me." Melanie smiled, pulled off her brown knitted hat and shook out her grey braids. "They say that he skates up and down the boardwalk because the school banned him from hanging around the playground. Even his own wife kicked him out."

"Wonderful! So he's a pervert as well as very rude." Ora squinted into the sun. Tyrone had shrunk to a small black dot in the distance.

"Forget Tyrone. You didn't hear the end of my story. Basil let the young man catch him, but he got his revenge."

Ora stiffened. "What did Basil do?"

"The guy shouts: 'Your dog's got his face in my pack.' So I said. 'Did you have food in there?' And he said, 'Yeah, a sandwich.' 'You don't any more,' I said. 'But it was wrapped in plastic,' the poor guy says. Honest to god, I couldn't help laughing. 'That won't stop Basil,' I told him, 'but it'll sure explain his weird poop and scoop tonight.'"

"Oh, for heaven's sake. You should have paid the man for his sandwich."

Melanie shrugged. "By the time I got Basil's harness back on, he'd left."

"Where did he go?"

Another burst of firecrackers made Ora jump. Shielding her eyes, she failed to pinpoint the source of the sound.

Melanie fiddled with her braids. "I missed you at the poetry reading last week."

"Sorry." *At least after today, I won't have to sit through another evening of suffocating feminist poetry,* Ora thought.

At the far end of the boardwalk where the path climbed up to the filtration plant, the dark outline of a man appeared. He was carrying a bulky pack by the shoulder straps.

And he was coming towards them.

"Let's go back to Queen Street for a coffee," Ora said, suddenly nervous.

"Can't you stop twitching? Where's Basil?"

Now Basil, too, had vanished. Ora shouted the dog's name. No sign of him. Where was he?

The man drew closer. He was wearing heavy black boots like the ones skinheads favoured. He looked like a skinhead, too, with his closely shaved head and baggy camouflage pants. Ora's skin prickled with tiny electric needles, the way it did whenever she had a near miss in traffic. Or last week, when her new boss had asked her into his office and closed the door.

Suddenly, Basil came hurtling out of nowhere, a gold cannonball. Where had he been? He flew past Ora to Melanie, who stroked and tousled his fur. "You're all wet, boy. What have you been doing?"

"For god's sake, Melanie, hold him." A dark, oily substance clung to the dog's chest and forelegs. "He's got blood on him!" she cried. "It's all over your hands."

"Oh, my god, is he hurt?"

"Basil, stay still." Ora pulled out the small plastic packet of tissues she always carried in her pocket and tried to wipe him off. In an instant, the papers were soaked a dark reddish brown, but with intense relief, she spotted no wounds. "He's fine. He hasn't cut himself. Here, give me your hands." She used the remaining tissues to clean her friend's fists, one at a time.

"Bad dog, where have you been?" Ora went on, glaring at Basil, who bounced out of her reach. "Rolling on a filthy dead seagull, I bet. And what have you got in your mouth?"

Basil tried to dodge her, but this time she was able to snatch the red disk free of his teeth. It was a faded Frisbee, pock-marked with threadlike tufts of worn plastic. Dark fluid had settled under the rim, streaking her hands as well.

Horrible, Ora thought. *How could the bird's blood end up there?* She chucked the toy onto the sand. Basil leapt down and scooped it up instantly. "Bad dog," she told him while she foraged through her purse, looking for a bit of paper, anything, to clean her fingers. She settled on her cheque book, tearing off the numbered pages, crumpling and tossing them to the wind, one by one, as she used them. *No value to me any more,* she thought.

Finished, she looked up. Her heart beat faster.

The man stood fifteen feet away. Motionless, he stared across the lake, his heavy shoulders turned slightly away from them. He dropped his pack on the boards. Ora felt the vibration through the thin soles of her shoes.

Basil bounded up to man, tail wagging. He nudged the man's leg and dropped the Frisbee beside him. The man's large fist hung down, unresponsive. The dog nudged him again.

"Bad dog," Ora called out. "Come here, Basil. Bad dog."

The man leaned down and picked up the toy. He stared at Ora. Smiled as he sensed her fear. With a sweep of his muscled arm, he flung the Frisbee out over the sand. Basil shot after it.

"Basil!" Ora sprang up. The dog caught the Frisbee in a white flash of teeth. He galloped over the beach, running round and round in a great circle, tail raised to the sky. "Here, boy. Come here, good dog." Ignoring her pleas, he headed straight back to the man who, with a coolly contemptuous glance at the two women, tossed the Frisbee again.

"For heaven's sake," Ora said. "Melanie, help me for once. Call your dog. He never comes to me."

"What's the big rush?"

"It's some man. He looks like a skinhead. He's using that mucky toy to play fetch with Basil."

"So let them play."

"Melanie…" Ora tried to rein in her voice. Her new boss had accused her of being loud and shrill. "I want to leave. He's making me nervous."

"Oh, stop it. Why do we always have to do what you want? You haven't changed since grade school."

"And you've never grown out of grade school," Ora flared. "You only survive because your friends and I look out for you. And who looks out for me? Nobody!"

"Why does it always have to be about you?" A dark obstinacy twisted Melanie's mouth. "If you're that worried, go home. I'm staying till Basil gets tired."

Anger charged Ora's courage. She crossed over the worn brown planks of the boardwalk until she was within striking distance of the man. He was scribbling in a notebook clipped to his belt by a thin brass chain. She realized that he was young, no more than twenty-five. In spite of the cold, he wore only a drab green singlet over his pants. Her new boss liked to call those tank tops "wife beater shirts", no doubt to fool his staff into believing that he was young, modern and full of ideas. He liked to show off his tattoo on casual Fridays, too, but his discreet Zen symbol looked laughably puny next to the vivid, diabolical patterns that swirled up the forearms of Basil's new friend.

Basil had returned, his pink tongue spilling blissfully from his mouth, the Frisbee an offering at the stranger's feet. The man looked up from his notebook.

She gasped. Cobra eyes, red diamonds on a yellow background, bored down on her. Contact lenses, she realized, recovering. She'd spotted similar ones in the window of a "Goth shop" that she'd passed on her way to a gallery opening on Queen Street West.

He dropped his notebook. It swung on its chain as his arm flicked out, hurling the Frisbee. Basil charged after it.

Ora's knees wavered. A metal tube with an oily blue sheen protruded through the top of his pack. *Oh, god, he has a gun.*

Heart pounding, she cleared her throat. Pretend everything's normal. "Excuse me, are you the man who helped my friend get her dog back?" she asked. The man ignored her. "If you are, my friend's sorry about your sandwich. I—I mean we—want to pay you for it."

"Doesn't your friend feed her dog?"

So it is him. Words rushed into her dry throat. "Of course Melanie feeds him, but Basil has an uncontrollable passion for bread. Today in the bakery café, it was so funny…" she pushed her fingers against her mouth to force the tremor out of her voice, "Basil stole four croissants when the owner wasn't looking. The minute her back was turned, up he went on his hind legs and plucked them delicately off the counter. She turned around, he ate one. She turned around, he ate another. Basil moves like lightning. He's quite graceful for such a big dog."

"And you didn't stop him. Just sat there and laughed," he broke in.

Ora blinked. "I paid the bakery back, of course."

"That's what you rich bitches do. Pay people off."

"I'm not rich, I'm broke." The words erupted, anger and humiliation overriding her fear. "The bank fired me last week after twenty-five years." *And I listened to investment advice from my cheating, incompetent ex-husband.*

"Oh, boo-hoo." He jerked the rifle from his pack. A military model with a mounted telescope sight. He braced it on his shoulder and scanned the horizon, squinting through the lens.

Act normal, just act normal. "Look here, I know it's none of my business, but isn't what you're doing illegal?"

"You're right. It's none of your business."

It's okay, she told herself. *That old hippy Tyrone skates up and down the boardwalk. He'll be back any minute. He can help us, even if he is a pervert.*

The barrel of the rifle swept back and forth along the water line. Where was Basil?

"Please put that away. You could hurt the dog—"

The roar of the rifle cut through her words. In the distance, a rupture of white feathers. Gulls shrieked, swirling in a mad white tornado. Their noise was intense, terrifying.

Basil! Where's Basil? To Ora's overwhelming relief, the dog stood frozen, tail down, halfway to the water.

"Ora?" Melanie cried back at the bench. "Where's Basil?"

"Playing."

"What's going on?"

"Nothing is going on," Ora bit out. Summoning every authoritative instinct she'd honed on the job, she brushed past the man and stepped down off the boardwalk. Cold sand poured into her shoes. She stumbled over fragments of bone-white shell, rusted bits of metal, and crumbles of Styrofoam, the urban detritus of a harsh winter, trying to keep the dog in sight. With every step, she felt the man's crimson cobra eye through the gun sight, burying into her spine. *Move, move,* she urged her legs.

She'd only covered a few feet when a piercing whistle drilled through the air. Basil trotted obediently over to the man, who lowered his rifle. A sharp click. He appeared to be reloading.

By the time Ora had staggered back to Melanie's bench, Melanie had wavered to her feet, the dog's harness jingling in her hand. Ora seized her friend's arm and said in a whisper: "Try not to react. He has a gun."

"What? Why is he shooting?"

"He's killing sea gulls. For now."

"What?" Melanie's podgy features spasmed.

"Listen to me! Get Basil over here and harness him up. I'll keep the guy talking. Hopefully, he'll think I'm a nattering, useless old woman like everybody else does. Haul your butt back up to Queen Street. Call the police."

"What?"

"Call your dog!"

"Ora!" Melanie's fists clutched her coat. "Don't leave me."

Ora broke free. Teetering on her heels, she forced herself back over to the stranger.

Watching the man's muscles flex under his thin shirt as he stared down the rifle barrel, she feared her bladder would give way. She was thin, suffering from the beginnings of osteoporosis. Physically, she didn't stand a chance. She waved madly at Basil, willing him to return to Melanie, but the dog uttered a low whine, crept forward, and nuzzled the man's knee. The man rested his free hand on the dog's forehead.

"Basil likes you," she managed to say.

The man ran a finger over Basil's head. The dog's deep brown eyes studied him as if he were the only human left in the world. The man lowered the gun, picked up the Frisbee. He tossed it in the direction of the seagulls. Basil shot after it. In an instant, the rifle flew back to his shoulder.

"For god's sake, what are you doing?" Ora screamed.

Instinctively, her hands clawed the man's hard arm to grab the gun. A toss of his shoulder sent her reeling.

"Fuck you, lady."

"And fuck you right back. How can you shoot an innocent animal? He trusts you, you damn coward!"

Turning, he fired. The cloud of gulls erupted. Basil, unharmed, dashed into the whirlwind of feathers. He chased the maddened birds, his barks echoing.

"I wasn't shooting at the dog," the man said, with a murderous look at Ora. He opened and closed the rifle with icy precision.

"Why are you shooting the birds? They have a right to live."

"I'm purging the world of vermin."

"That was you shooting earlier, wasn't it?"

He shoved the rifle under his arm, grabbed his notebook, and began writing. Back at the bench, Melanie slumped over, sobbing.

"You've upset my friend," Ora said, her fear burning away. "She thinks you shot her dog. He's not just her pet, you know. He's her life."

No response. He kept on writing.

"The Lions Club didn't want Melanie to have him, because Basil is, well, unfocused, that's how they put it. They were going to put him down. They'd just lost $25,000 and two years training him. But Melanie was so attached to him, I talked to my contact there, my former brother-in-law…"

"Shut up, lady. I know what you're doing. "

"Oh," Ora stammered. "What am I doing?" She waited a moment. When he didn't reply, she said, "You're right, I'm not good at establishing rapport. I can't talk people into anything. Or out of anything. In meetings, I can't spell out what everyone's thinking. Or should be thinking. My brain doesn't work that way."

"Your brain doesn't work at all."

"My ex-boss would agree with you."

"You don't know who I am."

"Yes, I do." She hesitated, then said, "I was waiting for you last night. And this morning." He raised an eyebrow. "You're Death."

"You're full of shit. You're pathetic, thinking you can trick me by acting all spiritual and New Age."

"I am not full of shit." Ora wrenched the pills from her coat pocket. "See these?"

"Tylenol," he snorted.

"Barbiturates. I was going to down them with a pint of vodka and get into the jacuzzi. The hot water opens your veins, makes the drug absorb faster. But I couldn't do it. I just couldn't."

"You're just whining because you're broke."

"You're young. You don't know what it means to lose your savings at my age. If only I'd been able to keep on working." The words cascaded out, Ora couldn't stop them. "So stupid to carry on like I was still thirty-five. Your abilities fade. Everyone knows it but you. And you learn that life has limits. The story ends. So much sooner than I ever thought possible."

Basil came loping back across the stretch of sand. He edged closer to the man and dropped the Frisbee, panting expectantly. The man dropped his notebook and fondled the dog's head with his free hand, ruffling his ears, rubbing his chin. "Life is a box, lady."

"I can't disagree with you."

Ora's legs trembled so violently, she collapsed and sat down on the boardwalk, dangling her legs over the edge. She tipped the sand out of one shoe, then the other. Melanie uttered a low keening wail, curled sideways on her bench. *She can't even save herself,* Ora thought in desperate frustration.

"What has made you so angry?" she asked the man.

"Stop the social worker shit." He forced the rifle back together. "Don't pretend you never wanted to blow someone to pieces."

"I did want my ex-boss to die with all my heart." She relived the patronizing, dismissive words he'd dispensed at their last meeting. They'd burned away the last illusion of her self-worth like acid.

The dog settled between them, resting his chin on the man's black boot. Ora curled a hand round Basil's leather collar. She swallowed and said, "You shouldn't give up in spite of what I'm planning to do. I'm old, I've run out of time. But you're young, you have decades to reclaim your life."

"No," he said with quiet finality. "I shot somebody."

She knew then that Tyrone wasn't coming back. And that Basil's joyous new dog toy must be Tyrone's Frisbee, soaked in the old hippy's blood.

"You shot Tyrone, the old hippy, didn't you? Out on the reservoir where the boardwalk ends."

His eyes narrowed. His bones seemed to harden as she watched.

"Did Tyrone collide with you? Is that what happened? Or was he just in the wrong place at the wrong time?"

"I was waiting for him."

"What?"

"He was my father."

A cry of horrified surprise escaped her. "He abused you."

"Shut up!" His fists looked like they'd break his gun apart.

"Ora!" Melanie sobbed. "Where's Basil? Tell me he's all right."

"Make her shut the fuck up."

Ora stood up, grasping Basil up by his collar. "I'll take Melanie home. We'll leave you alone."

"Go sit on the bench. The dog stays."

"My friend needs her dog."

"The dog stays."

His rifle was pointing directly at her face, inches from her chin. She stared into the two black pitiless holes in disbelief. Death, even though she'd longed for it, still astonished her.

"Are you deaf? Go sit on the bench."

"What are you going to do?" Ora asked, though she knew very well.

"Don't you ever stop talking?" he asked wearily. Ora released her grip on Basil's collar and backed away from him.

"Wait!"

She froze in her tracks.

"You're old. You'd know. He's dead, but he's still in my head. How long before he goes away?"

"Your mind is keeping Tyrone alive." She thought of her ex-boss. She'd let his odious words destroy her spirit, had nearly let them kill her. And now when she knew that only she could save herself, it was too late. "Your hatred is too strong. He'll never leave unless you get help."

"Fuck you."

"I know it isn't what you wanted me to say, but please, don't do this. "

"Forget it, lady."

"Shoot me if you want, but please don't hurt my friend." To her shame and dismay, tears streaked down her cheeks, dribbling off her chin. "My friend has never hurt anyone in her life. All she wants is to write bad poetry and live out her life with Basil. Please, I'm begging you, leave her alone."

"Go sit on the bench."

Ora dropped onto the seat next to Melanie, her limbs numb. "What's happening, Ora?" Melanie whimpered. "What is he going to do? I can't hear Basil."

"Basil's fine. Everything is going to be all right."

Melanie wiped her eyes. "I should have listened to you. And not just today. I'm sorry, Ora."

"Don't apologize. Everything is absolutely fine." Ora reached over and gripped her friend's hand tightly.

She felt Basil brush past her leg. He padded over next to Melanie, sighed and sat down. Sobbing, Melanie plunged her hands in his fur.

Ora heard the man's heavy boots on the boardwalk, then a dull clump as he stepped off into the soft earth beside it. *He's going behind us. He's going to do it from behind.*

She closed her eyes. Waited.

Why is he taking so long? Why doesn't he just do it? We're all together, she thought. *It'll all be over in the wink of an eye. We're here and in the next instant, we won't be. Here and not here. Here and not here,* she chanted silently.

The explosion, when it came, was the loudest sound Ora had ever heard. Light burst into her eyes. Melanie clutched her arm so painfully, she cried out.

She felt icy cold, but she could still see. She could still breathe. Slowly, the sounds of the world seeped back: the clang of the streetcar across Kew Gardens, the whistling of wind from the lake, Melanie's deep sobs, Basil's frenzied barking…

Melanie's face and parka were peppered with red dots. Her own face and hands were wet from a soft scarlet rain. She turned to look behind them.

"What's happened?" Melanie choked out.

Ora stifled a ridiculous warning not to look. "Hold onto Basil," she said.

She staggered up, stumbling down off the boards onto the grass to kneel next to the crimson nightmare behind their bench. His notebook had fallen open, its stained pages rustling in the wind.

She couldn't help herself. Her fingers reached for the brass chain and pulled the book over. Heart pounding, she took the edge of the last page. Made out the words "dog" and "soul". Underneath he'd scrawled, "Dog needs blind lady. Only way."

She bent her head and cried.

Madeleine Harris-Callway is a longstanding member of Crime Writers of Canada and Sisters in Crime. She has published mystery short stories in both print and electronic media. In 2004, she won the Crime Writers of Canada Golden Horseshoe Award for her story, "Kill the Boss", and in 2005, her entry, "The Land of Sun and Fun", was long-listed for the Debut Dagger Award. She and her husband share their Victorian home with two spoiled cats.

Mad Scientist

Linda Hall

I've suspected for some time that I should go to the authorities about Lewis. Why haven't I? Fear, I suppose. Even anonymous calls aren't anonymous. Both my landline and my cell phone could easily be traced to me. Even a payphone is out of the question. For example, if I used a payphone, the call would be tracked back to that particular phone. And witnesses would come forward, witnesses who could identify me making a call at the phone booth at that time. These people have their ways.

Plus, I have the idea that he suspects I know something. So, that's why I need to be circumspect in my dealings with him, and hope (and pray) for a window of opportunity.

Lewis, you see, is a terrorist. Lewis is the worst kind of terrorist, because Lewis is leading a classroom of high school aged children down the Taliban path. That's the sad part, the part that makes me know I'm shirking my responsibility by not going to the RCMP immediately with the information I have gathered about Lewis and the goings on in his classroom.

Lewis is a chemistry teacher in the same fairly renowned private school where I am employed as a mathematics professor, and my classroom is located directly across the hall from his. So, you see, this gives me an opportunity to note everything that goes on in there.

I have studied these things on the Web. I know the chemicals one must have on hand to build a bomb, and in what proportions. I know the paraphernalia required, the supplies needed. Lewis has all of these in abundance, in locked cabinets in his classroom.

You may wonder at my interest. My wife of only three years was killed in 9/11, and if this has sharpened my senses to terrorist activities, then so be it.

Lewis knows my history. I note the way he looks at me when he thinks I'm unaware he's there. I see the way he regards me across the hall with that pouty mouth of his, one eyebrow raised, hand on one hip. The way he stares at me in the staff room and addresses me with, "So, Maurice, you're young. When are you going to think about getting married again?"

That he would bring up the subject infuriates me!

I've chosen not to remarry. Terrorists like him would like me to. They would like me to get on with my life, but I won't give him or the terrorists the satisfaction. When I told him that, when I told him I hated all people, everywhere, of Arab descent, he seemed taken aback.

"I'm shocked," he said, eyes wide. "Many of them are good people. How can you say that?"

How can I say that? After what happened to my wife, how can he even wonder? It was then that I began to observe him. I live my life carefully looking for that window. But while I wait, I am forced to endure the smells from his room, the inane chatter, the music that he insists on playing. There are times I can almost taste the various reeks of the bomb-making chemicals in there. More than once I have gone home sick to my stomach at the stench of it all. Plus, my dreams are filled with his high-pitched voice calling to his students, "Measure carefully, kids, or you'll blow us all to kingdom come. Heh, heh." That chuckle and those words should tell you everything.

In my dreams I watch him sashay between his classroom tables on tiptoes, as if in dancing slippers, his grey-streaked pony tail whipping from side to side. In one recurring dream, he leans over and smirks at me, his lab coat falling forward to reveal a chest full of bombs.

Dreams or no dreams, I tell you, sometimes I am downright terrified of the man. I truly am. If you could see the gleam in his eye, I know you would agree with me. Plus, I have done a little digging. I have learned a fact about Lewis that few people know. One evening after everyone had gone home, I was able to get into the school's confidential files.

I discovered something profoundly unsettling. Early on in his career, two students suffered minor injuries when a chemistry experiment in his lab went horribly wrong. According to the report, it was not Lewis's fault. Two years later, the same thing happened. Again, he was deemed not culpable. Students had stayed after school, unsupervised while they worked on a science fair project. At the end of it all, he felt responsible (as well he should), took a year's leave of absence and spent some time in a psychiatric hospital. Psychiatric hospital, my foot. I know how these terrorist cells work. I know what he was really doing during that time.

Since I discovered Lewis's past history, something strange has happened. Somehow he has figured out what I know, and his rampages have become increasingly personal, directed at me.

This morning I came to school to find my entire desk in disarray. I always keep finely sharpened pencils in the rectangular compartment in the middle drawer of my desk. These are laid side by side next to the mechanical pencils and the ball point pens, all with their sharpened ends toward the left. I have arranged them thusly, so when I pick them up with my right hand, they are ready for immediate use. Next to them are my mathematical instruments, the compass, the protractors and other accoutrements of my profession. Beyond them, in the larger compartment, I keep boxes of staples, notepads, sheets of graph paper and an assortment of rulers, including a slide rule and a number of scientific calculators. To find the pens in disarray, to find them interspersed amongst each other, to find three of the number two lead pencils blunted, I was, frankly, horrified. The effect was one of violation, not unlike, I imagined, that of being raped. I immediately went to the headmaster, who asked me if anything had been taken.

Taken! No, nothing was taken. Nothing except my security, my safety. My sanctuary. When I suggested that it might be Lewis, he said, "Why would Lewis do that?"

"Because he's a…" I almost blurted out the word, terrorist! But I held my tongue.

I made my way back to my classroom, and there was that scoundrel standing in the hallway arranging student science fair displays. This is supposed to be a high school, yet these displays look as if done up by pre-schoolers. This is science? This is what parents pay for? I remind myself that this isn't where he shines; his expertise lies in bomb making, and what a perfect cover, a chemistry teacher.

"Morning, Maurice," he called to me. He was up on tip toes, taping a picture to the high wall. I merely nodded. *He will ruin the walls with that tape of his,* I was thinking. I was going to make a comment, there and then, but thought better of it. Time enough to bring it up at the staff meeting.

He came down to flat feet. "Just thought I'd brighten up the old halls of learning."

I turned away from him.

Plus, his classroom! I need to describe that room. Through his door—which he insists on keeping open at all times—I note the disorganization; students walking willy nilly, jars perched precariously on mucky tables. How can anyone live like this? No wonder two students almost died. My own classroom, by contrast, is orderly, and my students know exactly what is expected of them. I glanced at the locked metal door to the bomb cupboard.

A week later, another incident: I had returned from my usual quiet lunch in the corner of the staff room to find that my class instructions, which I had meticulously written on a corner of the blackboard—Homework, Chapter 18, Sections One and Two, Including the Bonus Questions—had been completely obliterated from the board. Lewis had done this to warn me. What he was saying was back off, keep what you know to yourself.

But I shall not! I shall not! I will wait for the window.

And this time I had proof. Moments before, I had seen Lewis emerging from my classroom. I walked over to his room, forced myself to enter that den of disorder and said, "Lewis. A word."

He strode toward me, all concern. "Yes, Maurice?

"You were in my classroom, I believe."

"Yes, I guess I was." He was rubbing his hands together. Well, of course he would, to get rid of the chalk dust!

"May I ask what you were doing in there?"

He raised his eyebrows. I stood waiting. He laughed. I hate that laugh of his, nervous and high-pitched, like a whinnying horse. Then he flipped his pony tail behind him and put his hands into his pockets under his dirty lab coat. I started. For a moment, I expected him to pull out a gun or reveal a chest strapped with dynamite.

But he pulled out his hands, scratched his nose and kept looking at me expectantly, like a child.

"You're serious," he said.

"Yes. I am. Most definitely." I stood my ground. It's important to stand one's ground when dealing with people like Lewis.

"I was talking to Anna Greene. She's your student, she also happens to be mine. We were discussing the set for the play."

I turned on my heels and walked out. The set for the play! And if you believe that, I have a bridge for sale. Back in my classroom, it took me several minutes of rearranging my things before I could calm myself enough to begin the mathematics lecture.

Lewis's torments increased after that. I began seeing him everywhere, hovering near my classroom, following me into the staff room. Once I even spied him bending over my car in the staff parking lot. I accosted him about that one, and here's what he said, "Your Austin. A beautiful car, Maurice. You've kept it in nice shape."

"Yes," I said, unlocking the driver side door and climbing in.

At home, I discovered that Lewis had even been there. He had actually come right to the front door of my home. There was a small pile of dog manure on my porch. Who but Lewis and his sick mind would have put it there?

"Is this what they teach you in Taliban school?" I yelled to the heavens. But I could not be sure this was just manure, so I donned a double layer of rubber gloves to check through it. It would be just like the terrorists to hide in the muck, a bit of plastic explosive. It seemed harmless, but what it gave me was a new revelation. Lewis expected me to think there was something in this and make me paw through it. He was probably at home right now, laughing at the whole ordeal.

Lewis, the ultimate actor, feigned complete innocence when I approached him the following morning. Chemistry? He should be teaching drama!

"Do you like shit?" I asked him quietly in the staff room.

"Do I like shit?" He turned slowly to face me and said the whole thing again, elongating the last two words, saying it loud enough for everyone to hear. "Do I like shit?"

"Yes. Do you think it's funny to put things in it, or not put things in it?" I kept my voice down while I stirred a sugar lump into my coffee. I watched his reaction carefully.

Lewis shook his head at me, sighed and walked away. But I could see it! I could! A tiny tic of nervousness, an anxious squinting at the corner of one eye. *I'm on to him!*

The last straw, the final straw occurred a week later, when I left the house one morning to find that one of the tires on my Austin was flat.

"Lewis, you have gone too far this time!"

I trudged back inside through the gathering storm and called a cab. I should have known when I saw Lewis admiring my car. I should have known he was planning something like this.

When the cab arrived, driven by a scruffy little man who smelled bad, I seethed all the way into town. It's a good fifteen-minute drive at the best of times, and the cabby seemed in no particular hurry, despite my protests that I'd better things to do than to sit in the back seat of his foul smelling vehicle.

By the time I arrived, school had already begun. It was raining heavily. "Lewis, you will pay for this!" I muttered as I slopped through puddles, cursing myself for forgetting my rubbers. I hurried down the hall, my shoes squawking with the wet. Outside of my still locked mathematics door, my students were lounging against the walls. Some of them were snickering.

"Mr. Schector, don't you know it's bad luck to have an open umbrella in a building," one of the girl students said.

"Thank you," I said, "for those words of consummate wisdom."

One of the tall girls tittered. I stared hard at her and unlocked the door. I was in no mood. Across the hall Lewis stood in his doorway and called cheerily, "Morning, Maury."

Maury? He was calling me Maury now?

A month after the car incident, fate handed me that window.

The two of us were at school late in the evening, when Lewis came into my classroom and right up to my desk. He was all smiles when he said, "I see the two of us are burning the midnight oil. How 'bout when we finish here, we go out and grab a beer?"

Grab a beer, indeed! I barely looked up when he said this but continued grading my papers. He was halfway out the door when I remembered the pipe and Bic lighter I always keep at the ready in my breast pocket and yelled, "Wait!"

He turned, clearly startled at my outburst.

"How about on the roof?" I said.

"Excuse me?"

"How about we go up on the roof. I was actually going to head up there in a bit to have a smoke." I patted my pipe and smiled. I actually smiled at him. "I'll make a pot of tea in the staff room and take it up to the roof and meet you there," I said.

"Well. Sure," he said stroking his ponytail. How I hate that man for what he did to my Mary.

There is a deck of sorts on the roof of this old school. It's strictly off limits to students, but staff use it, and there are several chairs and a picnic table up there.

I made a pot of tea, carried it up the steps to the roof and sat in the cool breeze on the top of the building waiting for him. I put the pipe in the middle of the table.

Then finally he was there, scraping his chair back and sitting down, flipping his pony tail behind him and chatting about how nice this was, just the two of us. And how he'd been looking forward to talking to me and he'd been wanting for a long time to clear up whatever it was between the two of us.

"Stop," I put up my hand. I could stand no more of this. "Stop right now."

He blinked at me and promptly closed his mouth. The pipe lay there between us. "Smoke it," I told him.

"What?" he looked at me aghast.

"I said smoke it."

"I don't smoke."

I leaned toward him and pointed to the pipe. "Pick it up. Smoke it."

His scrawny Adam's apple bobbled up and down as he swallowed rapidly. "What's going on, Maury? What's this about?" A tiny tongue of spittle snaked down his chin. The wind lifted his ponytail. I could tell he was nervous. Good.

"You know exactly what this is about," I said. "Consider this revenge. For the death of my Mary."

"Mary? Your wife, Mary? What do I have to do with Mary?"

"Take the pipe."

"No, thank you. I don't know what this is about, but no thank you." He got up, and I grabbed the pipe and my lighter and went to the railing, where he was leaning against it, looking out over the city. It was on to plan B, but that was okay.

"I don't understand it," he said turning to face me. "Why you seem to hate me. I've tried to be nice to you, I've gone out of my way…"

"Why do I hate you? Now there's a question." I leaned far over the railing. Up the road, a garbage truck was rumbling its way down toward us. I smiled. Fate was indeed on my side tonight. I leaned over farther, tried to calculate when the truck would thunder past to mask the sound…

"Maury, I wouldn't exactly trust that railing." Lewis was quite close to me now and was touching my jacket. To pull me to safety? With one quick motion, I pulled the pipe from my pocket, lit it, and shoved it deep within his shirt pocket, so quickly, so suddenly that he didn't have time to react. In one motion, I heaved him over the railing. He screamed, looking back at me in shock as he fell.

"Fly! Fly!" I called after him. As the truck roared past, covering the sound, the pipe bomb exploded. He had blown into a million pieces before he hit the ground. I watched the truck. It didn't stop. They hadn't seen anything, or if they had, they would merely have thought it was a light flickering in a window…

* * *

I was back home in my own house, drinking tea before anyone realized he was gone.

The following morning, when I entered the staff room for my morning coffee, a group of sombre faces looked up at me from around the table. The fresh out of college girls' gym teacher was there and her head was down, her shoulders heaving.

"What's the matter?" I asked cheerfully. "Somebody die?" My voice was jocular, full of gaiety.

She looked up at me with red-rimmed eyes. "Haven't you heard? Lewis is dead."

I raised my eyebrows, attempting to look concerned.

The biology teacher said, "As near as anyone can tell, it was suicide. His body was found this morning beside the school. He made a homemade bomb with chemicals from his lab then jumped off the building last night. Who would have ever thought he would do that?"

"He was working here late," another said.

I held my coffee cup steadily in my hand. Not a drop would spill.

The little lady gym teacher said, "He was going through a rough time recently. His wife left him and took their daughter. It was hard on him. But I can't believe it came to this."

"The students all loved him. This will devastate them." This came from the Home Economics teacher.

The police came. They questioned me intensely. Yes, I was here last night. Yes, working in my classroom the entire evening. No, I never noticed anything out of the ordinary. I keep my door closed, you see. Yes, I knew Lewis quite well, and yes, he had been going through a rough time of late. His wife had left him. Taken their daughter. Yes, I would say he did seem suicidal to me. Yes, most definitely. We were all concerned for him, all of us. And yes, several times I'd seen him working late on something in his lab. When I would go in and ask him about it, he tried to hide it, not that I would know anything about bombs. No problem at all, officer, glad to be of assistance.

I realized that I couldn't tell the authorities that I'd just killed a noted terrorist. Most of these local authorities are in bed with the Taliban. But I knew what had happened. There was one less terrorist on the planet.

Already news cameras were filming students hugging each other on the grounds, tears coursing down their precious cheeks. Oh, this will make for maudlin television, I thought. Hello, Oprah.

And suddenly I was thinking about fingerprints that I must have left on the door to the roof. Casually, ever so casually, I made my way up the stairs to the roof. A uniformed policeman was there, a young nervous looking man with darting eyes. Before he could stop me, I ducked under the yellow crime scene tape and grasped, firmly, the doorknob to the roof. I made sure he saw me do that.

"Sir," he said, "Sir, no one is allowed up there. This is a crime scene."

"Oh, dear, of course. I didn't realize. I'm so sorry. I'm not myself this morning. Lewis was a dear friend, you see. You'll have to forgive me. I wanted to put flowers at the site." And I held up the scraggly bouquet of weeds I had just scrounged from the cracks in the pavement out front.

*   *   *

A year has passed. There is a new chemistry teacher at school, a large woman who wears denim jumpers and Birkenstocks. I ignore her and she ignores me. But Lewis has found a way to torment me from the grave. At night I hear a sound like a roaring in my head, a choir of Lewis's voices, as if Lewis has become many Lewises, hundreds of Lewises, all calling out to me in unison, "Fly. Fly, fly Maury. Come back up to the rooftop and fly! Burst into a thousand pieces like me and fly."

I have taken to sleeping with the radio on at night, tuned between stations, but Lewis has found a way to speak through the white noise. "I can fly. Watch me. Watch me..."

"Quiet!" I cover my head with my pillow. "Leave me alone!"

But the voices have only multiplied. I hear them when I am in the middle of a mathematics lecture. I hear them when I am pushing a cart in the grocery store, the wheels squeaking on the tiled floor, "The rooftop, Maury...the rooftop, Maury...the rooftop, Maury." I can hear them when I am stopped at a red light or driving through traffic, or sitting in a staff meeting. "Come to the roof...come to the roof...come to the roof. Watch me fly...watch me fly..."

His harassments, also, have not stopped with his death. Little things. Always little things, he does. My toilet paper roll placed wrong way on the holder. My toothpaste tube squeezed from the middle. Fruit I have just purchased, spotted and withered in my fridge. Fresh cheese replaced with old bluing blocks. Milk in my fridge, not even my brand, soured and with lumps. Homework erased from the board. Students coming in with the wrong assignments. "Section Twenty-three!" I yell at them. "I assigned Section Twenty-three, but all of you have done Section Twenty-four! How is it that you have all done Section Twenty-four?"

"You assigned section twenty-four," they tell me, looking at each other in wonder. "You wrote it on the board yesterday."

I didn't, of course, but there is no use in arguing. It is Lewis who is doing this to me.

Tonight as I sit here at my desk, my classroom is in shambles. I am writing, writing, but the lead in my pencil keeps breaking. Papers are strewn across the floor. Books are upside down. Students' desks are upended. The chalk board is full of nonsensical scribbles. I cannot clean up fast enough from Lewis's tirades. They are getting worse.

He is above me now, dancing on the roof, prancing in those little black shoes of his. I yell loudly for him to stop, stop, but he does not. The dancing continues. I must go up there. To tell him to stop. To make him stop. I must do this. Must go... Must go up to the roof and make him stop. Fly with me,

Maury, Fly with me. I pat my breast pocket, where I have made another bomb, and ascend the stairs.

Linda Hall is the award winning author of fifteen novels and a number of short stories. She has received the Word Guild Award five times, and has been short listed for a Daphne Award and a Christy Award. She loves writing short crime fiction. When she's not writing, she and her husband enjoy sailing. She invites readers to her website: http://writerhall.com

Bad Chef

Joy Hewitt Mann

There was a bad chef named Lang
Who wished to go out with a bang,
But his bomb packed the punch
Of his abominable lunch
And he ended up in meringue.

Decked

Lou Allin

As Evelyn stared into the churning cement mixer, she made three vows about her life in the next world. First, forget graduate school. Second, marry a plumber or an electrician, someone useful. Finally, have fun. None of these tenets related to her marriage with Eliot.

At a turning point fifteen years ago, she could have followed her friend Becky to a private prep-school teaching position on Vancouver Island. Kayaking the Pacific surf, exploring Haida villages, feasting on salmon. But the University of Toronto had offered her an assistantship in English Renaissance literature, and her parents in St. John's, who had been fortunate to finish high school, were so proud. "You can never have too much education. Think of the choices, dear. Dad wrecked his back working at the warehouse, and I'm on my feet all day at Canadian Tire." Old saws for old times.

Plain as a wren and too studious and shy to have had many dates, in graduate school she had met Eliot Bracebrook, who was studying eighteenth-century French political philosophy and living in a garret with a leaky waterbed and ten dead plants. His witty banter and dark Byronic looks melted her heart. Every time she saw that sweet curl nestling at his temple, she longed to twine it around her fingers. After a dizzying year of foreign films, cozy ethnic restaurants, and evening strolls along Lake Ontario's beaches and through the quiet footpaths of the Don Valley, they reached a mutual understanding beyond the plebeian nature of a proposal. She still shuddered at the roseate kaleidoscopic tone of their woodblock wedding invitations:

On the sunlit rocks of Georgian Bay, Evelyn
and Eliot wish to celebrate with you. Barring
some misgivings and calming a few fears, we
believe that we will be good for each other
for a long time to come. Bring a favourite
food to share and a drinking vessel for soft red wine.

She could have wept for the gullible romantic she'd been, a keeper of scrapbooks and photographs. All for a career, then all for love, and where was she? Five hours north of Toronto in Sudbury, a roasted rock mining town where astronauts had trained for the moon walk. The trees had gone south to rebuild Chicago after the Great Fire; then open-pit nickel smelting had rained sulphur until the smaller growth had surrendered and the very earth had washed away. Progress towards regreening had been made, but the giant pines and lofty oaks would never return to an area the size of New York City.

Snatching an assistant professorship at the local university, Eliot had been the soul of logic. "Professional couples have to make tough choices. We need to go where the better job is. You'll get on here if you're patient," he promised, stressing his budding friendship with his chairman. "Bernard can pull some strings, and besides, English doctorates are flexible." So flexible that she had been lucky to crawl into a rundown junior high, with large, unruly classes, gargantuan piles of marking, and no fat sabbaticals such as Eliot was planning for this fall. He had his plane ticket for Rouen, where he intended to consult documents on the political ramifications of one of Montesquieu's trials. "A half-decent offer on the continent, and I'm out of this deep freeze," he had told everyone at the faculty Christmas party, as if he were a carefree bachelor. "We" was not a word that passed his lips.

But this summer, there was the deck to finish. Last year, for investment purposes, he had insisted that they build a cedar home on a large wilderness lake miles from the city. Land was reasonable, and since a new nickel mine was underway in the area, property values were due to skyrocket for the well-paid white hats who wanted to live near their job.

Suddenly an angry yell broke through the hum of the mixer. "Evelyn, get over here!"

She leaned her shovel against the gravel pile and looked toward the boathouse, where her husband held up several bundles. "What a mess. Boxes of your junk and an old suitcase. Come and get this stuff. I need room for my tools."

He tossed everything into a heap, settled into a lawn chair and lit a cigarette while he watched a loon dive for minnows. A few minutes later, he went into the house and brought out his boyhood BB gun, seeing how close he could come to spraying the frightened bird with shot.

Evelyn felt her neck muscles tighten as the poor creature fluttered down the lake to safety. During the months of construction, she had developed a non-specific arthritis. It hurt like hell, jumping from the hips to the knees to the feet while leaving her knuckles perpetually sore. How odd that it didn't run in her family. Maybe those weeks of clearing brush in the cold fall rain. Or cleaning up debris after the work crews: broken shingles, scrap wood, drywall, electrical and plumbing trash layered in chronological fashion like the cities of Troy. He'd made her responsible for tamping the basement earth with a gut-wrenching machine, as well as the parging and interior painting. "Subcontractors are ripoff artists," he would say. "Top dollar, and there's still a crack in the foundation. Drunken bastard. Good thing I know the meaning of the word 'backcharge'."

Instead of pitching in, Eliot made a more comfortable home at the university for research with his twenty-two-year-old blonde teaching assistant, Tammy. Next year, another nubile candidate would take her place.

Eliot's Rhodesian ridgeback Monty (short for Montesquieu) chugged into view and observed Evelyn's movements with a suspicious growl. Their dislike was mutual. It wouldn't have bitten her but considered her a poor third in the pecking order. The large, beefy dog forced her to the perilous edge of the king-sized bed and barked when she sat in Eliot's recliner. Evelyn remembered with a lump in her throat how her husband had made her get rid of her two cats, Merlin and Gunner, claiming that he couldn't tolerate the smell of the litter box. No matter how often she scrubbed and refreshed it, he persisted until she had finally given the animals to the humane society and hoped they wouldn't be put down. Monty, however, was necessary for security. "A small price to pay for peace of mind out here in the boonies. Worth his weight in gold," Eliot had said with a scoffing gesture when she had showed him the shreds of her sheepskin slippers.

Down by the boathouse, she picked up the books, old friends almost warm in her hands again, Tucker-Brooke and Levin, her leather-bound *Tamburlaine* bought at Marlowe's Cambridge on a graduation trip to England, underlined obsessively, each colour a deeper analysis. They smelled musty but were in good shape, merely needed some dry air.

Then she opened the suitcase her mother had given her for college and found her dissertation, its pages spotted with mildew. She turned to the preface:

Ever since Marlowe was "rediscovered" in a Romantic age ill-equipped to understand him, critics have reeled in horror at the atrocities of this Scythian shepherd, rejoiced in his painful ending, and cited Marlowe's own atheism as a bellwether for the play, yet could it be that the young poet, well-skilled in the duplicity of his role as a British spy, was playing a joke on his audience, limning a satire to which he planted clues throughout the ten acts?

Limning? Her thesaurus had been too well-thumbed. Evelyn placed a hand over her mouth to avoid laughing out loud. And what a preposterously long sentence, typical for a young doctoral candidate, foolishly confident that the fiery hoops through which she was faithfully jumping for her stern professors would deliver the keys to an honoured career. The realities of a crowded market had hit home when the rejection letters poured in, fresh wounds every day the postman arrived. "Barring an attack of the Black Plague," one read, "there will not be an opening in our department for another twenty-five years." How cruel, snug in their tenured nests. She recalled the single offer she had received from a small college in southern Alberta. "Really, my dear," Eliot had chuckled, inking a New York Times crossword. "A one-year appointment in a hick town full of rednecks. Trust me. You'd be miserable."

But once she had left academia, Evelyn's career had suffered the same fate as virginity in Marlowe's "Hero and Leander": "Jewels, being lost, are found again, this never. 'Tis lost but once and once lost, lost forever." Or in the more modern phrasing of one of her eighth graders when he returned from the bathroom to find his books missing. "You leave the room, you take the risk." The Alberta job might have opened up connections in

Calgary or Edmonton, but it was too late.

A scuffling startled her. Eliot strode toward her, tapping his watch, his florid face contorted in scorn. "Jesus, that trash stinks! Stop maundering around in it and get back to business. Don't you dare bring it inside. Evelyn, do you hear me?"

She rose painfully from her knees, swiping at a blackfly which had nestled into her neck and inspecting the blood on her fingers. The oily repellent was wearing off. "I'll take my books to school."

"You haven't missed them in years. Why get so attached now?" He flipped a cigarette onto the lawn, where it joined a collection. "I'd better not see them in the house. And don't try to sneak them into the basement."

As he walked away, Evelyn returned to her treasures. On the bottom of the suitcase, a note from her advisor appeared. "I'm distressed that you cannot take the assistant editorship of the *Elizabethan Quarterly* next winter. It would have been quite a feather for your resume, but you must do as you see fit." She had needed the extra time to edit and type Eliot's five-pound dissertation. What had a wise feminist said? That learning to type enslaved women? That chore had been a first step in trying to please Eliot. But no sooner had she learned one rule, mastered one task, than another took its place. It had taken her years to discover how clever he was at keeping her off-balance, at manipulating her self-doubts and making her feel unworthy of his slightest attentions.

After locating the Deep Woods OFF and spraying herself from head to toe, she returned to the droning mixer. The seven support pillars were ready to be filled. Only a hellish week ago, though it seemed like a lifetime, Eliot had rented a Bobcat backhoe, a "gravedigger," to excavate the massive holes, leaving piles of boulders as large as bowling balls. Evelyn had been dispatched with a fifteen-pound mine pry bar borrowed from their neighbour to hack down the last foot since the machine couldn't reach the deeper clay and rock of the Northern Ontario lakeside. Finally, with a small trowel, she had chipped away a quarter-inch at a time, Eliot sipping a frosty lager in the cab of the machine. Then the rain had begun.

"The water is filling the hole. I can't go any further, farther, whatever," she had said, her dripping glasses blurring the fine line between rock and clay.

"I told you over and over that the code says five damn feet, so get something to bail with. A margarine container or an old pot. Then grab a sona tube. We're ready to go on this one."

When the hole had been scooped to satisfaction, Eliot held each huge cardboard tube while she shovelled gravel to anchor the base. Then he called the rental agency to send the float to take away the expensive backhoe, so most of the excavation had to be refilled by hand, and the heavy, settled clay did not yield easily.

"Throw the bloody rocks back down, Evelyn. We're not farming here," he called as he headed for his Audi. "I have a lunch date with my new grad assistant. Tammy got on my nerves."

The last hole had been filled yesterday, just before they took Monty to town for his tooth cleaning with an overnight stay in case there was a reaction to the anaesthetic. Now the empty tubes waited for cement. Evelyn put her books and luggage into the trunk of her rusty Neon and returned to work. Her job was to combine the ingredients, not too thin or it wouldn't harden, and not too thick to pour into the wheelbarrow. Eliot's careless placement of the gravel pile forced her to walk backwards to hoist the shovelfuls over her shoulder into the mixer. He refused to relocate the cumbersome machine. "Too much trouble. People make such a big deal about ergonomics. Just don't trip. All I need is a broken ankle for you at this critical point. I'll be sitting for twenty-four hours in the Emerg."

She added a slurp of water from the hose and paused to see if the cement was dropping off the blades with the right hesitation. Eliot stomped over, huffing at the delay. "What kind of a mess do you call this?" he asked with a contemptuous grunt. "Aren't you being scientific? I said, and I said distinctly, five shovels of gravel and sand to one of cement powder. Do I have to write it down? And you should be measuring the water, not just hosing it in." He removed his canvas hat and wiped his brow. "I'm going for a brew. Fool around with this until you have it right. Then come and get me."

Three beers and several sandwiches later, Eliot was holding the wheelbarrow ready and still frowning. "Too thin. It's gruel. Never going to set. Do I have to mix this myself? Are you stupid or something? Don't you have a Ph.D.?" After adding a shovel of cement powder and nodding in satisfaction, he trundled the barrow to the waiting tubes, poking up a foot above the ground. Evelyn's shoulders ached as she eased each lumpy mass down the hole, hearing the smuck as it hit bottom far below.

"Hurry up!" he yelled. "Shovel that stuff faster, or it's going to harden in the wheelbarrow."

Biting her lips against the pain, Evelyn guided the cement down the dark hole. "More, more," Eliot called. "Move it!"

She thought of the work to come. The rest of the support pillars. And then the gigantic deck. Endless piles of cedar waited under tarps to be cut, stained, and hammered. Eliot had insisted that they could do the work themselves, with a few neighbours to hoist the main beams. The labour would continue to the end of her summer vacation and Eliot's happy departure for Europe. Her joints flamed up; her eyes brimmed with hot tears. As Eliot looked down the tube and sneezed, she smashed the heavy shovel quite decisively on his bald spot. He had always been so artistic in arranging his thinning hair.

The rest wasn't that difficult. Evelyn remembered how Eliot had told her to dress a doe he had shot on Manitoulin Island. From the rows of tools in the boathouse, she selected a coping saw for the finer work, then deposited some of Eliot into each of the seven sona tubes. Good thing they were twelve-inch, she thought, but her husband never stinted. "Build for strength," he always said. Cleaning was a breeze with the hose handy.

Evelyn returned to her cement, whistling "The Ghosts' High Noon" from *Ruddigore* as she filled the tubes. Eliot never let her play her Gilbert and Sullivan on his elaborate compact disc system. "Lollipop music," he labelled it, preferring Bach cantatas. Seven batches, seven pillars of wisdom. T. E. Lawrence seemed a good choice for bedside reading tonight. She finished as the sun dipped through the maple trees behind the house, shadowing it against the still lake. With a satisfied smile, she smoothed each grey concrete top and inserted a large screw and nut, carefully greased, as Eliot had decreed.

Then she went inside, showered with kiwi body gel, and cooked a batch of chicken enchiladas with Five Alarm salsa. Eliot disdained Mexican food. "How anyone can cobble together a cuisine out of the ingredients of poverty, I'll never know," he once said with a sneer. "Tortillas and refried beans, my god!" She went to bed among cool and soothing sheets, sleeping for ten hours without the slightest twinge of pain.

The next day she collected Monty and visited an auto wrecking business where Eliot had bought a hubcap for his Audi. The dog had been in the car, and the owner had been very impressed with the muscular ridgeback. The large property was the perfect place for him to exercise his nasty talents with abandon. "My husband is going to Europe on an extended trip, and I'll be travelling myself. We were very sad about Monty, but then I thought of you," Evelyn explained, smiling as she handed over his toys and a fifty-pound bag of premium chow. The dog was already roaming its new territory, lifting a leg at each post.

As for the sabbatical, it would be easy to arrange a message from Rouen saying that Eliot would be staying on. With his well-known contempt for the shortcomings of a backwoods university and general unpopularity, no one would question his decision. And when she returned, the sale of the house, in her name thanks to a tax shuffle, would finance her move to British Columbia. Becky was now head of the English Department and had mentioned an opening due to retirement.

Not long after, when the workmen had finished the deck, her neighbour strolled by to admire the job. Taking off his cap, he looked at the six hundred square feet of burnished gold. "Wow!" he said. "B.C. cedar. Must have cost an arm and a leg."

Evelyn blinked and smiled proudly as she looked across the glistening lake to admire the silken fog rising off the North River. So benign, so beautiful. And six months of winter on the doorstep.

"Yes," she answered. "It certainly did."

Lou Allin is the author of Northern Winters Are Murder, Blackflies Are Murder, Bush Poodles Are Murder, Murder, Eh? *and* Memories Are Murder. *The Belle Palmer series is set in the Nickel Capital of the World. Retired from teaching Criminal Justice students, Lou lives in Sooke, B.C., on Vancouver Island, overlooking the Strait of Juan de Fuca. Underway is a series starring RCMP corporal Holly Martin. The first title in the series is* And On the Surface Die *(2008). Visit her website* www.louallin.com *or contact her at louallin@shaw.ca.*

P(oisoned) M(y) S(pouse)

Joy Hewitt Mann

I know I threaten suicide
When I get PMS
And cry much too easily
And I know I look a mess
And I know that taking my own life
Is not something that you dread,
So I'll stop being emotional
And take your life instead.

The Good Lie

Sandy Conrad

There's nothing quite so awkward as a conversation with your lover at her husband's funeral. As her parish priest, I was in constant attendance, hovering protectively, dispensing platitudes and shabby comfort to the mourners, seamlessly guiding the proceedings from formal, ritualized grief to less formal mingling and tea drinking. I tried to catch her eye from time to time, gauging her weariness, but the gleam of excitement she beamed back at me was disconcerting, and I flinched every time. Lydia was a better actor than that. We'd had plenty of practice, and today was not the day for honesty.

I'd loved Lydia for eight years. She was my favourite secret, and I had no desire to make her a permanent part of my daily life. Every meeting with her was fraught with excitement and passion and a sense of stealing moments from ordinary days. We wasted no time discussing dull life details. I read her love poems, and she told me her dreams. We analyzed symphonies and prepared exquisite dinners together. We'd never eaten a meal without candles and soft jazz; never watched an entire film without pausing to make love. Few people got even a year of nerve-end passion, and we'd had eight.

I watched her hugging her grown up children, her friends from work, her neighbours. None of them knew the Lydia I knew. They saw her beauty; they saw a former high school bombshell who married well, and lived happily ever after. They asked awkwardly when she planned to go back to work and she, marvellously, looked sincere when she said, "Soon—it will take my mind off Harold." Her daughter Kelly had an arm around her shoulders. Her son Evan stood nearby. Lydia was a woman sated with creature comforts and love, but I knew that only I made her truly happy, and that without me, her easy life would be unbearable. That's what she told me. I believed her.

"She's holding up well."

I recognized the voice before I looked at the face—Madeleine Parker, president of the WI. I liked most of the women in my church, but Madeleine was without assets in the personality department. She was nosy; she was bossy, and she behaved like a schoolyard bully with the women who called themselves her friends. I wouldn't play with her, but I did fear her. She had power, and she sensed my disdain for her games. I had no intention of being nudged out of this parish. I was good at what I did, and even if my heart, or my faith, wasn't as naïvely pure as it once had been, I could still write a mean sermon and still incite some measure of intellectual stimulation in my parishioners. Madeleine made life interesting, especially when I had such important secrets to keep.

"She's a strong woman," I replied.

"Must have been a shock, him dying like that. Apparently he'd just had a check-up too."

"Unexpected death is always shocking, Madeleine. She'll need time to heal." I said this for Lydia's benefit. Madeleine's idea of comforting the grief-stricken was to push them onto every committee and keep them so busy doing good works that they had no time to remember their losses.

"I don't know why she keeps telling people she's going back to work. They're well off, and his business was booming. Surely she's not going to try running the dealership. I'm not sexist, but that would hardly be a job for a woman like Lydia."

I knew that Madeleine was trying to goad me. Even someone as thick as her knew that Lydia and I were friends, and that if she could get me irritated enough, I might blurt out some tidbit of new information that direct sympathy would never have drawn. "I guess we'll just have to see, won't we," I said, enjoying the pursed lips of my nemesis as she sensed my snub. "Won't you excuse me? The women have done a lovely job, by the way. Doesn't look like there will be much food left over."

Lydia was watching me disengage myself from Madeleine. I smiled to let her know that I'd won another round, and she winked. In a split second of unpriestly thought, I wanted to shout across the room—what the hell are you doing, Lydia? Behave yourself, my dearest. Grief was making her a little crazy, but it was her husband's funeral. Who was I to judge? Maybe she was more upset than I'd given her credit for. Harold had been a kind man, and I'd always appreciated his no-nonsense approach to church matters. The fact that he'd been embarrassingly fundamentalist in his Christianity didn't lessen his effectiveness as a deacon.

*　　*　　*

"You aren't really okay, are you?" I asked her later in my tiny kitchen.

"Please give me a real drink. I will die if I have another cup of tea."

I glanced out the window. No cars pulling up. It was late,

indecently late to be dropping in on the priest, but also bordering on inappropriately late to have a grieving widow in my home. As much as I loved her, she needed to go. "One drink, okay, then it's time for you to be on your way."

"My kids are here. What's wrong with me taking comfort from the rector?" She grabbed my hand and leaned toward me. "You are so sexy in a cassock."

I pulled away and went to the fridge for wine. I loved furtiveness too, but not with her son sitting on the other side of a thin wall and shutter doors. Plus, my curtains were open.

Lydia looked annoyed and gulped back the wine as soon as I set it in front of her. I stayed standing at the counter. "So, what did our favourite bitch have to say about me at my husband's funeral?"

"Lydia, please. Language." I hated it when she swore. She did it rarely, thank goodness, but it didn't suit her. I refilled her glass. "She wondered what you would do with the business, I think. Can't believe you would go back to work if you don't need to."

"Well, I have to admit, Madeleine is smarter than most of that gullible flock you shepherd. Why would a woman who just inherited over a million dollars in a business she loathes, do anything but sell out and put her feet up?"

"It seems in character for you though, to go back. People think you're dedicated and hard-working. You should be flattered."

"I'm tired actually, honey. It's not flattering to fool all of the people all of the time."

"I'm not fooled." I stared hard into her eyes. "I know who you are."

She stared back. "You don't know everything." She finished her wine. "I should go. You don't want to touch me, do you? Because that's what I really want right now."

"I will touch you everywhere, my sweet dear Lydia, when it's time. I will cover you with kisses."

"When it's time? Days, months?"

"I was thinking maybe this weekend. I could get away Friday night and meet you in Owen Sound. I'm doing a wedding on Saturday and staying at George's cottage."

"That's the best you can do? Make me wait four days for my lover?"

"Four days is nothing, hon. In our world that's a second and a half of time."

"That's right—'our world'—that special, special place. Well, I'll take what I can get for now, but let's put our world on the table for discussion shall we—this weekend we'll do kisses, then talk." She stood up and called into the other room. "Kelly! Evan! Time to take mom home."

* * *

I woke up that night with two phrases piercing my restless sleep—"you don't know everything" and "I'll take what I can get for now." There's a terrible clarity that can crash through the muddle of the mind's business at two a.m. The brain tucks the detritus of the day into files till it discovers the niggling viruses lying there. Full consciousness was now required. Lydia was not content with our delicate arrangement. Did she expect me to date her publicly? Then marry her? Was this what I wanted?

I tried to tell myself that I was panicking unnecessarily. Maybe she wanted to move to Toronto, or Vancouver. Maybe we would be long-distance lovers. That would be acceptable. I could live with that. But I'd been married once, for only two years, and that had been one and three quarter years too long. My life was not meant for intimate, relentless closeness. So much of my time was spent talking to parishioners, giving advice, sitting in hospital rooms pretending there's a better world ahead, and, worst of all, meetings. I'd chosen a profession where large blocks of my life were public property, so the blocks that were mine were mine absolutely. Silence, or sleep, or hours of reading, these were my private pleasures. I loved routine; I loved tidiness. Yes, I loved Lydia, but I loved even more the way she fit into my existence without spoiling one minute of it. I hoped she wouldn't make me choose.

I sat up in bed and reached for the lamp switch. I always had my laptop nearby. I flipped it open and pressed start. "Choice" would be a good topic for this Sunday's sermon. The text was on the Transfiguration of Christ, and my question was whether epiphanies made choices easier or more difficult. When you've seen the light, so to speak, do you really have a choice any more? I sat contentedly typing ideas till the pink dawn broke the semi-darkness of the street. I put Lydia away for the time being and got up to make my first coffee of the day with a light heart.

*   *   *

Lydia unpacked groceries while I arranged the roses in the only vase I could find in the tiny cottage kitchen. "So, tomorrow… Are you staying for the reception? Are we doing supper here?"

"There's no meal after the wedding. Finger foods. A glass of champagne. I should be back by five thirty."

"No meal? People want gifts that cost hundreds of dollars, and they don't even give the guests a decent dinner."

"Weddings do seem to be getting more extravagant for the bride and groom and less generous toward the guests. I'm not sure why. I hate to join the general consensus that the young are more self-centred than we were, but sometimes I wonder." I was happy to encourage Lydia's disdain for weddings.

"Not my kids."

"No, your kids are great. Is Evan going to finish this year?"

"I had to talk him into it. He thought he should take a year off and stay with me, maybe run the business. I had to tell him the business is going. So is the house. I'm making some serious changes in my life."

This was it. I'd been ambushed by the discussion I dreaded, thinking I had till tomorrow evening to divert her. Lydia was pouring sherry into the crystal glasses that she'd brought with her. She passed one to me. "Are we going to sit down for this?" she asked.

"You promised kisses first."

"Why don't we save that for the celebration?"

"What are we celebrating?"

"Truth. Freedom. No more lies."

I sipped the sherry. I was prepared for this. "First of all, you have to know that I love you."

"Good. That will make it all easier."

"Second, Lydia, is that I also love my life just the way it is."

"Not good."

"What we have is perfect."

"No, it isn't. It was okay while it was necessary. It was what we had to do. I hated it."

"You didn't hate it, my love."

"Stop calling me 'love' and don't tell me how I feel."

Escalation of intensity. Already I remembered what it felt like to be married, to have someone think they had a right to be contradictory, unpleasant. I was torn between asking Lydia to go home till she could be civilized or tearing off her silky outfit and making love to her divine body. "You are so beautiful. Let's go skinny dipping and watch the sun set. Let's sip wine on this quaint porch. I need your flesh on mine." I reached for her.

Lydia stepped back, not so easily distracted by lust as I. "For eight years you've enjoyed this affair. You cuckolded a man you knew and liked. You made me an adulteress. Now you have a chance to declare your love for me to the world. I will accept no less."

Libido shrivelled. My hand froze, then began to shake. I'd just been given an ultimatum. This was no choice at all, because I was being offered something I didn't want in exchange for something I valued more highly than gold. Did Lydia think for one second that I would choose her? Did she even know me at all?

"You'll have to say something eventually. Your silence is terribly revealing." Lydia refilled her sherry glass and rinsed a thick bunch of green grapes in a brass colander to carry to the porch. She sat on the oversized Muskoka chair, pointedly not looking at me. I stood behind the screen door, unwilling to be any closer.

"I don't like ultimatums."

"Right. And that's why you're going to dump me. Because once in all these years, I've asked something of you."

"So this is over if I don't marry you?"

"You don't have to marry me. Just publicly acknowledge me as your partner."

"That cannot happen."

"Isn't love supposed to make you brave?"

"Don't be naïve, and don't pretend that what we had wasn't love."

"Apparently it was a very fragile bond we had."

"But I do love you as much as I have ever loved anyone." I walked onto the porch and leaned into the railing looking over Georgian Bay.

"Maybe I should sweeten the pot a bit then? I am going to be quite rich. I'll never have to work again, and I can buy us a gorgeous house in any city you want to live in. I'll keep you in the manner to which you've become accustomed—tea, crumpets, sherry and trips to the theatre. How's that for happily ever after?"

"But I'd have to resign."

"Please spare me the hypocrisy. You are no priest. You're an actor who's good with words. I know who you are. I'll take you as you are. But I won't hide any more."

I hated it when people tried to analyze me, even someone whose skin I'd tasted with my own tongue. No one knows anyone completely. "I am a good priest. And I like the job."

"No you don't. You like parts of the job, and you loathe parts of it. Why not like parts of your life with me? Join me in the light, babe. Let the truth set us both free."

"The truth? You mean now that you've inherited your husband's wealth? Where was all this integrity while you were working at the board office making forty thousand dollars a year? Didn't want to come clean then? You waited him out. You won. You know very well that Harold would have divorced you if he'd found out about us."

"Who says I waited?"

"What?"

"You said I waited him out, and I said—"

"I know what you said. What do you mean?"

"You think you know me."

"Yes."

"Good. But I'm going to tell you more than you want to know, because I did what I did for you."

I felt like running very fast into the cold water, putting my hands over my ears and singing while I submerged.

"Harold had just been given a clean bill of health, you know, apart from the high blood pressure. I was so pissed off. His father died of heart failure; his mother died two years ago of a stroke. But Harold got a reprieve. So he decided to quit smoking and cut back on red meat. He said he felt like he'd been given a second chance—no more taking his health for granted. He'd always been so sure that he'd die young. It was one of the things I loved about him."

The smile she smiled at that point made me feel sick. There was no moral centre here, and the high ground for me was fast disappearing. "Why do I have to know this?"

"I played it your way for all this time. If you're going to love me now, you're going to love the person I really am, even if I'm only beginning to know who that is myself."

"You think I can possibly love you after this?"

"I don't know if I care, because from now on, I am who I am for better or worse."

"But you'll keep me out of it, right?"

"Not necessarily. It would be for your own good, of course, but I can blaze the trail that sets us both free."

"Or maybe you'll be in jail?"

"Why do you like your secrets so much?"

"Why can't you keep any?"

"You'll be my partner in crime…one more horrible sin for the parson to bear."

"Do not tell me anything. What if I go to the police, Lydia? I may not believe in God any more, but I still believe in law and order."

"What if I tell the world about us?

"Then I would hate you." I turned away, so she couldn't see the tears of blind frustration. She moved to the railings and pressed herself into my back. Her body was warm, so warm.

This woman was so much more than I'd expected, and so much less. But my hands had a mind of their own, and they still wanted her. She whispered against my ear, her tongue flicking the lobe. "I showed him pictures of us."

I wrenched my body around to face her. "Why?"

"I couldn't wait any longer. I'm not young; I don't have all the time in the world. I've only got a few good years left in this skin you love so much."

"And that killed him?"

"He trusted you."

"People don't die of betrayal, Lydia. You cannot make this my doing."

"Well, I did exchange his medication with Meridia, my diet pills—not good for people with high blood pressure. It was probably a combination. But he looked at the pictures, screamed a lot of obscenities at me, pulled out a cell phone to call you, and bam. He was on the floor sputtering and gasping for air. I just had to wait it out. I called the ambulance as soon as he stopped breathing."

Lydia's hair was red and gold, and her eyes were blue. I stared at her face, reconfiguring the elements into someone I recognized and had feelings for. She kissed me, and I kissed her back, once again letting my body speak for me. "You can still love me, can't you?"

"I don't know what I'm feeling," I replied.

She threw her head back and laughed. "You clearly know what you're feeling," she said as she redid the buttons on her pale shirt. She kissed the inside of my hand and each finger. "Let's have dinner. I'm starving."

I didn't move. "Lydia, can I just get this clear. You're blackmailing me into an open relationship. Have I got that straight?"

"You wouldn't want it any other way."

"And I'm an accessory to murder."

"Oh, what a tangled web we weave."

"And this is the truth that is setting me free?"

"Okay. Here's the truth. You're a shallow, materialistic agnostic with illusions of grandeur because you're the rector of a backwater parish, and a few unimportant people care what you say once a week. But I happen to find you endlessly amusing, and sexually thrilling. I know I can make you happy for a long time, because I have lots of cash and lots of yummy dreams to share with you. I feel no guilt at all, not for Harold, and not for you. Now pull yourself together and let's get on with getting on. Light the candles and put on some dinner music while I make you a meal you will never forget."

I could walk away now and phone the police. But, I wouldn't have my lover, and I wouldn't be able to live in this parish wondering how much everyone knew, my precious privacy breached. The real choice was a swim that never ended or life sentence in the jail of Lydia.

I never did forget that meal. While she was sautéing and chopping, I sat on the porch with my laptop and reread my sermon for Sunday. I guessed it would be my last. I'd called it "The Illusion of Choice". Appropriately ironic, I thought. I made a few amendments, tweaked a sentence or two, but overall the sermon was ready. Maybe there was choice after all. I closed the laptop.

The waters of Georgian Bay were aquamarine blue. The sun was low in the sky, and clouds promised a brilliant sunset. It would be a glorious backdrop for my final act.

The smell of garlic and butter floated across the porch. Lydia was working in a pale pink camisole now, her thin blouse tossed over a wooden chair. I was hungry. I felt lazy. Could I live with evening after evening like this? Would granite countertops, and gardens and a pool of our own compensate for the stigma and a permanently guilty conscience? Would Lydia get on my nerves the way my husband had?

The tinny sound of the "Hallelujah Chorus" broke my reverie.

"Mary, your phone's ringing."

I ran to my briefcase and checked the call display. Madeleine Parker. It must be church business. Maybe not my business any more. I didn't answer. I joined Lydia at the counter and slipped my arms around her. She froze.

"What choice is there really?" I answered. "I love you."

"Can we do this?"

"Did you really watch him die?"

Lydia put a lid on the vegetables and measured rice into a cup. "I'll answer that question if you answer mine."

"Okay."

"Does it make any difference now?"

Would it make any difference? Could I live with a cold-blooded killer? What would she do to me when the passion waned? "Yes, it matters."

She laughed. "Oh, Mary. Look at your face. Of course I didn't kill him. He died of a heart attack, and I had nothing to do with it. You know me better than that. "She lifted a platter of gruyère and stuffed olives toward me.

I took one olive and placed it on her lips. She chewed slowly, her eyes locked on mine. I backed away to light the candles and fumbled with my iPod till Norah Jones broke the silence. "I'm thinking Niagara-on-the Lake, a small perfect house close to the water. We've had such wonderful times there."

"That's my girl," she said, and blew out the candles I had just lit. She pulled the pale camisole over her head and reached for my hand. "Now, for kisses."

There, in the orange glow of a Georgian Bay sunset, we made our vows. I told her that I loved her many times. I told her I had been a fool to doubt her. My words were all bloated and adoring. She wanted to believe them, I'm sure, and I wanted them to be true.

Sandy Conrad lives near Paisley, Ontario with her husband Ian and numerous pets. She teaches high school English. Her short story, "The Eulogy", won first prize in the Scene of the Crime contest on Wolfe Island in 2005, and her Christmas story, "How Silently, How Silently", was published in Blood on the Holly *in 2007.*

Going Out With a Bank

Mary Jane Maffini

As banks go, it's nothing special, Harry. Small potatoes. Not like the good old days when we were the toast of London. Not like Lloyds job. Or Midland. Couldn't hold a candle to the romp at Barclays."

"Stay in the moment, Nev. Have you learned nothing from our yoga for geezers class?"

"Ah, but the past has its appeal. We were the best. I'll never forget the split-second timing, the sweet smell of explosives, and all that lovely lolly afterwards. It's hard to think that's gone forever."

"In the moment. Otherwise, I'll never get that knee replaced. Twenty-six weeks is a roundabout way of saying 'get used to your pain for six months more if you're lucky'. How many six monthses do you think I have left, Nev? Now watch this."

Harry was right. I knew that nothing lasts forever, especially geezers and their bodies. And that was as true for the proceeds from internationally renowned bank jobs as it was for handsome Harry's knee. The dwindling pile left after a life full of wine, women and song was being sucked into the coffers of Laurel Woods Retirement Home. That's the trouble with a life on the lam: not much by way of pensions and supplementary health benefits. All to say, just when we should have been settled to enjoy our nicely anonymous life in Canada and be learning to love lawn bowling, we had two good reasons to sharpen old skills and reconsider options.

Harry was at his most professional. He checked me over. "Try to look a bit sicker, will you? Hunch your shoulders. Maybe you should moan a bit more. Work on your green complexion. Try to drool."

"Easy for you to be funny. You're not the patsy waiting for the johnny shirt."

"Put a cork in it, my lad. Here's our chance."

Harry had shaved before we left Laurel Woods in the official van. He was wearing a crisp white shirt, tailor-made jacket and a cloud of pricy aftershave. He'd had his splendid wavy white hair trimmed the day before and had seen the dentist to perk up the pearly whites. He was as splendid a geezer as you could ever imagine. The wheelchair just added to the mystique. I was in my ratty silk dressing gown and well-worn slippers and working hard to look like it was my last day on earth due to intestinal unreliability.

His hand brushed the arm of a plump, frazzled nurse as she whizzed by with a squeak of white shoes. She glanced down at him, irritation flitting across her face and vaporizing at the sight of Handsome Harry in his wheelchair. He pointed to me and moderated his baritone boom to a whisper. "We can't reach our own doctor, probably marooned on the fifteenth hole, but he's already told poor old Nev here he's not long for this world."

He turned his head to gaze at me sorrowfully. I did my best to look terminal.

Harry swivelled back to the nurse and sighed. "Nev'll never complain, but if you ask me, it's a terrible terrible time we live in when a World War II hero gets to spend what may be his last day in the world without a place to lie down."

"I'm sorry," she said, "I know it's awful, but there's nothing I can do. The emergency room is always blocked right up on Mondays for some reason. People procrastinate on the weekends, and they all show up at once. Now it's like three days trouble in one. We just don't have the beds. Did you speak to staff at the desk?"

"I can see that you're under duress here, my dear. And I understand you're doing your best. I've been back and forth to the triage nurse pleading the case, but for old folks, it's hard to get attention. It's just that Neville here gets godawful diarrhea."

Harry raised his voiced at "godawful" and continued it through "diarrhea", putting emphasis on each syllable and rolling his r's—as if anything needed emphasis. Wouldn't want anyone in the waiting room to miss out on that scrap of information. Heads snapped up around the room. The pregnant woman next to me heaved herself out of the plastic chair and waddled to a seat at the furthest end of the room.

Harry's mouth was still working. "And with his condition, that could be the end of him, not that he gets any sympathy from the dragon at the desk. Diarrhea, that's an awful way for a hero to leave this world."

Thanks a lot, Harry.

Her mouth tightened, and she shot a look of sympathy my way. Oh, that Harry can pick them. She was exhausted looking, pushing fifty with dark-circles under her eyes, but she was still drop dead gorgeous in her rumbled purple scrubs.

I glanced around at the motley crowd of sneezers, coughers, bleeders, ranters, moaners and sleepers, mouth-breathing and otherwise. Most of them were staring back at me with unconcealed disdain. Harry and the nurse had eyes only for each other. I tried not to roll mine.

Harry added for good measure in a voice that sounded

magnified by a megaphone, "You wonder what's happened to our country when a vet can't get a simple bedpan for hours."

He'd played the vet card first. No time to waste. You never know what will do the trick. But Harry never hits a wrong note.

She hesitated and stopped before she could repeat the party line drilled into them by the administration. She bit her plump pink lower lip and gave me a long look. I clutched my bulging overnight bag in gratitude. She swivelled and delivered a luminous smile to Harry.

"And you?" she said, with an eye on the wheelchair as well as the handsome ham sitting in it.

"Me? Nothing wrong with me, my lovely. Just waiting for the new knee. No trampolines until then, I'm afraid. And you know how long the waiting lists are for that. At this rate, I guess I'll just have to soldier on without poor Nev here."

Harry has a way with nurses, even when they're thirty years younger. He's like a nurse whisperer. They're fascinated by him, calmed, ready to follow him anywhere. He gave her a wink—jaunty, wicked—a wink that said she was the best thing about this entire hospital, maybe the whole town, and he recognized that.

I raised my hand weakly in a salute. I smiled bravely, considering I was supposed to be dying and that diarrhea bit was a low blow and there wasn't a soul in this purgatory of a waiting room who hadn't heard about it. They wouldn't be likely to forget that either, which was good.

Harry said, "He's putting up a good front. You learn that in the war. He has some terrible heart condition. Don't ask me what it's called, lot of Latin mumbo jumbo. Valves snapping shut or something. On top of that tragic reality and this other intestinal situation, a long wait will kill him for sure. But we've all got to go sometime."

I like plump blonde nurses too, as my gal Pearl can tell you, and it was hard not to sympathize with this kind and beautiful creature. Was it her fault that half the town had arrived by ambulance on a Monday and stayed for the duration? Now she had fallen into Harry's clutches.

"I'm sorry," she said sympathizing. "We are trying to deal with the influx as best we can. It's..."

"Overwhelming," I said, bouncing back from death's door.

"And getting close to a shift change."

As if we didn't know.

Harry broke up the rapport. "Be that as it may, old Neville here's sick and he's tired, and this could be the end of him. He's gotten so scrawny, I fear he'll never make it out alive at this rate. What's this country coming to, that's what I want to know. There's never a reporter around when you really need one."

Well, that gave her an idea as it was intended to.

A small smile played around the nurse's pink lips. "I'll see if I can get him on a gurney. We'll find an alcove behind a curtain somewhere. He won't see the doctor one minute faster. We're overwhelmed here, but it will be more…"

"Dignified," Harry offered, adjusting the old school tie he'd borrowed from some unsuspecting chap years ago.

* * *

"That went well," I said, as I hopped onto the bed. "I hope she's not going to hang around after she goes off shift. In case she didn't believe you about that trampoline possibility being out of the question."

Just as I dropped the duffle bag, the curtain was swept open with a crisp grasp, and our nurse saviour beamed at us. "You'll be more comfortable here, Mr.—"

Harry said, "Colonel. Neville was a Colonel, although you'd never know it now, the shape his poor old body's in. Because of his condition, he has to have access to the bathroom quite often, it goes without saying. There should be some dignity."

You'd think.

She smiled, rosy and sympathetic. "You're in a good spot here. There's a toilet right across the hall and another one right down the hall."

"If you are looking for us, we'll be in one or the other. Can you let the staff know for us, there's a love? I won't let him hobble off on his own, even if he did have the strength," Harry said. "Even so he's a proud and private man, so I hope…"

"Of course," she said. "Privacy. Never easy to get in a hospital. I'm going off shift now, but I hope everything goes all right for the Colonel. And you too, with your knee. Take care."

"What can I say? Six months minimum. I'd head south if I could, but that takes…"

I gave Harry a quick kick and hoped our lovely lady didn't notice. I squeezed her hand in gratitude. Harry stopped blabbing and gave a courtly bow of his leonine head.

"Okay, Harry," I said as soon as the coast was clear. "Time to get the lead out."

In our line of work, timing and optics are everything. Less than two minutes later, an old couple lumbered along the hospital corridor, by-passing the Emergency Room, in case the day shift triage nurse was working overtime and noticed something familiar about the faces of the pair whipping past, the old fellow wheeling the wife's wheelchair. The heavy set husband had a full head of rusty hair and moustache that could have won a competition. He peered through a pair of horn-rimmed bifocals that had last been fashionable in the seventies. The wife was more attractive, if I do say so myself.

A slender, angular face with a silver bob and black glasses that gave her the look of an aging artiste. Not a speck of five o'clock shadow. She clutched an overstuffed shopping tote on her lap and dabbed at unseen tears with a fresh tissue. She hissed, "Slow down. We don't want people to look too closely."

"What are you on about? They wouldn't glance at me if I slapped on a feather boa and danced out every scene from the Kama Sutra. I'm old, in case you haven't noticed, Nev."

"I have noticed, Harry. You're also a fool who likes attention. And we are counting on not blowing this job by getting the wrong kind. Watch out for that pillar."

"Yes, dear."

*　　*　　*

In just over two minutes, we'd rolled to the nondescript Ford Focus parked in the handicapped parking lot, and the game was afoot. Twenty minutes to the bank, one hundred and twenty seconds more to keep on going around the corner. One minute to park the car in the handicapped space. The public bathroom in the small mall was a perfect place to change wigs, gloves and bags on the way. It's not like people pay attention to elderly people when they're not dancing in feather boas. Seven more minutes, and we were on our way again. I left the wheelchair carefully tucked behind a row of garbage cans, ready for our return trip.

Harry said, "You haven't lost your touch, Nev. Still got the split second timing."

"You better hope I haven't lost it."

*　　*　　*

It was just before closing time when the two ancient ladies teetered up the front door of the bank. They were a vision in tweed and polyester, with strong overtones of Phentex. Their hairdos were firmly rooted in the roller sets of the early sixties, only the colours had kept pace with the time: one pinkish, one bluish, both sprayed to a hard shellac finish.

The chunky one walked slowly with a pair of canes, the other's manoeuvres were quite stylish and elegant, if I do say so myself. Harry may be a dashing devil, but he makes a spectacularly ugly woman, particularly with that blue-toned wig and the bulldog jowls. At least he'd shaved. Just be glad your granny looks nothing like him. I was quite taken with my pink roller set and ancient cat's-eye glasses, also pink with small rhinestones at the tips. I had leather gloves to match. There's nothing like vintage to make an impression, and I'd been thrilled to find a pair that fit. You never know what fingerprint info might have made its way across The Pond.

"Whatever you do, resist the urge to flirt," I cautioned in a low voice. "It's not womanly."

"Don't worry," Harry said, making sure the camera caught the back of the wig and the get-up, but not the face. We'd practiced that during reconnaissance. They can do so much to enhance images now, and who knew what images of Harry and me might surface. Facial recognition technology has created a lot of new wrinkles. All to say, they'd have a good shot of my backside and welcome to it, but I kept my head averted.

Harry's teller looked up, and smiled condescendingly. "And what can I do for you today, dear?"

Harry warbled in his ugly old lady voice. "You can do this," He slid his note across the counter and let the barrel of his Glock show. "And don't hit the alarm, missy, because that would be a very bad idea. It's only money. And may I remind you, it's somebody else's money at that. Not really worth taking a chance."

Her face drained of blood. I only hoped that Harry didn't mess up by feeling too sorry for her and admitting his so-called Glock was nothing but a replica. The supply of weaponry wasn't that great at Laurel Woods.

Face to face, that wasn't the easiest. I'd been worried about Harry, because it must be obvious he has a soft spot for the ladies. Didn't we both spend a spell in Wormwood Scrubs because of a slip with a playful widow in the old days? But that's another story. Then there's the fact that pain can make him unpredictable, although he was dosed to the ears today in order to walk with those canes.

My own teller was younger, a bit more panicky. "Be calm, child," I said, soothingly. "I certainly don't intend to shoot you. You remind me a bit of my own lovely granddaughter. I wouldn't want anything to happen to you. Of course, you don't want that either, do you?"

She shook her head, lower lip quivering, her huge black eyes not leaving mine for a second. I reminded myself that there was a serious purpose to this activity, and I took no joy at this poor child's emotional trauma.

"Money in the bag, please. Everything you have. No dye packs. No pressing silent alarms. No holding back. No tricks. This will be a rough day for you, and you'll want to be home having dinner with your family tonight, alive and in one piece. Probably have your own granny to see you and give you a hug. You look like a smart girl. You should get a better job than this, afterwards, something less risky. I would certainly advise that."

Harry was transmitting the same message to his teller. I only hoped he hadn't already fallen in love with her.

Anyone who knew us in the old days would be stunned.

The pair of us got up like old girls, and not too stylish at that. Willing to take a chance for the takings at the cash of a bank branch in an unremarkable Canadian city. Us! Neville and Harry. The villains who'd looted the vault at the Merchant Bank, the job they still talk about in hushed voices in London. Harry and Nev, who did the job at Barclays. The digging, the dirt, and the flash of acetylene torches, the dust it took a week to get out of your skin, the months of planning, the watching, the waiting, the thrill of the drill into those safety deposit box doors. The final touch—the fountain of champagne we poured straight into our mouths. Those were the days for sure.

But, of course, we couldn't get to the vault this time. So close and yet so far away. As they say. Our days of digging a tunnel from a nearby building to the vaults on the right long weekend were gone forever. It's not like we could leg it if we were rumbled. We need our naps at this stage of life. We need our footstools and our tummy medications. We needed our nurses. Wouldn't want to miss movie night or bingo. And how could you ever get a gang together these days? Hard to recruit the type of person with attention to detail, even if you could find one with loyalty. You'd be hard-pressed to find a driver you could trust. What the hell, there was something splendid about walking right in the front door, getting it over with, no muss, no fuss. No grabby colleagues to roll over on you to get themselves a better deal the first time some copper flashes them a dirty look.

You'd rarely rake in more than twenty large, but at least you could take the money and run.

*   *   *

The Irish couple plowed along the hospital corridor, again disappearing somewhere along a long green corridor and into a washroom, after a quick glance around making sure that no one was watching. Five minutes later, I emerged in my ratty silk dressing gown, nudged back to my curtained gurney by my guardian angel, Harry, in his wheelchair. I wobbled down the hallway, just in time to see a young doctor in scrubs that suggested he'd been on for more than twelve hours. He was peering into my alcove and scratching his head.

"Here we are. Hold your horses. Don't go scampering off after we've been waiting all this time," Harry boomed.

"You two back again?" he said with a tired grin. "What is it this time? Malaria?"

I liked that. It meant he remembered us, and he'd recall us if it ever came down to that.

Harry went into fake whisper mode again. "Worse. The galloping trots. And we've been here for hours. Badgered the people at the front desk to no avail. Had to use the facilities. Let me tell you, Nev's colon waits for no man."

*　　*　　*

"Welcome back, fellas," the night nurse at Laurel Woods said as the medical transport driver deposited the two of us at home.

"Long night for these gentlemen," the driver said. "Emergency was backed up the worst I ever saw it."

"It was hell," I said, not too cheerfully, I hoped. Trying not to smirk. The sack of money in my overnight bag was unaccountably amusing. Harry would be heading south of the border for a new knee, and I'd had my fourth thrill of the month. The outfits were long-gone in a dumpster on the outskirts of town. The pilfered Ford Focus sat stranded in the parking lot, the phony license plates tucked away for future need.

"I hope the hospital wasn't too rough on you. We heard it

was a false alarm about your heart at least, Neville. That's great news. Sorry to hear about the tummy bug."

Bad news obviously travels fast.

"We don't know what we'd do here without you. But it's a terrible thing that it takes so long. All those hours, just stuck there."

"No one pays a bit of attention to you," Harry bellowed.

I said, "Ah well, that's the health scare system for you."

Harry winked. "Look at the bright side. We don't get out much. Have to take our fun where we get it."

The night nurse's eyes were bright. "Did you hear that a pair of old ladies robbed the bank?"

"You're kidding," I said. "That's shocking!"

"Girls will be girls," Harry added. "See, Nev, we miss all the fun."

She shook her head. "But that's the fourth time. The fourth! They got fifteen thousand this time. Elderly women! All different ones. It must a gang of them. And then they just vanish. Imagine that. You can't count on anything these days."

"Not so, my darlin'," Harry said, with a wink just this side of salacious. "If you spend enough time in the hospital, you'll find you can always count on wait times."

Mary Jane Maffini is the author of the Camilla MacPhee (RendezVous Crime), *Charlotte Adams* (Berkeley) *and Fiona Silk* (RendezVous Crime) *series. Among her acclaimed titles are* Speak Ill of the Dead, The Cluttered Corpse *and* Lament for a Lounge Lizard. *She lives in Ottawa, Ontario and can be visited on the web at* www.maryjanemaffini.ca

A Priest, a Cop and an Undertaker Walk into a Hunt Camp

Vicki Cameron

In Margaret's red and purple living room, we resembled white stamens in an exotic flower: five women in white terry robes with white towels wrapped around our heads. Our intrepid leader Samara fussed around at the CD player, loading disks of mantra-inducing new age music. Our helpful hostess Margaret delivered our personal china pots containing kelp deep cleansing and erasing mask.

Connie slathered hers on her face with several more fingers than recommended. "This feels great, getting away from the house for a while. I left Ashley minding my brood. She's old enough now to baby-sit, so I told her, kiddo, I am going to be your number one client. Just because I'm your mother doesn't mean I don't get to hire you. So, Elizabeth, I hear John has the pharmacy up for sale, and you're moving to the city. Is that true? Is it?"

Elizabeth's brow furrowed just a hair. "John enjoys new challenges. One cannot hold a man back from an interesting career move." She dabbed another layer of the green goop on her flawless cheeks. "This tingles, doesn't it? Almost painful."

"We can't eat these wonderful lime nacho chips with this stuff on," Lois said.

"No, you can't, and you can't talk either," Samara said, her voice low and breathy. "Relax. Close your eyes. Let go of your mind. Allow your skin to absorb the treatment and push out impurities. Allow yourself to become a new woman. Relax."

The new age music floated into the air like poisonous gas in a mine shaft, sneaking up on us and erasing our will to move.

Relaxation was not going to be my strong point today. Brian was out of cell phone reach as of six this morning. Yesterday, I could have called him home. Today, he was on the float plane on his way to the hunt camp.

He'd left The Room in readiness, as insurance. He always said if you're not ready, something happens. His stainless steel table glistened, his embalming tools stood in formation on the counter beside a brand new box of surgical gloves. Despite his attempts to outwit Chaos, something always happened when he was away. If he was at a four-day conference, I'd run into a glitch, solved by a scoop of panic and six phone calls. This time, two weeks, and I expected the worst. Funeral service is a team sport. If the coach is away, the equipment manager has to run the game.

I felt a breeze float around me, the kind you get from a peasant skirt wafting into your personal space. Gentle fingers began massaging my shoulders.

"I can see you are not relaxed, Hilary," Samara whispered in my ear. "Your worry lines are showing through the mask. Let go. Let it all go."

My skin started to itch and burn. I wondered if I could politely race to the bathroom and stick my face in the toilet bowl to cool it down. The creeping discomfort totally occupied my brain.

Until Elizabeth started shrieking "Margaret, Margaret, Margaret," and I opened my eyes to see Margaret on the floor tangled in a gate leg side table with a bowl of salsa and chips trickling over her white terry cover-up.

And so it starts, I thought, as Elizabeth wailed, Samara felt for a pulse, Connie flapped in circles and Lois dialled 911. *The entire first string players are off moose hunting, and I'm left to call up the bench.*

*   *   *

The paramedics, Constable Sanjit Dharwarkar, and Elizabeth's husband John arrived in rapid succession. While this team huddled in the living room, I dove at the bathroom sink like a person about to vomit. The green stuff came off in shale-like wafers but softened quickly and rolled down the drain. Connie and Lois elbowed me out of the way and madly scraped at their own faces. I had a half-glance at my face in the mirror before I retreated into the hall. Puffy blotched skin, swollen nostrils, fat lips.

I stood in the hallway, trying to be unobtrusive, and watched the activity in the living room, with a partial view of the kitchen. The paramedics loaded Margaret on a gurney and trundled her out the door. John clutched a wailing Elizabeth and eased her out to his car. I hoped he wouldn't take her to the hospital in her terry robe and green face. Samara in multicoloured cotton flitted around the fridge like a butterfly headed for Mexico without a compass. I guessed from the package in her hand she was trying to make a calming pot of Tao Relaxing Herbal Infusion. Connie and Lois squabbled over the sink. Their faces were a mess, too.

Sanjit paused at Margaret's kitchen door, notebook in hand and stared at us. "Wait here," he said. "I will interview you in the kitchen." He frowned at his notebook as if he wished it was his procedure book, and he could flip to the page that dealt with distended faces. "I will start with Ms Samara."

Samara, who was normally my rock in tense situations, abandoned her tea mission when she saw me. "What happened? This isn't right." She pushed Sanjit out of the way and felt my face. Her fingers were cool, like icicles on the eaves. Her eyes flooded with tears. She made a move as if she were going to run out the door and chase the ambulance down the street.

With a snap of his notebook, Sanjit blocked her escape and waved her to a chair. Connie, Lois and I retreated to the bathroom.

"We're a mess, aren't we?" Connie said, fingering her newly bulbous chin. "Samara's stuff doesn't usually do this." She pulled on her jeans and shirt and tossed her bathrobe into the tub. "I'm not getting interviewed in my underwear."

"Do you think Margaret will be all right?" Lois asked. "She never moved, after she stopped twitching. Elizabeth was some upset. The nachos were ruined."

I said nothing, just stared at my face and wondered how much makeup I'd need to make myself presentable for the funeral.

Samara fled the scene in her hand-crocheted shawl four seconds after the conclusion of her interview, leaving her entire beauty invigoration kit behind. Connie leaped forward to take her turn, saying she was anxious to get back to her children. I suspected she was more anxious to get back to her telephone, but what do I know, I'm the undertaker's wife and not welcome to hobnob with the regular folk.

After slipping into her street clothes, Lois wet a face cloth and held it to her flaming cheek. "Did it look like a heart attack to you? Their mom died young, you know. Margaret left town soon after. Ran off to the city to some art college. Got herself a fancy job decorating hotel rooms coast to coast.

That's why she's hardly ever here. This was her parents' home, although it wasn't decorated like this when they were alive. Elizabeth got the money, and Margaret got the house. Poor Margaret. Not much of a deal. The house needed a lot of work, and Elizabeth invested the cash. Did okay on it too, so I hear."

We heard the front door open and close. Lois went to the kitchen for her turn under the interrogation spotlight, and I waited alone in the bathroom, splashing cool water on my face and getting dressed. Lois slithered out when her interview was over, with the briefest of pauses at the pile of donuts on the dessert table, where she filled her purse.

I settled on the zebra bench seat in Margaret's kitchen. Sanjit was trying to look professional on a purple swivel chair, notebook square on the table.

"Could you tell me what happened?" he asked.

"Margaret invited us for a ladies' spa day. We had some snacks, listened to Samara's lecture on "The Benefits of Omega Three in the Micro Universe of the Soul", and changed into the white terry. That green gunk can destroy your clothes. We were to sit with eyes closed, relaxing, for twenty minutes. Samara put on some music and massaged shoulders." I rubbed my face. "This is itchy. Sorry. Then Elizabeth started yelling. I opened my eyes and saw Margaret on the floor with the salsa. Lois called 911. Elizabeth was so distraught, Lois phoned John. The room filled up with paramedics."

Sanjit sighed and stared at his notebook. "That's what everyone said. What now?" He flipped to a fresh page in his notebook and smoothed it.

His first year on the force, first month in Maudlyn Mills, and he was already known as a cop who went by the book. No reduced speeding fines if Sanjit caught you on his radar. He was the only rookie on my bench. Why did the police sergeant think it was okay to abscond on a moose hunt and leave the new guy in charge? Because Sanjit was a vegetarian? Or because, having grown up in Mississauga, he didn't know a moose from a UPS truck?

"It's not our place to say, but you and I have both seen dead people before. Normally the coroner calls the tune, but he's gone hunting." I said. "Doc Payne is on call. I know he's retired, but he's still got a licence to practice. He'll probably have a pronouncement for you by the time you get to the hospital."

Sanjit scribbled that down.

My interview over, I trudged home to call up the rest of the bench.

*   *   *

Margaret's family would call me soon enough. We were the only game in town. With an ice pack on my lips, I hauled out the vacuum cleaner and did a quick pass around the viewing rooms while I ran through a mental list. Half the town would show up, partly because John was a twenty-year fixture, and partly because Connie would be spreading the word about the circumstances and the salsa. I'd need to suggest the Level Three package, the local caterer in the Blue Room. I didn't think Elizabeth would open her perfect home to the masses, and she wouldn't want the church basement either, with its pervasive aroma of mould and competent women dishing out egg salad on white, boiler coffee and slab cake. Elizabeth would choose Menu A, the tiny perfect pinwheel sandwiches, the exotic olive tray, crudités and petits fours. None of this would be Margaret's choice, but funerals are for the living.

Someone pounded on the door. Florid-faced Connie, with one of her numerous children in hand, pushed her way into the lobby. "I know you're short-staffed. This is Ashley. She's fifteen. She needs some part-time work. She'll be good. Honest. Ashley, say hello. Ashley? Ashley!"

Ashley pulled a little bud from one ear. "Hello," she said, pushing the bud back.

"I know she'll be a great help to you," her mother said. "She's smart and quick and will do as she's told. Smile, Ashley, you're at a job interview. I told you to smile." She jabbed her daughter in the ribs. Ashley pulled her lips back in a weak replica of a smile, black lip liner over tiny teeth.

I looked at Ashley, from the long hair in layers of black, white and red, past the multiple piercings to the bare navel and tiny jean skirt over black leggings on stick legs.

"Well, I'll leave you to it, then," Connie said. "How does your face feel now? Mine feels like I was run over by a bulldozer."

She pushed Ashley one step further into my hall, dodged through the door, and slammed it.

Ashley stood like a statue of a slender half-naked goddess. I motioned to her to follow me upstairs into the kitchen of our apartment above the shop. She sat at the table and adjusted the volume on her iPod.

I called Samara. "What's wrong with my face? It's all red and puffy."

"I don't know. I mixed the blend myself. Something went wrong."

"What can I do about it?"

"I don't know. I don't know what caused it. One person, maybe an allergic reaction. All of you, well, no."

"I'm going to need you to help with the funeral," I said. "I don't have dates, but you know the drill. Probably Wednesday for visitation and Thursday for the service."

"I can't. No. I can't. I got such bad vibrations from Margaret's living room. From her. I can't take any part of her funeral. I can't touch the terry robes, can't collect my kit. It's all tainted. Drenched in bad spirits."

"Hey, relax. Give it a few hours. Do some yoga. Call me tomorrow, and we'll go through the arrangements."

"No. Are you listening to me?" Her voice was rising. I could almost feel her blood pressure going with it. "I'm telling you the vibrations around that woman are pure evil. I think she was murdered."

Murder. If Samara thought it was murder, she wouldn't come to my place until Margaret had been carried away and she had done a cleansing ritual around the building. I was short another member of my first string.

I looked at Ashley, sitting with skinny legs crossed and feet tapping. I was so deep on the bench, I didn't have uniforms to fit the players.

* * *

Doc Payne went through the paperwork in record time, probably because the golf season was winding down, and a day spent on an autopsy was a day not spent on the greens. Margaret was delivered to my basement.

Deeper and deeper I reached onto the bench. There was no avoiding it. I had to call Stockton Heath. Stockton had an embalming licence, and he also had an assistant, the divine Thelma. Apparently on their wedding day in 1962, he had told her she was the most beautiful girl in the world, and she resolved to remain such.

They arrived two hours later. Stockton always came to work in a suit, white shirt and pencil-thin tie. Thelma glowed in pink shirtwaist with shawl collar and crinoline. Her hair stood high in a bouffant with flipped up ends. Today she wore a pink daisy on her hair band, marking the line between her smooth bangs and upper pouf.

With a familiar sinking feeling, I followed them downstairs and paused at the door to The Room while they went in and took up their stations. He did the dirty work, and she did the cosmetics.

Stockton flipped back the sheet. Margaret lay bundled in her terrycloth robe, hair towel askew, and bits of green flaking around her face. Doc Payne had done his usual thorough job. "What's this green stuff?" Stockton asked, picking clods off with two fingers and rolling them around on his palm. "Looks like she was allergic to it. She's red." He turned and looked at me, as if he hadn't noticed before. "So are you."

"It's a face mask," I said. "We were having a beauty makeover when she died. It's supposed to make you look younger. Twenty minutes to a new you."

"It's been on way too long. Not that it matters, seeing as she's dead."

Thelma smoothed her bouffant, an entirely unnecessary move as it was shellacked to withstand a Force Ten Cyclone. "Gonna cost extra to cosmetize all that redness and swelling. You know that, don't you?"

I nodded. "Understood. We can't leave her like that. Open casket."

Stockton hung up his suit jacket and donned a rubber apron. I shrank back from the doorway.

"And, um, Margaret was proud of her curly hair. I hope you can recreate her style." It was faint hope, but I had to try.

Thelma gave me a withering look. "I'll make her the most beautiful girl in the world."

I was afraid of that. Margaret was in her early forties. She was born after the Beatles. She was a teen during the Heavy Metal years. She set her own style in the Lilith Fair days. Hair spray was a dim memory. She had long, luscious, naturally curly hair. "Do your best with those curls," I said, with fainter hope. "She liked them cascading down her left shoulder."

Thelma opened the new box of gloves and snapped a pair on. "You got any clothes? I'm gonna need some clothes."

*　　*　　*

Ashley lounged at my kitchen table nursing a coke and staring into space, her toes tapping to her private music. Once the phone had stopped ringing and the arrangements had started falling into place, I pulled the buds from her ears.

"Okay, Ashley, here's the deal. You're here to work, not amuse yourself with music. You'll put that thing away. We need to arrange the chairs for the visitation and set up the coffee room and the Blue Room. I'll need you on the door during visitation. You'll be greeting people, pointing out the washrooms, and the office for donations. You will not smile at people. This is a funeral home, and people don't expect smiling. You can look pleasant without smiling. You will not look bored. You will lose the body jewellery. I require a certain standard of dress, dark pants or a skirt that comes to your knees or lower, and a dark top. There are some jackets in the staff closet. I hope one of them fits you. Those are the rules. I didn't make them up. That's the job. Take it or leave it."

Ashley blinked. "Do I have to touch the body?"

"No, you don't go anywhere near the body."

"Will there be kids, like my screaming little sisters?"

"Not likely. People don't usually bring small children to funerals."

Her eyes did a tour of the room like she was sizing up a jail cell. "It's quiet here," she said. "How long can I stay?"

*   *   *

I hadn't expected to find Constable Dharwarkar at Margaret's house. He was taking pictures of the living room from every conceivable angle. I paused outside his range until he lowered the camera and frowned at the coffee table.

"What's up, Sanjit?" I asked. "I thought Doc Payne had ruled heart attack."

"He did and signed off on the need for an autopsy. But Ms Samara has been pestering me about bad vibes. I have to agree, it doesn't feel right to me either. So I thought I'd take enough pictures and notes about the scene that the sergeant would not be able to criticize my work when he gets back." He snapped the lens cap back on the camera. "Can I help you?"

"I came to get some clothes for her."

"Shouldn't the next of kin be doing that?"

Always by the book. "Yes, but Elizabeth has withdrawn to the fainting room, and I know she'd select a cashmere sweater and simple strand of pearls. That isn't how Margaret would want to make her entrance through the Pearly Gates."

"Did you find out what's wrong with your face?"

"A reaction to the green stuff, I think, although I don't have any allergies."

True to his quest to provide the sergeant with every possible piece of evidence, Sanjit rearmed his camera and took a photo of my face. I imagined it pinned on the memory board at my own funeral, we knew her when.

I excused myself and wandered into Margaret's bedroom. Navy and purple walls, like sleeping inside a grape. Huge walk-in closet, possibly formerly a small bedroom, commandeered by a single childless woman to serve her needs.

The closet was packed. One small section contained kilts and cashmere sweaters in muted tones of heather, with strands of pearls looped on the hangers. I swear I saw cobwebs on them, and one sweater had a scrap of wrapping paper stuck to it scrawled To Margaret from Elizabeth, Merry Christmas. Conservative Elizabeth seemed to think her sister ought to be her clone.

Free spirit Margaret had not bought into this way of thinking. The remainder of her wardrobe ran a riot of rich colour and exotic fabric. I thumbed through some wild and wonderful outfits, and settled on a red and gold one-shouldered sheath in silk chiffon. I picked a pair of sequined sling backs, not that Thelma would bother jamming shoes on Margaret's feet, but it felt like the right thing to do.

With my selection folded over my arm, I strolled back into the living room.

Sanjit still sat there, brooding. He glanced up. "You were here. What's wrong with this picture?"

I sat down beside him. "I dunno. What did you have in mind?"

"Where was everyone?"

"Samara was in charge, helping everyone, so she was everywhere. I was in that easy chair. Connie sprawled on the couch. Lois had the rocking chair, and she got up twice and went to the bathroom. The chair squeaked. Elizabeth and Margaret had the love seat. They were up and down. Margaret, as hostess, kept running to the kitchen for punch and pretzels. Samara mixed the green stuff in the kitchen and put on the music while Margaret delivered the pots."

"Did you hear anything?"

"Samara rustled around. I think she went down the hall to

the bathroom; I heard the tap running. She helped Lois, so she probably got green stuff on her hands. Someone else moved, too, but I don't know who. I just heard a softness of bare feet on carpet."

I stared at the coffee table while he wrote notes to himself. Individual pots of green concoction sat beside green-streaked facecloths, stained by us wiping our fingers after application. The whole lot had been pushed to one side of the table by the paramedics, who had left their latex gloves scattered around in the drippings of salsa. The green stuff in the bowls had hardened like concrete. "I guess I should clean this up. Samara won't come in here, and Elizabeth is a basket case."

Sanjit nodded. "Yeah, sure. I'm done taking photos."

I dragged Samara's kit out from its hiding place behind the couch and gathered the detritus. I bunched the facecloths into a plastic bag and tossed the stir sticks. I paused at the little green pots. "You know what's wrong with this picture? There were five of us getting facials." I pointed at the table. "There are only four pots."

*   *   *

Sanjit searched the house. He didn't find the missing pot. I left him talking on his cell phone, requisitioning fingerprint tests for the remaining pots, to see who had used each one, and thus discover which pot was missing.

Visitation Day at my command post, one hour until showtime, and my next player from the bench had arrived. The spiritual leader from the Holiness and Grace Congregation sat in the coffee room swilling down his fourth cup while he communed with a Higher Power and munched his way through a tray of cookies. I caught him reviewing crib notes to remember the name of the deceased.

Ashley had done a commendable job on her grooming. She had toned down her makeup and tuned up her fashion sense. The house jacket wasn't too huge on her, and she managed to carry it off with a surprising level of dignity. Perhaps it was the no-smile requirement. She stood by the door with a stoic demeanour, directing traffic as if she had been doing this for years. She only faltered once, when Sanjit arrived, resplendent in full dress uniform, and she quivered like an aspen leaf in a breeze.

My makeup was too thick, but I looked the right colour, if not the right facial proportions. I drifted into the crowd, waiting for the roof to fall in.

John and Elizabeth arrived half an hour late. Elizabeth wore her hair in her usual tight French roll, and her grey tailored suit was exquisitely correct for the occasion of losing your sister, if it was a smidgen tight on all fronts, especially the front. Not this year's model, apparently. The shoes were a little odd for Elizabeth, though. A touch too pink.

Her face was a disaster, bloated and blotchy like mine, but her concealer was not doing an adequate job. Her mascara had smeared under one eye so it made her look like a Kiss fan. I hardly recognized her.

John cupped his wife's elbow with a great deal of solicitation and led her to the head of the receiving line. Elizabeth patted her hair again and again, a new nervous tic, and who could blame her. When they reached the casket, both looked down.

Elizabeth fell apart. She burst forth in a torrent of hysterical laughter. John hugged her shoulder and led her away to the Quiet Room to recover herself.

The guests snickered behind their hands. I mean, you just had to laugh. You didn't expect a dead person to look really good, especially not one whose face had suffered irreparable swelling. But Margaret had prided herself on her voluptuous hair, and Thelma had turned her into a clone of herself. Thelma did that to everyone, which is why she was on the bench. Thelma only knew one hairstyle, a bouffant with bangs and a shoulder-length flip.

Margaret's hair was teased into a stiff pouf. The bangs were neatly cut at her eyebrow level. The hair-sprayed flip narrowly missed her shoulders. In the one-shouldered sheath, she looked like a 1962 pin-up girl.

A pox on the moose hunt. I hoped they came home empty-handed. No, worse, I hoped they bagged a 1300-pound bull moose with a colossal set of antlers, about a mile away from camp, and they had to carry it back through a swamp.

*　　*　　*

Connie stopped beside me and scratched her face. "How long do you figure until this redness goes away? Elizabeth's a wreck, doesn't hardly look like herself. John's holding up well, don't you think?"

"John?"

"Yeah, John. He used to date Margaret, you know. Before he went off to pharmacy school. When he came back, he went to pick up with her again, and she was off at art college. Elizabeth sunk her artificial nails into him right fast. I always thought he'd be better off with Margaret. So did he, I reckon."

"How's that?"

She lowered her voice. "John and Margaret were, you know…"

I remembered my social position and merely raised an eyebrow.

"Oh yes, for a few years now. Whenever he's at a conference, she's out of town on some job. That's the rumour, anyway."

She stepped away and joined the line that was shaking hands with the family.

I looked at John, speaking to someone, holding Elizabeth's waist. Elizabeth patted her French roll with one hand and dabbed a lace hanky at her nose with the other.

Lois finished making the circuit of relatives and waved at me. I joined her in the office. She wrote out a cheque for the charity of choice and shook her head. "Poor Margaret, she had so much going for her. She looks wonderful in that dress. But that hair, she doesn't even look like herself. Promise me you won't let that happen to me, when I end up here."

I promised. Although I wanted to remind her not to die during moose hunting season.

The main room filled up and a line formed, trickling down the steps and along the sidewalk. As I predicted, half the town had come out. The Blue Room was set up with enough chips, dip, sausage rolls and donuts to keep them all happy. As the line snaked around the room, Elizabeth patted her hair and fumbled a stray wisp into the big toothy clip. She kept her hanky near her swollen nose. She barely said three words.

I closed the office door behind me and sat down for a moment, fingering my lumpy face. Samara had mixed up this concoction which had disfigured us all. Margaret had delivered the pots to us. Margaret had died.

Samara was the last person I could imagine who would take another's life on purpose. She was a card-carrying holistic, entrenched in the sanctity of life and natural order. If Sanjit suspected her, and he would once he studied his notes, she'd state unequivocally that she alone had mixed the green solution.

I picked up the office phone and called Stockton. Thelma said he was ill and she'd had to take him to the hospital. Just as I thought.

Sanjit hovered near the front door, making Ashley ripple. She appeared on the verge of spontaneous combustion. "Excuse me, Constable, if I might have a word."

*   *   *

Sanjit joined me in the Blue Room. I frowned at the bowls of party food, all Margaret's favourites, from the sour cream dip to the chocolate dipped donuts. He frowned at the row of coffee cups like a man who does not drink on duty. "What can I do for you?"

"We were talking about what's wrong with this picture. What's wrong is the priest, the cop, the coroner, and the undertaker all walked into a hunt camp. And everyone knew they'd be gone for two weeks. Timing is everything."

"I don't follow."

"Elizabeth and Margaret are sisters. They look much alike, except Elizabeth is a bit thinner and Margaret has naturally curly hair. When Brian is away, Stockton does the embalming and Thelma does the hair. She always gives ladies the bouffant with bangs, no matter what they normally wear. You can count on it, and someone did."

A light bulb flickered over Sanjit's head. "Go on."

"You've noticed Elizabeth fiddling with her hairdo. Women do that when they have a new style they're not used to. Tugging at bangs, flipping wisps out of the way, or pushing a bit behind the ears, then remembering and pulling it out. Maybe we should enlist Ashley. She's young, and she knows about those big hair clips, like the one holding back Elizabeth's French roll."

The light bulb blinked full on. "Let's do it."

We strolled back to the door. "Ashley, you've been doing a

great job here with the door. I hope you can come back tomorrow for the funeral. I could use more of your help."

Ashley almost grinned, but caught herself. "Yeah, sure, whatever."

"There's another small job you could do right now. Elizabeth is having trouble with her hair and that big clip. She was probably upset when she did it up. I wonder if you could go over there and offer to help her with it."

"Okay."

We watched Ashley work her way around the room, as far from the casket as she could manage. She paused beside Elizabeth and whispered something. Elizabeth nodded. They both dropped out of the cluster of mourners and slipped down the hall to the Ladies. We followed. As the door was swinging closed behind them, I caught it and held it open. We had a clear view of the big mirror over the sink.

Ashley pulled a comb from her hip pocket, and with the quick hands of youth, unclipped the plastic thing, releasing long curly hair. She whipped the comb through the sides, pulling it into a tamed clump.

Sanjit maintained his post at the door while I stepped in the room. "I'll take that clip, thank you Ashley. Did you really think you could get away with it, Margaret?"

*   *   *

Later that evening, in the blank spot that should have been evening visitation hours, Sanjit dropped by.

"How did you figure it out?" he asked, placing his notebook neatly in front of him on my kitchen table. "Was it just the hair, or do you have some other evidence that will hold up in court?"

"More evidence? The shoes were wrong. Elizabeth would never wear pink shoes, especially to a funeral. If you go down to Brian's workroom, you'll find the pair of shoes I collected from Margaret's closet. They won't fit on the body. I think Elizabeth and Margaret wore a different shoe size."

Sanjit bent over his notebook, scribbling.

"That green stuff we had on our faces is still on the counter where Stockton chipped it off her face. I think it contains a skin-absorbed poison, courtesy of John the pharmacist. Samara mixed the stuff up, but Margaret delivered the pots. I think she slipped a trace of poison into each pot, just enough to irritate our skin and make us all look unrecognizable."

"I see. To help with the disguise. But enough in one pot to kill."

"Stockton didn't use gloves when he cleaned her face up, and now he's sick. Brian put a new box of gloves on the counter, but Stockton never uses them. It was still sealed when Thelma opened it to get herself a pair, and you'll find only one pair in the garbage can. John and Margaret didn't know that, so they don't know Stockton is sick, and the poison can be verified through the hospital's tests on him and the remaining green bits."

Scribble, scribble, scribble.

"You probably won't find the missing pot used to apply the goop at the party, but 'Elizabeth' wore her robe home, and must have taken the pot with her. There might be a trace in the pocket. John is having an affair with Margaret, so there's your motive. Swap the wife for the mistress, and keep the wife's inheritance to boot. He's got his business up for sale, and I'd guess they planned to skip town as soon as possible. And if Doc Payne had ruled anything other than natural causes, they had a backup plan. Implicate Samara."

"Another coroner is coming out from the city to review Doc Payne's decision," Sanjit said, turning a page.

"The food is wrong, too. The survivors always order comfort food, not the favourite food of the deceased. Elizabeth favoured exquisite food, Margaret liked fast food. You saw the Blue Room tables." I glanced out my window. Outside, Samara traipsed around my lawn, chanting and sprinkling herbs.

In the distance, I heard the fire siren, followed by an ambulance. The box on Sanjit's shoulder beeped and issued the garbled chant of a dispatcher saying something about a fatal shooting. Sanjit leaped out of his chair like a sprinter from the blocks and vanished out the door.

Right. Every time Brian goes away.

Vicki Cameron writes novels for young people and short stories. Her work has been nominated for several awards, including two Arthur Ellis and an Edgar. Her middle grade novel Shillings *features Colonel By's children during the building of the Rideau Canal. Her short story collections* Clue Mysteries *and* More Clue Mysteries *are each fifteen short stories based on the board game Clue. Her stories appear in the Ladies' Killing Circle anthology series and* Storyteller Magazine. *Her inspiration for this story came from dining out with funeral director friends.*

Peace and Quiet

Joy Hewitt Mann

The sound gave me blinding headaches,
His snoring drove me insane.
The snorts of my sleeping husband
Gave me a southerly pain.

I tried everything on the market,
But the pills just addled my thought
And you could deafen a country
With the earplugs that I bought.

Ten years of noise was the limit;
By then I had gone quite mad.
A hundred earplugs down his throat
Gave me sleep I'd never had.

Hostile Takeover

Sue Pike

Nora stood in the Arrivals Lounge at the Manaus Airport waving a sign with the words "Tranquility Eco-Tours" etched on it, feeling anything but tranquil. Only eleven of the twelve-member tour had arrived. She'd watched for the missing woman at the departures gate in Miami but hadn't spotted her there either. And now it seemed certain she'd missed her flight.

Nora asked the man standing beside her to hold the sign up while she pulled a pencil from the pocket of her cargo pants and checked the list on the clipboard again, ticking off for the third time the names on the tags of the impatient men and women gathered around her.

"Serenity Sims?" She peered through her smudgy glasses at the motley group surrounding her, but they shook their heads. "Anyone know her?" Shrugs.

"I hope this is not a portent of things to come on this tour." A burly, bull-necked man with a shiny shaved head glowered at Nora and tapped the face of his wristwatch with the nail of his index finger. His speech was clipped and guttural. She looked at the tag hanging from his neck. "Gunther Schwartz", it said. And underneath the words, "Bonn, Germany".

"We'll just wait a bit longer," she said, trying not to

wheedle. She could feel the familiar signs of panic creeping over her—sweat breaking out on her forehead, her heart pounding in her chest. She tried to remember the drill if someone missed a flight, but her mind flitted about, unable to light on the subject long enough to make a decision. And since she'd bought the tour company six weeks ago, there was no one to call. She was on her own.

Nora wiped her glasses on the tail of her shirt and stared through the grimy airport windows and along the tarmac through the gathering dusk. Her group was supposed to be on board the riverboat before nightfall, but that hope was drifting away like the vapor trail they'd left behind them in Toronto.

"Yoo hoo!" She spun around and stared as a middle-aged woman in layers and layers of pink and lilac silk swept toward them, waggling her fingers and dazzling them with her white teeth. A porter staggered in her wake, loaded down with three very large pieces of Ralph Lauren luggage and a huge backpack.

"Sorry." She ducked her head and made a little face. "American Airlines gave me a hard time about my carry-ons. I had to catch the Brazilian airliner instead." She flashed the impossibly white teeth. "I hope you haven't waited long."

"Exactly two hours," Gunther Schwartz consulted his watch, "and three minutes."

"Oh, well." Her laugh tinkled merrily. "I'm here now. What are we waiting for?"

Nora clamped her mouth shut and led the way to the parking lot and the bus where she and the rest had already stowed their bags. Serenity waved the porter toward the open luggage compartment and disappeared up the steps, leaving Nora to deal with the mutinous man holding his open palm in front of her face. She reached into her belly-pack, extracted a handful of bills and watched while he threw the luggage into the hold.

She boarded the bus to find Serenity dusting off the front seat where the sound system was installed.

"I'm sorry, that's my seat," Nora said with as much authority as she could muster. "I have to be able to use the microphone."

"Oh, my dear. You don't look old enough to be leading a tour." Serenity put her arm around Nora's shoulder and turned the younger woman to face the others at the back of the bus. "Now I ask you," she raised her voice, "does this sweet thing look old enough to be our leader?"

Nora could feel a blush spreading over her face. "I'm thirty-two," she stammered. "Almost thirty-three."

"That old?" Serenity raised her eyebrows in mock horror. "Why, you're practically ancient." Laughter filled the coach as she sank into the disputed seat. "I'm sorry, but I absolutely must sit at the front. Otherwise I get sick."

Nora glanced back and noticed everyone still watching, waiting to see how this would play out. "But there's another front seat," she indicated the one across the aisle.

"Oh, I would sit there, truly I would, but that window is so dirty, and the upholstery is torn." She shuddered.

Eleven heads swivelled back and forth. Nora heard the familiar tapping and saw the German glowering at her, the nail on his index finger beating out a tattoo on the face of his watch.

She nodded to the driver and braced herself in the aisle between the two rows while the bus lurched out of the parking lot. There is strength, her therapist Dr. Bernstein had told her, in knowing when to retreat from battle. "Can everyone hear me?"

Silence.

"I'll just point out some of the sights on our way to the boat."

"What about the Opera House? The brochure said we'd visit the Opera House." Gunther Schwarz glared at her from his seat three rows back.

"I'm afraid we got off to a late start. We'll just have time to get to the boat before it gets dark." She smiled, but her cheeks felt made of clay.

Gunther frowned. "It's all that woman's fault," he muttered, thrusting his jaw in Serenity's direction. But Serenity was in another world, humming softly to herself and staring out the side window.

"Oh, leave her alone, for heaven's sake," said a stout woman seated in front of him. She was wearing purple shorts and a faded T-shirt with the Tranquility Tours logo. Nora thought the woman was probably sizing her up, comparing her to other leaders she'd toured with.

She pushed her glasses back and began the speech she'd rehearsed until she knew it by heart. "Early in the twentieth century," she began, "Manaus was a thriving port, the centre of the worldwide rubber industry—" Gunther suddenly leapt to his feet and began twisting knobs on the ceiling above his head. "Mr. Schwartz? Is there a problem?" She tried to keep her voice steady.

"We must turn off this air conditioning. It is deadly." He stabbed at the roof a few more times before pounding on the vent. "Thousands of germs reside in these ducts."

"We're almost at the equator here, Mr. Schwartz. It's forty-five degrees Celsius outside." Nora's voice definitely squeaked this time. She closed her eyes and swallowed hard, whispering the mantra Dr. Bernstein had taught her to use whenever panic threatened to overwhelm her.

"Legionnaires' disease!" Her eyes flew open. "Norwalk! SARS!" Gunther was shouting at the others. She saw flecks of spittle flying from the corners of his mouth. "They all lurk in air conditioning units."

A fat lady in yellow shorts lumbered to her feet and started wrenching at the buttons over her head. Others muttered to one another. An elderly couple half-rose to their feet.

"No!" Serenity's shriek ripped the air. "We'll die in here with the air conditioning off. The heat will kill us." She turned a pathetic face to the people behind her and wiped imaginary sweat from her flawless brow. "Please."

"Excuse me." Nora tried to make her voice heard above the babble. "Please, let's just try to stay calm. If you look out the left window, you'll see the fish market." But no one was listening. She'd lost them.

The bus trip lasted another twenty minutes, and she watched helplessly as the ranks formed behind Serenity on the one hand and Gunther on the other. People who hardly knew one another were arguing the pros and cons of air conditioning.

By the time they arrived at the riverboat, it was dark, and the impatient captain glared at Nora and hurried them through the safety drill in halting English. He gave them their room assignments during a cold supper of salad, ham and the inevitable deep-fried manioc. Nora and Serenity would share a cabin, he told them, as they were the only single women on board.

The cabin was only big enough to turn around in. It had dark mahogany panelling, a couple of portholes, narrow bunk beds and a diminutive closet that Serenity immediately filled with her flowing garments, forcing Nora to leave her clothes stuffed in the duffel bag under the bunk. The older woman couldn't possibly sleep on the upper bunk with her vertigo, so Nora scrambled up a narrow ladder, bumping her head on the low ceiling. She lay awake, trying to control her panic. It was all going wrong. Dr Bernstein had said that owning the company could give her the control she so desperately needed.

But that wasn't the way it was working out at all. She pounded the mattress and wept silently into her pillow. It was nearly dawn when she finally fell asleep to the rumbling of the motor and the sound of water lapping against the hull as the riverboat made its way up the Rio Negro in the dense Amazonian night.

Sosa, the Yanomami guide, pounded on the cabin doors at five thirty in the morning for a dawn tour of the flooded rainforest. Serenity shot into the bathroom, and Nora jiggled on one foot then the other while waiting. After a quarter of an hour, she heard the others making their way up the stairs to the dining room, but still the bathroom door remained closed. Finally, just as Sosa called her name, the door opened and Serenity appeared in full makeup and a trim safari outfit. Nora was finished in the bathroom in four minutes and tore up the stairs two at a time but found her charges muttering to one another and glaring at her accusingly. Gunther tapped his watch.

Two wooden launches lay against the side of the boat, bumping together softly in the early morning mist. Nora began to help the more elderly of the tourists down the ladder while Sosa held the launch steady with a boat hook and the second guide, Eddie, led them to their seats.

Suddenly, Serenity grabbed Nora's elbow and squeezed it hard. "I absolutely refuse to sit in the same launch with that German brute," she hissed. Nora's cheeks burned as she held Gunther back for the second launch.

She climbed onto the seat next to the German, hoping to smooth over the insult, but he only muttered darkly and turned away from her. The guides pushed off and started the outboards. As they putted among the trees of the flooded rainforest, they listened to the dawn chorus of thousands of birds and watched as pairs of brightly hued parrots flew squawking overhead. Howler monkeys began their morning chant, sounding like snow tires on a distant expressway. A couple of large Cayman slipped under the water as the launches floated by, and a Collared Aracari hopped out of sight behind a rocky outcropping.

Nora explained that successful bird watching demanded quiet, so they wouldn't frighten the shyer birds, but she could hear peals of laughter coming from the other launch and Serenity's voice, strident and raucous. She was in full storytelling flight, and the words "Nazi" and "Herr Schwartz" skipped easily across the water towards them. A pair of scarlet macaws, startled by the noise, flew away into the jungle.

Nora didn't dare turn to her seatmate, but she could sense the tension in his body as he pressed binoculars to his eyes. Her own panic mounted as she met the accusing looks of the other four people in the boat.

"You must speak to that woman," said the tall man who had held the sign. The others nodded silently.

When the sun was fully up, the tour returned to the riverboat, climbed out of the launches and sat down to a meal of scrambled eggs and toast. Nora stood to announce she would be conducting an orientation talk in the dining room right after breakfast.

"Oh, but I've promised to give the women a yoga lesson on the top deck." Serenity's voice cut through the announcement, and Nora watched helplessly as four women followed Serenity out of the dining room, not one willing to catch her eye. The men scraped their chairs back and skulked off through the door into the lounge. Gunther led the pack, tossing a box of poker chips from hand to hand. Only the stout woman with the faded Tranquility T-shirt remained behind. Nora thought perhaps she had an ally until the woman frowned at her and said, "Either this tour improves, or I'll be demanding my money back." She flounced out of the room, leaving Nora behind with the dirty dishes.

She sighed and climbed up to the forward deck, where she leaned on the rail and stared into the dark water. Her life was a mess. This trip was a mess. And it was all so unfair.

This was the only work she'd ever wanted to do. The only work she was suited for. She'd grown up in the Brazilian rainforest with parents who were ornithologists. Her only friends had been native children from the villages along the riverbanks. Her formal schooling was patchy, but her command of Portuguese and her knowledge of jungle flora and fauna was second to none.

She'd landed a tour leaders job at Tranquility Tours, but they'd fired her after her first excursion. She was a gifted naturalist, they said, but lacked people skills. She tried other tour companies, but none of them had worked out. Then, when she heard that Tranquility Tours was on the market, she sold the Victorian mansion she'd inherited from her grandfather and put in an offer. It turned out she wasn't the only one who wanted the company, and the sale had developed into a bidding war between Nora's lawyer and the lawyer for a numbered company. It took all her resources from the house and the sale of her parents' Brazilian artifacts for Nora to come out on top. And now it was all going so dreadfully wrong. She could feel tears burning her eyes.

She clutched the worn mahogany railing and resolved to try harder. The tour members seemed to like Eddie and Sosa. Perhaps if she enlisted the boys to handle the bird checklist this afternoon, that would engage the more competitive members. And surely even Serenity would be lulled into silence during the evening tours in the launches. If they could pick out a sloth or two in the spotlights, perhaps even Gunther would stop scowling. Things might yet turn out all right.

But then Nora's stomach clenched as she remembered that both Gunther and Serenity had paid extra for the Tranquility Tours special feature—to spend Thursday night in a tent in the jungle. The thought of managing those two enemies filled Nora with terror. Could she cancel, she wondered? No. They were already furious with her. That would just add fuel to the fire. She would simply have to go through with it and hope against hope they wouldn't do anything rash.

* * *

After dinner on Thursday evening, Sosa helped them down from the riverboat and into the launch, and Eddie steered it across to the near shore. Serenity and Gunther sat at opposite ends of the boat, ignoring one another, and Nora sat in the middle, whispering Dr. Bernstein's mantra. Her glasses slid down her nose, and without thinking, she pushed them back in place. The launch bumped up against the bank, and they climbed out, following Eddie's spotlight to the campsite. After only a few metres, he stopped abruptly and threw his arm out to hold them back.

The snake lay along the lowest branch of a young cacao tree, unmoving except for the forked tongue flicking in and out. Its eyes glowed amber in the spotlight. Nora leaned closer to get a better look at the pattern on its back, brown chevrons edged in white.

"Get back," Sosa hissed without taking his eyes off the viper. "A bite from a fer-de-lance kills in minutes."

She stepped back a foot or two but continued to watch. Snakes have poor eyesight, but this one would have known they were there. Its tongue would smell the presence of humans, taste it in the heavy heat of the Amazonian jungle. It appeared alert but unperturbed in the face of four hovering humans. Nora peered over her shoulder at Gunther and Serenity who had fled behind the buttresses of a huge kapok tree. Given how much they hated one another, it puzzled her they would choose to stay together.

"Kill it," Serenity screeched from her hiding spot.

"Yes," shouted the German, "use your knife."

"We kill nothing," Eddie, the senior guide, said in his ponderous and heavily accented Portuguese. "We leave everything as is. It is our rule."

"But I'll never be able to sleep if you don't." Serenity's voice trembled on the verge of tears.

Eddie reached for a burlap bag at his feet and handed Nora the spotlight. "Hold this."

The big light was heavier than she expected, but she managed to rest it on her shoulder with the beam trained on the viper. Snakes, even such a deadly one as the fer-de-lance, held little fear for Nora. It was the humans who terrified her.

Eddie picked up two sturdy branches from the leaf litter at their feet, and with a stick in each hand, lifted the sides of the burlap bag and held it a couple of inches under the snake. He nodded at Sosa, and the young Indian used the tip of his machete to flick the fer-de-lance off its perch and into the bag. Eddie swung the bag up, dropped the sticks and caught the strings with both hands. He pulled the bag closed and dropped it to the ground and with his boot nudged a large stone over the opening to hold it secure.

"There. It will stay trapped until morning, and when Miss Nora and Miss Serenity and Mr. Gunther are back on the boat, we will release it into the jungle again." Eddie pulled the red bandanna from his neck and wiped his forehead, a few drops of perspiration the only indication of his stress.

Nora nodded and called across to the others. "Okay. It's safe." She hoisted the spotlight back to Eddie and picked up her backpack. "We should get into our tents. It'll be too dark to see anything in a few minutes." She flashed her penlight on the nearest tent. "Gunther, you sleep here. Serenity, you and I are in the one over there," she pointed the light at a second tent.

She waited for the usual arguments, but Serenity and Gunther picked their way silently across the clearing, their flashlights aimed a foot or so in front of each footfall, their arms held tight against their sides. Eddie had warned them about bullet ants lurking on the cecropia trees, and neither one wanted to risk encountering an insect that could give a ferocious sting from either end of its body.

Nora tried to lead Serenity to the tent, but she held back. "What about the guides? Where will they be?" She looked at Eddie and Sosa.

"I will go back to the boat to take care of the others." Eddie said. "Sosa will sleep in the hammock—just here." He pointed the big spotlight at a piece of cloth tied between the trunks of two trees. "He will have his machete with him and will watch over you. You will be safe."

"I'm not so sure," she balked, digging her feet into the jungle soil. "Maybe we should go back to the boat."

"Look, Serenity." Nora took a deep breath and tried to control her frustration. "You and Gunther requested the jungle night. You insisted. Tranquility Tours doesn't normally offer this, and we've gone to a lot of trouble to accommodate you."

"Gunther!" she spat. "Don't even mention that horrible man's name." She wrenched her arm away and bent down to crawl into the tent.

Nora heard Gunther hiss the word "bitch" in their direction but managed to push Serenity inside the tent before she hurled another insult at him.

Serenity wrenched her boots off and threw them into the corner of the tent. "I could kill that man," she said. "I'll never be able to sleep with him in the next tent and that snake out there. And what are those hideous noises?"

"That's the jungle you were so anxious to experience." Nora said. The shrieks and whistles were straight out of a Tarzan movie, but she found them familiar and comforting as she settled into her sleeping bag.

Serenity rummaged inside her backpack. "I need a tablet to help me sleep. Do you want one?" She pulled out a plastic container and dropped two tiny pills into her palm. Nora shook her head but the woman insisted. "Oh, come on. It'll do you good to relax for a change."

Nora took the pill and popped it into her mouth, but as soon as Serenity turned away, she let it fall onto her pillow, where she palmed it. She wondered briefly what the woman was up to but soon fell asleep to the sweet sounds of the jungle.

*   *   *

Nora's eyes flew open in the velvet blackness, and she wondered what had wakened her. Then she heard the sound again—the snuffling of a peccary exploring the perimeter of the tent. She rolled over to go back to sleep, but something was wrong. It was eerily still inside the tent.

She sat up and shone her penlight at the other sleeping bag. Empty! Nora felt the familiar flutters of panic like a small bird trapped inside her chest. Perhaps Serenity had gone outside to relieve herself, she thought, but after a few minutes realized that couldn't be it. No one as afraid of the jungle as Serenity was would linger outside the safety of the tent for so long.

Another thought struck her and filled her with an even greater fear. Serenity had looked mad with fury when she talked about the German last night. What if she had gone to his tent to hurt him, kill him even? She'd certainly threatened it often enough.

Nora pulled on her boots and glasses and reached down to undo the tent, but the flap was already hanging open. She slipped out and stood listening, trying to distinguish individual sounds in the cacophony of the jungle night. She heard Sosa snoring and shone her thin light on his inert form in the hammock. Then she heard something else that sounded almost like stifled laughter.

She crept toward the German's tent and heard voices. That was good. At least they hadn't killed one another. She moved nearer. In the dappled moonlight she saw that the zip was half open, and she could hear their voices clearly.

"Well, you'll never get an academy award for that performance." It was Gunther's voice, but it was all wrong. What had happened to the German accent?

"Oh, I don't know," Serenity giggled. "She bought it, didn't she?" There was some rustling of fabric. "Mm. Do that again."

"What if she wakes up? Won't she notice you're gone?" This wasn't the voice of a German at all. Norah shook her head, wondering if she was in the midst of some nightmare.

Serenity snorted. "I gave her a sleeping pill. We won't hear from her until morning."

Well, of all the nerve. Nora reached for the tent flap.

"I think we've got her where we want her," Serenity said. "If we put the offer in again the minute we get home, she'll jump at the chance to get rid of the company."

"But we'll offer less this time, eh?" Nora sat back on her heels. Gunter's accent was Canadian, plain and simple. "She'll be grateful to have us take it off her hands."

"Mmmm. That feels good," Serenity groaned. "I've missed you."

"How about this?" The German grunted, and Serenity sighed.

Nora felt the panic in her chest harden into hot coals of rage.

She turned, shielded her penlight with her palm and made her way over to where Eddie had left the burlap bag. She didn't even bother trying to be quiet. The sounds from the tent would cover any noise her footsteps made in the soft jungle soil.

She kicked the rock away, dragged the bag to the tent opening and undid the ties. When the snake had slithered out of the bag and into the tent, she carried the empty bag back to where Eddie had left it, tied it up again and pushed the rock over the opening before going back to her own tent. Under her pillow she found the pill that Serenity had given her. She popped it into her mouth and settled down to sleep until morning.

A riverboat trip along Brazil's Rio Negro inspired Sue Pike's story. Sue is a founding member of the Ladies' Killing Circle and won the Arthur Ellis Award for Best Short Story in 1997. In 2007, she launched Deadlock Press to publish fiction set on the Rideau Canal. Locked Up, *tales of mystery and mischance along Canada's Rideau Canal Waterway, is a celebration of the 175th anniversary of the opening of the canal and its designation as a UNESCO World Heritage Site.*

Thinking Inside the Box

Kris Wood

I'll have me jars of the good stuff along with me. Saint Peter'll let me into Heaven, sure. I'll have me own good brew with me in me box."

The Old Man's quavering, senile bletherings would have been just an irritation to Liam if they had been alone. But they were not alone, and not content with trotting out his own daft plan for a safe eternity, the old fool had spewed the carefully guarded family secret to this new priest, of all people. Liam's fist clenched as he fought the urge to silence his father's maunderings with a clout. He slid a glance at Father Grayson, who stood rigid with disapproval at the bedside.

"Sacrilege!" the cleric hissed, "Blasphemy! I won't hear another word. This is a house of sin!"

Liam thudded down the steep wooden stairs behind the black back of the priest.

Even from behind, Liam could see the man's fury. Liam fought to keep his own anger in check. For one brief moment on the top stair, he considered the possibility of giving the cleric a shove. Surely crashing into the sharp dog-leg at the foot of the treacherous slope would break even a neck as stiff as the priest's? Liam rejected the idea almost as soon as it surfaced. Way too iffy.

How could his father have been so foolish? Liam knew that his father wandered in his mind some, but to blab! After all the rants Liam and the others had endured over the years from the old man, rants reinforced with slaps—repeating the treatment that he had received from his own father. A legacy of strict secrecy passed on with the unlawful skill of making moonshine. They could talk about the fishing. They could talk about the wood-lot, but the real family business, the one that put money into the special account in the Charlottetown bank, far from prying local eyes, must never be discussed.

Then the old man himself went blurting out his crazy plan of salvation, along with the family's private business to the priest. And not a priest like old Father Cullum who'd likely have laughed at their dad's foolishness, then sat down at the kitchen table while you poured him a shot. Liam stifled bitter laughter. No, it had to be this priest—this newcomer, a narrow, humourless creature; as down on drink as a Presbyterian.

Liam stretched out his hand to grab the man's sleeve, sure that once the idiot left the house he'd go straight to the RCMP. Liam felt himself sicken at the thought of getting nabbed now. He made less than a couple of dozen jars a year these days. Just a bit for their last few faithful customers, most of them as far on their way out as Dad. It wasn't as if he even had the knack for brewing the good stuff. The old man could hardly choke down a glass of Liam's making. Only the determination to keep the last two quarts he had made himself in the days when he could still get down to the hidey-hole under the chicken house, for his planned free pass to Heaven, forced him to drink the inferior stuff produced by Liam. That, and a life-long reluctance to give the government a cent more in taxes than he must.

Liam didn't care. He had no liking for homebrew. Give him a glass of beer any day. White lightning had scarred his childhood, and he'd devoted too much of his adult life to obeying his father's bellowed orders in the boat, in the woods and in the still hole to want to continue with any of it after the old man went.

He wasn't good at quick thinking, but he needed to think now. Something to say that would stop the priest; deflect him from reporting the facts behind the old man's ramblings to the cops.

As he rounded the foot of the stairs, he heard the back door open. Thank the Lord! Florrie was home from Montague.

"Why, Father Grayson! What a lovely surprise!" she said, ignoring the priest's preoccupied scowl. "You'll have come to see poor Dad. Isn't that just like you, as busy as you are? Kindness itself, driving all the way out here on such a miserable, cold afternoon."

Florrie's soft voice stopped the angry priest in mid-stride. "Now there's no way I'm letting you leave this house without a nice hot cup of tea to warm you, and a big piece of my lemon loaf. I know how you enjoy it. You said so many nice things at your welcome party. I was some flattered; Liam can tell you."

As Florrie spoke, she whisked off her coat, tied on an apron, pulled the kettle forward on the stove and began setting out china on a tray. The priest hesitated.

"I know it isn't really the thing keeping you here in the kitchen, Father dear, but it's the coziest spot in the house on a day like today. Just sit yourself down there by the stove in poor Dad's old rocker," she eased the reluctant man into the waiting chair, "and I'll have the tea brewed in a wink."

All at once the room became a welcome place, full of warmth and harmony, fragrant, comforting—impossible to leave. The tension began to ebb.

"Shake up the stove, Liam." Florrie turned to her brother, her eyes full of questions. A ticked-off priest in the house needed explaining, and Florrie could be counted on to ferret out the answer to any mystery. Two lifetimes of kinship, of conspiring against parental tyranny and hiding the family secret from a nosy neighbourhood had tuned the powers of silent communication between brother and sister to concert pitch.

Liam indicated that their father had created a problem by a slight upward glance and down-turned mouth. He managed to tilt his hand and raise an elbow to denote that booze was involved as he thrust sticks of maple into the roaring stove.

Florrie's eyes widened as she gathered there was something seriously amiss, something concerning their father and the new priest's hatred of liquor. She didn't know the half of it, Liam thought as he pulled a kitchen chair into the space beside the big old rocker.

Florrie poured the tea. "Poor Dad," she sighed. "I'm afraid he's really failing. For sure he won't be sitting in his chair again." She glanced at Liam as she offered the cake plate to the priest. He nodded approval of the direction her conversation was heading. "I notice the difference in him every day I get in from the store. Fading fast he is, and his mind! Well, Liam can tell you even better than me. Liam looks after him all day while I'm at work. I feel bad about leaving him, but there's nothing to be done. The way his mind is wandering, it would almost be a mercy for the Good Lord to take him. He was always so sharp. It's pitiful to see him so brought down. When I think what an active man he was."

Liam bit back a snort. Active, all right! Active with the back of his hand and the rough edge of his tongue when anyone upset him, and back then, they'd all managed to upset him every blasted day. Even Brendan, his eldest, favourite child, felt it when the old man was mad. A "parlour angel", that's what poor Mam used to call him—some wonderful host, life and soul of every party, but like a bear with a sore head with his own family. No wonder the children had mostly left home as soon as they could. Florrie would have gone too, if Jim Fleet hadn't been lost with the *Magdelena*. Liam didn't blame any of them—except for Brendan—the old man's golden-boy, the son and heir. It should have been Brendan staying home, following in the old man's footsteps, not Liam. But in the end, he'd turned out too much like his father for the pair of them to work together. The fights between them gave Brendan a good excuse to get away to greener pastures. Prince Edward Island wasn't big enough for the two of them.

In other circumstances, Liam would have rejoiced to get shot of Brendan's bullying, overbearing presence. Most days back then, it was like having two bosses in the bush, two captains on the boat for Liam. How he'd longed to be rid of Brendan. But when his brother had gone to Ontario back in the early seventies, he'd taken Marie with him, and Liam's heart had gone with her. After Marie was gone, Liam slid into the role of his father's slave. He could no longer even dream of escape. The years that saw Brendan prosper slid past Liam, polishing his resentment as they rolled away. The anger with Brendan still burned in his chest. Liam made a huge effort to set it aside and concentrate on the present crisis.

He lowered his eyes so that the priest wouldn't see how little he cared for the old man and tried to copy Florrie's sad tones. They might just be able to keep Father Grayson from letting the Mounties in on the family secret if they played on the "wandering mind" theme that Florrie was busily talking up.

"I'm sorry to say that Dad upset Father Grayson, Florrie."

"No!" Florrie's hands flew to her face.

"He got back in the past, like he does. Talking about Grandad, and the old Prohibition times." This wasn't strictly true, but the last thing he wanted to do was remind the priest of the old man's daft maunderings. Liam shook his head, feigning shame and sorrow by keeping his head bent. He mightn't be such a good actor as Florrie, but he was doing his best.

"Oh my soul! It's like he was back in those wicked days when he gets that way. Going on about them taking the homebrewed liquor into the States when he was no' but a boy. We must have heard Grandad tell those old tales a million times when we was little." She leaned forward to gaze into the priest's face. "I do hope that you'll forgive poor Dad, Father dear," she murmured. "He lives in the past. He would be some mortified to think he had offended a priest—if he was in his right mind and all. Dad's always been such a pillar of the church."

Liam barely bothered to listen while the priest mumbled a string of platitudes about his duty to forgive. Florrie had saved the day. She must have been as stunned as himself at the old man's letting the cat out of the bag, but look how she'd turned the thing around, and she still didn't know that their father had told Father Grayson about the family's secret business while going on about his stupid scheme for getting through the Pearly Gates.

Florrie stood up and refilled the cups, smiling and full of gratitude for the priest's forbearance. "I'll just pop and check on Dad," she said, whisking her wiry little body off to trot upstairs, "Give Father some more loaf, Liam."

Liam admired the speed at which Florrie operated. Off to see the old man, getting the tea ready, thinking up a good story. She was a marvel. It was because she was like Mam— small, skinny and sharp. His younger brother Ken was like that too, and Agnes, years gone to B.C. Ken was big, like the old man and his other two sisters, married and living in New Brunswick, and like Brendan. Not that Brendan was just big now. Brendan might be long gone to Hamilton, but, Ken's wife Jeannie was Marie's sister. The sisters kept in fairly frequent contact by phone. Jeannie loved nothing more than a good gossip. Every word she heard from Marie was passed on to Florrie. Even though Liam would have liked to never hear Brendan's name again, it was impossible not to learn all the Hamilton branch of the family's news, and the news was that Brendan's girth had grown at a rate of knots this last while.

Florrie's footsteps clattered downstairs. She was going some, even for her, Liam thought.

"Oh, Father," she gasped, "Come up quick. Dad's breathing sounds so strange. Liam dear, I think you'd best call 911."

*   *   *

"He was gone 'fore the ambulance got there." Liam leaned against the side of his pick-up, his hands thrust into his pockets. He kicked at an icy ridge on the body shop forecourt, speaking in the general direction of his brother Ken's backside as it jutted from under the hood of a battered red Toyota in the first bay. Apart from Ken's oldest, Scotty, who could be heard cursing to the accompaniment of muffled rap music from bay three, they were alone.

"Brendan and Marie'll be here tomorrow." Ken groped for a wrench and banged at something inside the Toyota. "I'm surprised you didn't hurry the funeral. Superstitious bugger won't fly. It's not like him and Dad was close." He gave a small snort of a laugh. "You could have fixed it so's he didn't have time to drive."

Liam, who had been doing a lot of serious thinking lately,

chose his words with care. Ken would wonder if he seemed to have abandoned his well-known dislike of Brendan. It'd be tricky getting it right. If he could fool Ken, he might be able to fool Florrie. That would be the clincher. Anybody who could get one past his sister would be home free.

"I thought about it," he said. That was good. Never lie when you don't have to. Disarm Ken with a show of honesty. He took a breath. Now came the lies. "But I couldn't do it. After all, there's been a lot of water under the bridge. None of us is getting any younger. I don't mind saying it shook me up some when the old man went so sudden like. The priest didn't have time to open his book. 'Course, he did the whole rigmarole anyhow. Still…"

Ken had emerged from under the hood and was looking at him with considerable surprise as he wiped his greasy hands on an old Moosehead T-shirt.

Liam ploughed on. Only semi-lies this time. "Anyway, the old man had Brendan down as a pallbearer. I had to take that into account. Don't need to give folks cause to flap their tongues about us more'n they do already."

"I can't believe you got Dad to arrange anything about the funeral at all. He was that superstitious about dying, and such." Ken seemed okay.

"Once I'd got him convinced that the government'd grab everything unless he made a will, he got the bit between his teeth, like. Wouldn't shut up about it. Going on about the wake, and the prayers, and the service till me and Florrie was half crazy," Liam sighed. "You remember. That was when he started up with his daft idea of taking the brew to Heaven. 'Saint Peter'll have to let me in the Pearly Gates if I takes along a couple of jars of me good stuff.'" Liam whispered, imitating the quavering tones of their failing father.

Ken laughed softly. "At least he didn't tell the world. People'd thought he'd gone off his head, sure."

"Fair makes me boil, always on at us kids to keep us from tellin' all those years when the still was going full tilt. Then he goes and blabs to the priest of all people! That uptight bugger? I never thought Florrie'd be able to get him calmed down. Course, when the old man croaked right after the blow-up, the poor devil got left feeling some guilty. Let's hope he stays that way."

"Oh well, no harm done." Ken clapped Liam on the shoulder. "It's not as if you'd really do what the old man wanted."

Liam gritted his teeth. This was it. How would Ken take it?

"What d'you mean?" Liam gazed at Ken, intent on looking and sounding utterly sincere. "Me and Dad had our differences, but I give him my word. You don't go back on your word, man."

"C'mon, Liam," Ken was still half laughing, unsure whether to take Liam seriously or not. "You've gotta be kidding! Nobody 'ud expect you to keep a daft promise like that. Put a couple of jars of homebrew in his coffin so he can bribe his way into Heaven! It's nuts!"

"Nobody knows about the promise, 'cept you, me and Florrie." When he'd shared the old man's stupid plan with Ken, it had been a joke. They'd snickered about it several times. Now he wished he'd kept quiet. "You didn't tell Jeannie, did you? I asked you not to tell a soul."

Liam had no need to fake his earnestness now. This was vital. If Jeannie knew, then so did all of Montague. More to the point, so did Brendan. His own plan was out the window if Brendan knew. Then he could be stuck following through on a dumb promise that no one in their right mind would keep, all for nothing. He certainly wouldn't be keeping it now, not with the Priest in on the business, if he hadn't suddenly realized the possibility that the old man's craziness had given him. Just as long as Brendan hadn't heard.

"You know me better than that. I didn't say nothing to nobody." Ken smiled and elbowed Liam in the ribs, "I'd not tell a secret to Jeannie. She's a good old lass, but no one can accuse her of keeping things in."

Liam gave a sigh of relief and risked a grin back at Ken. Now all that mattered was that Brendan hadn't changed. Last news from Maria, via Jeannie, was that he was up over three hundred pounds, still smoking the big cigars, eating the expense account dinners and knocking back the booze. He was also still engaged in all-night, hardball negotiations for the union, and ignoring everything Marie and the doctors said in favour of his lucky rabbit's foot, and the same obstinate belief in his own superiority that he'd got from their father. Jeannie seemed to think that Marie was pretty fed up with Brendan's bad habits. Liam was confident that Jeanie would have been hot off the press with any news that Brendan had reformed. He soldiered on with the task of getting Ken on board.

"Look, I know it was crazy to swear I'd carry out Dad's getting into Heaven idea, but it's done. I can't change it. If you, me and Florrie just keep Dad's daft little plan under hatches, nobody'll ever know. Okay?"

"But, how'll you work it? Douggie's got the old man now, hasn't he? How'll you square putting something extra in the casket?"

"Douggie won't know nothing. Nobody at Monahans'll be any the wiser. The old man wanted the prayers and the wake at home, not the funeral parlour. He hated undertakers— more unlucky than a woman on the boat, to hear him talk. Douggie'll deliver him home tomorrow for the prayers and wake. I'll be the one to sit up with him overnight. Florrie's beat, and Brendan'd have a fit if you asked him to sit beside a dead body. Him and Dad always more'n half believed them ghosts and hauntings tales."

Ken nodded. The old man's superstitious beliefs had lasted a lifetime. From all reports, Brendan's were just as deeply ingrained.

"I'll wedge the jars in so's they don't show when Douggie comes to screw him down before we head out to the Point. Then it's just the short service round the grave, we cover him up, and it's over." Liam could see that Ken was almost on side. "It's a piece of cake, Ken. Stop worrying about it, and worry about all the money you'll lose while the shop's closed on Thursday."

They laughed together a little, cuffing and shoving one another, engaging in the same friendly horseplay that had defined their relationship since Ken was weaned. Liam felt huge relief that the task of getting Ken squared had gone so well. There was still a lot to mull over—a lot of "what ifs". He'd thought and dreamed about ways to kill Brendan for thirty years, and this plan, the only one that had even a hope of working, was far from foolproof. It might not pan out, but at least he was more confident now that he could pull it off.

$$* \quad * \quad *$$

Liam had steeled himself to be civil meeting Brendan, but it was Marie who shook him the most. He hadn't seen her for years. Not since Mam died. He knew she was no longer the laughing girl he'd loved and lost. He expected her to be like Jeannie, comfortably middle-aged. Better dressed maybe, since Brendan was a big-shot union boss and pulling down a lot more money than Ken, but instead she looked like someone on TV. Slim, young, and her clothes had a look that even he could see was a far cry from the local womens' finery from the catalogue.

Brendan, enormous and purple-faced, seemed exactly as Liam had hoped. His superstitious edging away from the old man's casket set up in the big bay window, his utter horror at the appearance of Florrie's black cat, until she showed him its white belly, the salt tossed over his massive shoulder after he'd frosted his potatoes at supper; all served to hearten Liam no end. Brendan wouldn't get near enough to the casket to look over the rim, let alone walk up and give it a close inspection. He'd be the last to spot any additions. It made it easier to bear Brendan's crushing hug and sentimental "reminiscences" about the "good" times they'd shared as lads. Liam didn't even care that Brendan took over as host of the wake. He was tired from helping Al McCourt dig the grave. Usually folks who died in winter weren't buried until spring, but everyone knew how superstitious the old man had been, and Al didn't mind a bit of heavy machinery work in the off season. He certainly hadn't noticed Liam's satisfaction at the churned up mess they'd made of the old cemetery laneway.

He sat quiet, perfectly happy to look at Marie who took little part in the noisy wake. How much would she really care about what might happen tomorrow? He could comfort her, if things went as planned.

Not a lot of the night remained after the wake. Liam found the time went very fast. It took longer than he'd thought to remove the padding from the foot of the box, and longer yet for the smell of burning it to clear. Arranging the two big old mason jars of homebrew took even longer. They were well sealed, but he had to get them positioned to stay hid while Douggie Monahan screwed down the lid, and to remain in place for the ride out to the cemetery at the Point. Monahan's boys could be counted on to keep the casket pretty much on the level in transit. It was going to be later when Liam wanted the jars to move.

Dawn came, and he opened the drapes. It was snowing. He almost laughed out loud.

*   *   *

The morning went badly. Brendan seemed to be feeling the effects of the wake. He and Marie argued. Marie kept up a string of complaints—the cold, the lack of cappuccino and melon slices, her hair, the snow. Liam couldn't help noticing that she looked somewhat haggard, older and overly made-up in the daylight, and her voice had lost the soft Island lilt. It sounded nasal and whiny. Brendan growled that he couldn't do anything about her problems and wolfed down a second plateful of bacon and eggs. Marie switched to criticizing him, his overindulgence at the wake, his barbarity in dragging her to such an uncivilized event, and the effect of a huge, fatty breakfast on his health and girth.

Liam almost felt sorry for his brother. The nagging was getting on his nerves. He was used to quiet and harmony with Florrie. Couldn't Marie see that Brendan was a bag of nerves about the funeral? He began to feel uneasy about his plan. It had all been going so well, but he was no longer quite so pleased with his cleverness in pulling it off.

He'd just decided to let Brendan in on the old man's getting into Heaven scheme when the undertakers arrived, followed by Ken's family and the New Brunswick lot. Douggie Monahan screwed down the lid of the old man's casket without a blink, and before Liam could say anything to Brendan, they were all hustled out the door and into the cars.

Liam and Florrie went in Monahan's new black SUV behind the ancient hearse. Then Brendan with his Audi, and Marie complaining that the short walk across the snowy yard had wrecked her four-inch heeled, suede boots.

The little old church out at the Point was no longer used, but many local families had plots in the cemetery up on the hill behind. The lane to the graves was in notoriously poor repair. Old ruts from ATVs and new ones from Al's digger plus years of erosion from rain etching out the gravel were now frozen solid and covered by three inches of snow.

The cortège drew to a halt. Just as Liam had so hopefully planned, the lane was impassable for Douggie's old hearse. Nor did Douggie want to risk the oil pan on his nice new SUV, four wheel drive. Marie returned to her seat in the car.

A neighbour with a half ton tried to drive up the slope with Douggie and the priest, but he fish-tailed so badly that he gave up, and they, like the rest, had to walk. Before they set off, Douggie got the six pallbearers plus two of his own boys organized to carry the casket. Liam had imagined this moment so well that it was almost like déjà vu, but now he realized what a fool he'd been to even think of doing such a thing. He hovered close to Brendan, ready to pull him aside and tell him about the jars as soon as everyone else got out of the way.

"The weight'll be to the back," Douggie told the men. "Liam and Brendan's the biggest…" He looked at Brendan's purple face, and faltered, struck by doubt.

"No!" Liam's anxiety sharpened his voice. "Brendan's not in good shape. Let Ken come behind."

Brendan turned on him. One minute he was standing there panting in the cold air, the next he was the old man reincarnated, a bellowing, snorting fury in an alpaca coat and gleaming city shoes.

"Who the hell you think you're calling 'out of shape', boy?" he yelled, balling his huge fists and spitting his fury into Liam's face, "I could beat you to a pulp when we were kids, and by god, I can do it now. I'll give you 'out of shape'!"

Liam froze. He could feel his face flame. He was horribly aware of the others looking on; of the neighbours crowding up behind, their ears flapping.

"Right," he muttered, "Suit yourself."

After that, Liam concentrated on nothing but keeping his footing and listening for the jars. Had he got them set right? Would they roll?

The pallbearers made slow progress. Without warning, the casket lurched to one side. Liam grabbed for a handle, yanking the casket hard against his own head. Scotty, in front of him swore, but managed to hang on. The brother-in-law, in front of Ken, had slipped and Ken had tripped over him. Liam felt a terrible urge to laugh. Imagine if they'd dropped the casket! The old man would have a fit. Nothing could be more unlucky. They got going again, but the pallbearers' confidence had taken a beating, and so, it seemed, had the jars. Almost at once Liam heard one move. No worry that Scotty might hear. He had one of his music machines plugged into his ears, as usual. Liam had spotted the wires under Scotty's upturned coat collar when they'd almost fallen. The only problem now was whether or not Brendan would hear the jars over the noise of his own steam-engine breathing.

There it was again. A rumble this time—not much padding in the bottom of Douggie's mid-price boxes, Liam thought, and thanks to a good night's work, none at all at the foot. Another rumble followed, then two loud, distinct bangs. Brendan stopped abruptly, letting go the casket as if it was red-hot.

"Get him out," he gasped, backing away. He couldn't seem

to speak properly. His words sounded garbled, and he clawed at his collar, his feet sliding from under him in the snow. "He's alive in there! He's alive! Get him ou…"

Almost everyone following clustered around in a vain attempt to assist the twitching mound that had been Brendan. Liam and the others carried on up the lane. With Douggie's help, they got the casket into place. The priest, who had rushed down the lane with his cell phone to call the ambulance and mutter last rites, soon returned and hurried through the committal service for the old man, aware that there was more snow coming, and he had an invitation to lunch with a friend.

Florrie patted Liam's shoulder as they were at last able to drive to the Legion Hall for coffee and refreshments. "It wasn't your fault, dear," she whispered, "you was just keeping your promise to Dad. Besides, you tried to stop Brendan walking at the back. But there, he always was that pig-headed. Just like his father."

"Yes," said Liam, "He always was, wasn't he?"

Kris Wood lives on the Eastern Shore of Nova Scotia with her husband John, mother, Ellen, and Rosie, the dog. She is a retired gerontologist who writes both alone and with her long time friend and projects partner, Pat Wilson. Short stories are her favourite thing to write, especially when they incorporate wild and weird Maritime happenings in the telling. She is the co-author, with Pat Wilson, of the Maritime mystery novel Lucky Strike.

A Really Good Day

Nancy McQueen

The Mouse and Donny had staked out a sunny spot on the steps of the Canadian Regional Bank on the corner of Queen and Bathurst. The Mouse watched Donny smile at no one in particular as he sat his enormous bulk on the second from the top step. The Mouse glared at the people they had just chased off the stairs—a middle-aged Indian man with hair in a greying, greasy ponytail, who was now standing undulating gently on the sidewalk, and an ancient Chinese woman with a stubbly chin and a pinchy mouth that held one protruding tooth. The woman clutched the handle of a rusty, crook-wheeled bundle buggy packed with several overflowing yellow garbage bags and a number of pointy objects wrapped in faded red cloth.

The Indian was holding up his dark, stained pants with one hand and gesturing vaguely with the other toward his possessions on the steps beside the Mouse. The Mouse kicked the man's filthy sleeping bag with the side of his ratty sneaker, then the torn cardboard box beside it. The sleeping bag tumbled down the steps and landed softly at the man's feet, but the box hit old one-tooth woman's buggy a glancing blow and tore a hole in one of her plastic bags. Bits of paper, freed from confinement, began to drift onto the sidewalk and were riffled away by a slight breeze. The woman started to shout at the Mouse in little singsong yelps. The Mouse made a rude gesture and sat down on the top step. As usual, when he got agitated, the iris of the Mouse's left eye began a loose rolling spin in its socket. He hated it when it did that.

Donny stared at the Mouse's spinning eye. "Are you mad, Mouse?"

"Shut up, Donny," the Mouse said, as his eye picked up a bit of speed. "And don't stare at me neither, or you can go sit somewheres else."

Donny dragged his gaze from the Mouse's face. "Donny likes this day, Mouse. This is gonna be a good day, a really good day."

"It'd be a better day if we had a coupla hundred bucks."

The Mouse had rolled a young guy the night before in an alley behind a club on Adelaide Street in the entertainment district, but the kid's wallet had only held a twenty and some small change.

The Mouse looked at Donny. "Maybe Tony needs us to do some collecting." The Mouse often hired Donny out as muscle. He looked huge and impressively intimidating as long as the target didn't realize Donny wouldn't actually hurt anyone. Hurting people didn't fit in with Donny's sunny disposition. Fortunately, a smile on Donny's meaty, uni-browed, ape-like features looked like a menacing growl to those who didn't know him.

Such a grin appeared suddenly on Donny's face as he looked over the Mouse's left shoulder, causing several pedestrians to decide to hurry across the street now and take their chances with traffic, rather than waiting for the light to change.

"Look Mouse, it's Drake-the-Snake. Hi, Snake!" He gave a cheery wave with one huge paw.

The Mouse whipped around, but it was too late to escape. Detective Drake, recent undercover cop, was already starting up the bank steps toward them, chewing on the business end of one of the carved toothpicks that the Mouse knew he extorted by the hundreds, along with other considerations, from the hole-in-the-wall Yung Fat Trading Company Emporium on Dundas Street.

"Donny and me aren't doing nothing," the Mouse said quickly.

"I can see that. So I'm gonna give you the chance to do something good with your day," Detective Drake said, rolling his toothpick to the other side of his mouth with his tongue.

The Mouse looked around quickly from under lowered eyelids. Even though Drake was dressed to fit in with the neighbourhood, ripped-knee jeans and a once-white t-shirt that read "Ontario—Yours to Discover", and had only recently started working this area, the Mouse did not want to be seen talking to him.

Drake scratched the stubble on his chin. "I need some information."

"What kinda information?" the Mouse asked shortly. He looked Drake in the face.

Drake grimaced. "Jesus, can't you do something about that damned eye? It gives me the creeps. One of your bad-ass friends should rip it out one day. Or maybe I should just do it myself, eh?" He grinned at the Mouse around his toothpick.

"Gee, Snake, Mouse don't like it when you talk about his eye. Do you, Mouse?"

"Shut up Donny. Whadda ya want, Drake?"

"Seems to me you should be glad to give me this information, Arthuuuuur," Drake said, drawing out the Mouse's real given name. "Seeing as how you owe me a favour and all."

The Mouse felt his rolling eye pick up its tempo. "Drake, you ain't never going to forget that guy! It was an accident. An ak-see-dent. How was I supposed to know he would breathe in his own puke and die?"

"Well, Arthuuuuuur, he was just a drunk, stoned club kid on his way home, and if you hadn't happened by to tap him on his skull while he was upchucking in that alley, he would still be here, and likely a credit to his family." Drake swivelled his toothpick then snapped it with a crack of his large front teeth. He spat it on the sidewalk and pulled a replacement from his back pocket, licking both ends before installing it in the corner of his mouth. "Way I figure, you owe me favours until you die."

The Mouse's left eye was now exceeding the speed limit. "All right, all right, whadda ya want?"

"With your underworld connections, Arthuuur, I want the name of a local exterminator."

The Mouse saw Donny's face crease in a frown. "You got roaches, Snake? Mouse's and my place's got roaches too. They're bad."

"Shut up, Donny. He ain't talking about roaches." The Mouse's could feel his eye reaching escape velocity. It made him feel dizzy and ill.

"Sure I am, Donny, a she-roach who's bugging me." His voice hardened. "Someone I need to disappear. And before you ask, it's none of your business why."

"You wanna hit on a woman?" The Mouse kept his voice barely above a whisper. His body tensed.

"Why, Arthuuur, you wanna protect the weaker sex or something?" Drake paused then grabbed the front of the Mouse's shirt, pulling him close, the carved end of his toothpick an inch from the Mouse's swirling left eye. The

Mouse cringed and tried to pull back. Drake's voice was deep, low and slow. "And if I hear anything—a peep, a whisper—about this little conversation, Arthuuuur, you will find yourself locked in a cell forever with the meanest, most perverted, drug-dealing biker I can find. Get it?" He let the Mouse drop, and only Donny's bulk behind him prevented him from falling down the steps.

"Get outta my way, Donny," the Mouse snarled. He broke Drake's stare and looked down at the sidewalk. He only hesitated a moment, and his voice, when it came, was low, but steady. "You wanna good job, Hecate's the best. She looks like an old gypsy lady—tells fortunes even, from her walk-up on Queen above the Budapest Bakery." The Mouse gestured further down Queen West. "The victim never suspects this li'l old lady, and next thing, he's bleeding on the sidewalk, floating in the harbour, or eating cement on a construction site."

"But Mouse," Donny said, his face puckering in a frown.

"Shut up, Donny, and I mean it! Don't say no more, or I won't let you hang around. Got it?"

"I got it, Mouse. But Mouse..."

"No more, Donny, I swear..."

Drake turned back as he began walking down the steps. "So Arthuur, remember what happens if I hear anything about our little chat. In fact, maybe I should give you a taste of jail time anyhow, just so's you can try it out."

"Nobody hears nothing from me," the Mouse said quietly, his eyes still on the sidewalk.

Drake turned down the street toward the Budapest Bakery.

"Can I talk now, Mouse?" Donny looked up at the Mouse, but the Mouse kept his gaze on Drake's back as the cop strolled up Queen Street.

"Yeah, what?"

"Mouse, Hecate don't do women! It makes her crazy mad even to ask her. Donny heard the last guy who asked her just disappeared."

The Mouse turned around. "Aw, Donny, that's just a story. We don't know that for sure. If Hecate don't do women, she'll just tell the Snake, and he'll find somebody else." The Mouse sighed and stretched his arms above his head. "Remember how you said this was gonna be a really good day? I'm thinking you're right. Tell you what, I'll pay for breakfast over at the Kowloon Chinese-Canadian Restaurant, I'm thinking it's gonna be such a good day."

The Mouse looked down at his friend and smiled. His left eye was rock-steady.

Nancy McQueen is a new mystery writer, although writing of the non-fiction (mostly) variety is part of her day job. She lives in downtown Toronto, quite near the location of her story, with a very cranky Quaker parrot named Malki, and Malki's pet budgie Pip. She is working on a novel-length historical mystery, and some short non-mystery fiction inspired by quirky characters in her neighbourhood (including herself, and possibly a loud, crabby parrot).

Dead Against Telling

Linda Wiken

S o, who did it? Who did the old babe in?"
Detective Julie Kellogg spun around to face the hoarse voice demanding an answer. She had to look down at the wizened creature propped up by a cane.

"You ask me, it was young Bulldog Face. Probably got caught humping Poodle Cut and knew the old dame had to go if he wanted to keep his paycheque. Old lady McGuire kept real quiet, looked like a Shih Tzu, all silk 'n bows, popping in and outta mass and rattlin that rosary around in her pocket. She wouldnta stood for having anything on the side around here. No sirree, she'da been sniffing around for secrets." He snorted. "Can't have any fun around here."

"Now, Mr. Sorens." A tall thin woman dressed in a pink uniform appeared from a doorway. "And, where should we be?"

"I'm on my way to my room," Sorens snapped, "but you sure as hell can't come with me." He shook an arthritic hand and continued his shuffle down the hall. Julie could just make out the tune he whistled, "I got my thrill on Blueberry Hill". She smiled.

The nurse's aide grimaced, shrugged her shoulders in Julie's direction, and ignoring the old guy's warning, followed him.

Life in the seniors' fast lane, Julie thought. She spotted the stairs, opted to bypass the elevator, and climbed the three flights. The start of a new case always got the adrenaline pumping. A murder, especially that of an older person, added a note of dread. Especially one in a seniors' residence. She'd been in a lot of them this past month, looking for the perfect new home for her mother, juggling the guilt she felt, even though her mom kept assuring Julie it was time.

She shook herself out of her reverie as she reached the door to room 310. It opened as if on cue, and two officers in blue—one a constable, the other, Sergeant Lorens of Delta platoon who'd called in the homicide to Criminal Investigations—backed out of the room.

"Hey, Kellogg…it's all yours," said the sergeant.

"Ident get started?"

"Not here yet. Dawson'll fill you in." He winked and strode towards the elevator. They'd gone through Police College in Aylmer together, and now, twelve years later, Ken Lorens was sergeant and Julie still a constable. Not that it really bothered her. She'd meant to take the sergeant's exam a couple of times, but life had a way of interfering. First, her no-fault, amicable divorce that turned out to be neither and had consumed her energy. Now, all the worry about her mom, not to mention time spent looking at places.

"What've you got?" Julie asked Dawson.

"Victim's name is Mary Margaret McGuire. Age seventy-nine. Took one shot right between the eyes. 911 got the call at 1720 hours. I arrived on scene at 1724."

"Who called it in?"

"One of the staff. A nurses' aide, Peggy Warden. Came to see why McGuire hadn't shown up for supper. Took one look then called us. Unfortunately, she used the phone in there, but, get this. She had to unlock the door to get in."

Julie opened her notebook and wrote down the details.

"Any sign of the weapon?"

"Nada. And I'll bet you my parking spot for a month that nobody heard or saw a thing."

"No bet, Dawson. Although the sound of a gunshot is usually hard to miss. You on watch here?"

He held up the yellow plastic "crime scene" tape. "You got it. Just going to start decorating the hall."

*   *   *

Julie found the administrator's office back down on the main floor, along a hallway that ran the length of the building. The door stood open, and a male, medium-build, in his late thirties, sat at the desk. She knocked.

"Excuse me, I'm Detective Julie Kellogg. You're Mr. Gant?"

"Yes, I'm David Gant, come in. This is a very sad thing, but I've got to start making some phone calls. Damage control. When this makes the eleven o'clock news tonight, there are going to be some very unhappy backers. I don't mean to sound crass, what with Mrs. McGuire just dying, but I have to face the reality of bad press. I've been at Ogilvy Manor for ten years, and nothing like this has ever happened before."

"I do need to ask you some questions, Mr. Gant. Now would be a good time. It won't take long."

Gant hesitated, then pointed to the chair. Julie remained standing.

"Tell me, as administrator, do the residents talk to you about their problems? Share confidences?"

"I hear about their financial problems, of course."

"How were Mrs. McGuire's finances?"

Gant shook his head and shifted in his seat. "I'm really not certain. She had been concerned just before Christmas, as I recall, but hadn't mentioned anything lately. And her payments were always on time."

"Does she have any relatives?"

"She has a niece who lives in Toronto. Here's her phone number. I'm not looking forward to this call."

Julie scribbled down the number. "I'll make the call."

"That's a relief. Look, I need to know how your investigation will affect the routine around here. The residents are creatures of habit, you know. Everything has to be right on schedule, or we hear about it."

"I can understand that," Julie said. "My mother's like that. Any changes, no matter how small, and we're into a crisis."

Gant nodded.

"The Ident crew could take a long time, and we'll need to keep her room unavailable until they're finished," Julie explained. "We'll need an office where we can interview the staff tonight, then in the morning, a couple of officers and I will be back to interview the residents."

"How about the photocopying room next to the library? There's a desk and telephone in there. And here's a copy of our monthly newsletter with the daily schedules in it. That might help."

"Thanks. And I'll need a list of the residents and their room numbers."

"Just let me know if there's anything else I can do," Gant said, handing over the list.

Julie left the office and headed back upstairs. Two attendants from the body removal service lounged against a gurney in the hall to the left of the door at 310. She nodded at them and knocked before entering the room.

"How you doing, Teddy?"

"Oh, same as usual, Julie, just frigging fine." Teddy used the back of his latex gloved hand to push his gold-rimmed glasses back up to the bridge of his nose. The only other visible feature was his greying black mustache. The rest of his body was encased in the standard white coveralls and cap of the Ident team.

"Okay, if I come in?"

"Sure. You know the drill. Grab a suit. Don't touch. Yada, yada."

Julie donned her outfit, complete with white hospital-style booties, and went straight over to the bed. It was hard to get an impression of what Mary Margaret McGuire had looked like. The bullet hole between her eyes had shredded the flesh, leaving a grotesque opening in its wake.

Julie looked the body over, noting the high-necked white polyester blouse, now stained with blood, the pale grey suedene jumper, the shrunken hands clasped at the waist, with liver spots creeping out from under white lace cuffs. She stepped back against the wall and made a sketch of the room. "Any wild guesses?"

"There should be a bullet somewhere in there, so you'll have one thing to go on. As for the door, lots of partials on the lock. We'll see what we can do for you."

"Any other prints?"

"Not many. Some fuzzy latents. Overlays mainly. Nothing's been wiped, just added to."

She took a couple of steps forward and looked around the room, trying for a sense of Mary Margaret McGuire's life. Light ash dresser and chest of drawers along one wall, Queen Anne chair, light coloured round end table and pink tub chair at the far end under the window, TV on a dark bookcase, and the bed.

The story was on the walls, every inch covered by frames, some photos, some paintings, others apparently poems cut from magazines. A closer look later on would give her an overview of all those years of living.

Julie checked the inside of the door, careful not to touch the handle and lock. She'd seen several like this model in her recent tours of seniors' residences. The lock ensured the privacy her mom was so insistent upon, even if the rules discouraged it. Doors were to be kept unlocked at all times, except when the resident went out.

Too bad. It meant an open invitation for the killer.

* * *

Julie took a few minutes to look around the garden before entering the residence the next morning. Lots of colourful flowers bordered several seating areas. Her mom would enjoy that. It would help take her mind off the growing realization of what she could no longer manage to do. Simple tasks, often. Her mom was right, it was time, but Julie's guilt just wouldn't quit.

Ogilvy Manor had been on Julie's list for a visit. What an introduction.

These were not thoughts for today's agenda, though. She'd read a copy of the ballistics report before leaving the station. The weapon in question was a .45, but the shell casing didn't have the usual U.S. markings. Possibly German. And it was old. She hoped there would be more answers by the end of the day.

But for now, all she had was questions. Why had no one heard the shot? And how had the murderer been able to lock the door when leaving? The two keys that McGuire had been allotted were found in the room. The staff keys were accounted for. And why bother to lock it? Unless the perp had wanted to buy time. A resident needing those extra few minutes to settle back into his or her own room. At slow speed. And wait for the heart rate to slow back down to normal.

Julie had timed her arrival for the end of the breakfast hour.

Several residents were already ambling along the hall towards the elevator. It took her a few minutes to track down McGuire's neighbour and several more to steer her into the interview room.

"Did you see anyone visiting Mrs. McGuire just before supper last evening, Mrs. Edgecombe?"

"Nope. That's the time I watch my show, *Law and Order.*"

Julie had to lean closer to distinguish the words from the slow exhaling of breath, almost a hiss. Fortunately, her mother could still be understood, when she so chose. Selective speaking, the kids had dubbed it.

Enid Edgecombe dabbed at her mouth with a handkerchief rolled in her right hand. "Watch it every day, and I don't like to be interrupted. You see the noise, the shooting and such, gets too loud, so I take my hearing aid out. Then I turn up the volume so I can hear the talking."

That explains why no one heard anything unusual, thought Julie. "Do you remember when you last saw Mrs. McGuire?"

"Yesterday afternoon, I think."

"About what time was that?"

"Right about when the afternoon's program was to start. They thought they'd treat us to a bunch of twittering schoolgirls trying to be a choir. I left when they were starting. I saw Mrs. McGuire, just didn't talk to her. She was going into the nurse's office to get her pills."

"Had Mrs. McGuire talked about anything unusual lately? Or if she was worried about something?"

"Nope. Just the chocolates. She was always looking forward to having a chocolate. She loved chocolate. But do you think she'd ever share? Two years we've lived here, right next door, and not once did she share her precious chocolates."

"Is there anything else you can tell me, Mrs. Edgecombe?"

"Only that if you were looking for the most likely dead body around here, it should be that snotty Mrs. Franconi," she wheezed. "Goes around with her nose stuck up in the air all the time. Talks about how famous she was, how much better than the rest of us. Wouldn't have surprised me one bit if she turned up dead one day."

Edgecombe sniffed into her handkerchief. "She says she was an opera star, you know. Tries showing off singing the high notes whenever there's a sing-a-long, but old Joe Park is always telling her to stuff it, and she gets all huffy and carries on about her days onstage, although she's never shown anyone a program book or newspaper article. Not that we'd pay any attention. She won't even invite anyone into her room. I'd sure like to get in there and have a peak."

"How did Mrs. McGuire feel about her?" Julie asked.

"How did she feel? Like the rest of us, of course. Thought the woman was hard to stomach."

"Did she tell you that?"

"No. She didn't need to. I could tell. Especially after the fight those two had."

"Tell me about it."

"I didn't hear what they were saying, 'cause they were out on the patio, standing in the cold wind, although the sun was out that day. But I could tell they were arguing, and it looked like McGuire got the better of her that time."

"When was this?"

"Oh, last month some time. Must have been late in the month, after the snow went, because Mrs. McGuire wasn't one for going out for a walk in the snow."

"Can you think of any other time you've noticed the two of them together arguing?"

Her eyebrows scrunched into two penciled lines. "No. It's only that Mrs. McGuire once said something funny about her. Real funny."

"What was that?"

"Oh, something about Mrs. Franconi was going to keep her in chocolate. Now, isn't that strange?"

*　　*　　*

Julie knocked on the door to room 209 and had to repeat it a few seconds later. "Mrs. Franconi, are you in there?"

The door opened inward a few inches, and a voice asked, "Who are you?"

"I'm with the police. I'd like to ask you a few questions, if you don't mind."

Maybe she did mind. She hesitated opening the door long enough for Julie to wonder about protocol with the elderly. She couldn't just barge in, but she sure as hell didn't have grounds for a search warrant.

Julie wasn't prepared for Franconi. The auburn wig was obvious, but only on closer look did Julie notice the masses of wrinkles woven beneath a layer of foundation. This wasn't a body withered with age but one with layers of padding wearing a very stylish coatdress. She commented on it.

"You like it, my dear?" Her accent was thick, Italian, but understandable. "I made it myself. I make all of my clothing myself because I have never bought off the rack. In my younger days, I travelled Europe as a renowned opera singer, and my gowns were gorgeous. Simply gorgeous, and always made by a seamstress. Now, I cannot sleep at night, so I amuse myself by making my clothes. I even design them myself."

"You're very talented."

"Oh, yes, my dear. I have many talents, but they are not appreciated here. These people have no culture. They cannot begin to know what my life has been about. The fame, the money.

231

Until the war came, and then I could travel no more. And my Guido, he was wounded by the Germans, so we came to Canada, then he got sick so I spent my years taking care of him. Until he died, ten years ago. I do not sleep through the night since then."

Julie murmured something intended to be comforting before proceeding. "I'd like to ask you some questions about Mrs. McGuire."

"Yes, but why me?"

"We're questioning everyone in the residence. Did you see Mrs. McGuire yesterday?"

"No."

"What did you think of her?"

"Think of her? I tell you this, she was not one of the nasty ones, looking down on me because I come from the old country or the others who are jealous because of my celebrity."

"Were you friends? Did you do things together? Take tea, go for walks?"

"No, I keep to myself these days. People here are too mean."

"Did the two of you ever argue?"

Franconi drew in a deep breath, as if to give voice to an aria. Julie braced herself.

"No. Not argue. I just tell you she was different from the others."

"Someone mentioned seeing you two arguing."

"That is all they do around here, make up stories and spread them. Probably upset that I talk to her and not them. Envy takes on many shapes, you know."

*　　*　　*

Julie tried Ernie Sorens' room next. She finally found him downstairs in the lounge.

"Mr. Sorens, remember me? I'm Detective Kellog. We spoke in the hall yesterday, the day of Mrs. McGuire's death."

Sorens looked startled, then took his time in giving her the once-over. "Sure, I remember you, doll. Those legs. The legs of a Great Dane you've got. Long'n lanky. Makes you a mite taller than me, but I don't mind."

She pegged Sorens at about five feet tops, which made her extra eight inches feel positively towering.

He moved his cane closer to her. "I'm kinda partial to blondes, too. Why don't you come along to my room and we'll, you know, have some fun."

"I am on duty, Mr. Sorens." Julie bit back a smile. "I need to ask you a few questions. I've got an office down the hall."

Sorens hobbled in front of her to the room and waited for her to precede him through the door. She thought she felt a light tap on her right hip as she walked past him, but couldn't be certain. Sorens looked pleased with himself as he eased into the chair across from her. He was whistling the same tune, "Blueberry Hill".

"Now, Mr. Sorens..."

"Wilfred, or Wilfie, doll."

She tried again, "What can you tell me about Mrs. McGuire?"

"Aw, she was a sourpuss. Probably hadn't got lucky in decades, that one. You can tell those around here that's getting it once in a while, and those who aren't. That's what keeps you young, you know."

"You mentioned last time that Mrs. McGuire would go sniffing around for secrets. What did you mean by that?"

Sorens kept one hand on his cane and scratched his chin with the other, watching her the whole time. "Need a shave. That's another thing that keeps on going or should I say, growing." He chuckled. "Anyways, I didn't mean anything by it, doll. I like to talk, that's all. We all of us in here have things that help pass the time. I talk. Some play cards all day. Joe Park, he's always sitting in the lounge, tinkling the ivories. Mrs. McGuire liked to snoop. Getting at people's secrets was her thing. Now talking, that's harmless. So are cards and the piano. But secrets, well you know, there's plenty of those, what with the…" He winked. "You know?"

"I imagine this isn't a place where secrets are safe." Julie tried a casual smile. "Why don't you tell me about this…you know."

Sorens let out a snort, which turned into a coughing fit. He pulled a creased handkerchief from his pant pocket and wiped his mouth once he'd gotten his coughing under control. "I can tell you, one has nothing to do with the other. Besides, talk is, it's one of those serial killers, and some of the guys have got a pool going as to who'll be next."

"You're kidding."

Sorens shrugged. "Gotta do something to lighten the time. That's what I call it, doing time until your number's up. So's you make it one hell of a party, and that's okay. Not even thoughts of murder can throw you."

Julie shook her head. "Okay, but I'd like to hear about what's been going on, even if you think it's not related. Why don't you tell me all about it, and then we'll be sure." She smiled and lightly touched his arm. She'd try it his way.

Sorens looked at her hand, squared his shoulders, placed both his hands on the handle of his cane and grinned. "So, do you think I'll need my lawyer for this?"

"Are you implicated?"

"Not in the murder, doll. And not directly in the service, although I do help with the flow of traffic, so to speak."

"You're welcome to call your lawyer, Mr. Sorens, but it doesn't sound too damaging so far."

"Okey dokey, then. Here goes. There's a male resident here, who shall remain nameless, who contracts the services of members of the fairer sex for other residents as needed."

"Are you saying what I think you're saying?"

"Sure am, doll. He knows several show breeds from the Seniors Bingo Centre down the street, and he lines them up, for a slight fee. In between games, you know."

Julie managed to shut down the images threatening to pour into her mind. "And do these women get paid for their services?"

"Not really. Cab fare mainly, and maybe some money to stake them to a few games."

He leaned towards Julie, lowering his voice. "You're not going to do anything about this, are you, doll? I mean, we aren't hurtin' anyone. Like I said, gotta have some fun. Gives ya something to look forward to, besides a nail clipping or the monthly birthday bash."

Julie sat in silence a few minutes, wondering what the hell she would do with this. Give it to vice? Not too likely.

"Who's running the service, Mr. Sorens?"

"Wilfie. Aw, I can't tell you that, doll. No matter how much I'd like to. I'm an honorable fella."

She decided to let it go for the moment. It did seem an unlikely scenario for murder. Unless McGuire had tried her hand at blackmail. A good motive for murder and maybe a little something for a sweet tooth.

*   *   *

Sophia Franconi was no faster in opening the door this second time.

"Sorry to disturb you again, but I have to ask you a few more questions. I hope you don't mind." Julie smiled and edged her way in, so there'd be no chance of refusal.

She looks flustered, Julie thought. A good start. "I got to

thinking about your opera days and what a glamorous time it must have been."

Franconi motioned Julie into a chair, suddenly the relaxed hostess. "Oh, my dear, it was. You cannot imagine how exciting it was. Nobility came to hear me. I was showered with flowers and romantic offers. That was the thing in those days, you know. I had the men adoring me."

"And then the war changed all that."

"Yes. We escaped from Mussolini, Guido and I, and with some help from admirers of mine, made our way to New York. And then, we go to Montreal."

"What did you do there? Did you resume your singing career?"

Franconi fumbled with the tissue box on the end table. At last, she found a tissue and an answer. "Not really. I teach singing for a while, and then, I nurse Guido. He had emphysema. A terrible time. And then kidney failure. My poor Guido." She used the tissue to wipe the tears from her eyes.

"Mrs. Franconi...what did Mrs. McGuire have on you?"

"What?" She paled, highlighting telltale age lines that she'd hoped to hide with makeup. "I do not know what you mean."

"I think you do. I think Mrs. McGuire found out something about your past and was blackmailing you. You see, she told someone you'd be keeping her in chocolates. You two argued, maybe she wanted more money, whatever. And you couldn't take it any more, so you used that old German handgun you've been keeping, and you shot Mrs. McGuire."

Was she right? It sounded logical. Mrs. McGuire's past history. The gun was a stretch, but possible. There could be other explanations, of course. It all depended on how badly Mrs. Franconi wanted to keep her secret. If there even was one.

"It's over now. You need to tell me about it, Mrs. Franconi. We need to put it all to rest. Please."

Franconi pushed herself out of her seat and stood there a moment, head bowed, gripping the arm of the chair. Her eyes brimmed with tears when she raised her head and slowly looked around the room.

"It is not much, is it? My son does not come often. His wife is jealous of our relationship. They have all my furniture, though. My fine crystals, the silverware. And this is all I have for myself. This and my memories."

She walked the few steps to the window and stood staring out. "My memories are all of Europe and my fame. How they loved me! And then, in Montreal, there was no work. My name was not known. In those days, there was not much money for opera. We needed money, to pay the doctor. Guido one day met a man who promised great wealth. He took the job but never let me know what he did. And then, the man offered me a chance to sing again."

She paused to dab at her eyes with her handkerchief. "On stage at a dance hall. And when the customers did not understand my voice was trained for opera, I become one of his showgirls. Oh, yes, I was once again in a costume. But not much of it." She made a sound, part laugh, part moan.

"Was that the secret you were protecting?"

She nodded and walked over to her chair. "Mrs. McGuire was nosy, mean person. She comes into my room one day when I am out walking and finds my metal box. The lock does not work so well any more. Like a lot of things. Like my voice." She swallowed hard. "Inside the box I keep old newspaper clippings—I should have burned years ago. One is of Guido when the police arrest him and his boss. I have lost so much about Guido, I keep all the clippings. He was not a bad man. He only did what his boss tells him. And for that, he goes to jail. There was a picture of me, too, in a *costume."* She spat out the word this time.

"Mrs. McGuire laugh in my face when she sees it, says I never was a real singer, only a dance hall floozie. She say she tells everyone about it if I do not give money." Franconi turned to stare at Julie. "I have some cash which I give her, and then she want more. First it is for chocolates, and then she say she need money to pay the rent. I do not have any more, not without asking my son. And his wife want to know why. So you see, I have no choice. I have to kill her."

"What about the gun, Mrs. Franconi?" Julie asked softly.

"Oh, it is old. From the war, when we leave Europe. We need it for protection, and my Guido hide it when we come into this country. I keep it with my music. No one ever know I have it."

She ran her hand through her hair. "I sew a dress, pink to look like a nurse, and I take Mrs. McGuire's key one day when she naps and take it to the shop to make another one. Oh, she fuss about where it is, but she look foolish when they find it in her dresser drawer. I plan that, too."

And that's probably why nobody had thought to mention it, Julie thought. How clever. How sad. This was one case Julie wasn't elated about closing.

Franconi sat back down and tried to smile. "I make good plans, yes? No one see me. I could just walk in without a costume. Still, it's good to have something to keep my mind and hands busy. She have to die. You see, no one can know. No one around here. They already laugh behind my back. I know. And especially not my son's wife. She already is embarrassed by me…by my looks, my accent. I'm not good enough for her. But in the old days, she would not have been good enough for my son."

*   *   *

Julie left David Gant's office feeling relieved. Her mother

could well manage the monthly fee at the residence, and the waiting list wasn't very long. Just one more item to deal with. She headed for the lounge.

"Ah, Mr. Sorens, just the person I wanted to see."

He looked up startled, then polished off the drink in his hand. "Why, it's the doll. Good to see you. You on duty?" He gave her an exaggerated wink and started whistling.

"Something more important," Julie told him, trying to keep a stern face. "I've come to see about my mom moving in here. But there's just one thing."

"Does she have legs like yours?"

"That's the thing, Mr. Sorens. My mom isn't..." She stopped. Her mom wasn't what? Able to watch out for her virtue? Capable of having fun? What right did Julie have to run her life? It's bad enough she was pushing her into a seniors residence.

Sorens leaned on his cane. "Yes?"

"I'm bringing my mom here on Friday to have a look around. I'd like to introduce her to you."

He wiggled his shaggy eyebrows. "I'd like that, doll."

"Just one thing, Mr. Sorens...remember, she's my mom."

As owner of Prime Crime Books in Ottawa, Linda Wiken gets the best of the mystery world—she buys them and writes them, too. Her short stories have appeared in the seven Ladies' Killing Circle anthologies, and the American magazines Mysterious Intent *and* Over My Dead Body. *She has been shortlisted for an Arthur Ellis Award for Best Short Story from the Crime Writers of Canada. As a volunteer with the Ottawa Police Service for over fifteen years, she has developed a strong, sometimes scary interest in police procedures.*

Chocolate to Die For

Joy Hewitt Mann

I'd priced it, put it on a shelf
And slowly walked her by it.
I'd put it in a gorgeous box,
Knew well that she would try it.
I'd glued the lid on really tight,
Made sure that she would pry it.
That kind of chocolate bomb-bomb
Will really ruin her diet.

Payback

Jean Rae Baxter

Carter sat in the booth closest to the door, warming his hands on his coffee mug. He would rather have met Jacob some place dark and secret. But it was too cold.

At the White Spot Grill, people come and go. Carter figured he wouldn't be noticed. He was not the sort of person that attracted attention. He was a blue-eyed man with dirty-blond hair cut close. He wore glasses. He was neither tall nor short. His black leather coat was neither new nor old. He wore scuffed brown boots.

When he saw Jacob through the glass of the White Spot's door, Carter put his right hand under the table, laying it on his thigh. He probably should have kept his right hand hidden all along. It was the only thing about him that people would notice.

Jacob Vogel opened the door and closed it quickly behind him. He was shorter than Carter, with a broad, snub-nosed face, and just as ordinary to look at.

He was wearing a windbreaker, jeans and dirty white trainers. Not dressed for winter. From the brown stubble on his cheeks and chin, he looked like he hadn't shaved for a couple of days. His eyes fixed straight ahead, he approached the booth and slid onto the bench facing Carter. Jacob's eyes were burning red, as if he had been crying. Liquor could cause the same effect. Carter smelled stale whiskey on Jacob's breath.

Seeing him so close, without a glass barrier between them, Carter started to shake. Under the table, he made a fist with his right hand. Wincing at the pain, he felt a year of rage boil to the surface.

Jacob leaned forward. "I gotta get away." His voice was a hoarse whisper. "I need money."

Carter grunted. "Sorry. I can't help you there."

"You've always come through for me."

"Christ! I've been out of work for six months. I'm broke."

"You can get it for me."

"How am I supposed to do that?" Carter snorted. "Rob a bank, maybe?"

"My mom will give it to you. I've already phoned her."

"Your mom! Get real. She doesn't know me from a hole in the wall."

"I told her you're the one friend who's always stood by me." Jacob paused. "She understands. My Mom's been through plenty of bad stuff."

Carter sat there taking it all in. Here's a guy thirty years old who runs to his mommy when he gets in trouble.

"Go yourself," Carter snapped. "Why send me?"

"People might see me," Jacob whined. "Neighbours know who I am. Look, I'll give you her address. She lives on Mill Street East, about four blocks from here. Get the money. Then we'll meet."

Without waiting for an answer, Jacob pulled from his jacket pocket a ballpoint pen and a crumpled cash register receipt.

"What makes you think she'll have money in the house?" Carter asked. "I mean, serious money. Fifty bucks won't get you far."

"She doesn't trust banks," Jacob said as he scribbled an address on the back of the receipt.

"How much is she good for?"

"Couldn't say. Money's her big secret. She hides it different places. Russians looted her house during the Occupation."

"What occupation?"

"After World War II. In Germany."

"You never told me your folks were from Germany."

"Didn't I? My father was a Panzerjäger."

"A what?"

"He knocked out tanks." Jacob's mouth twisted in a bitter smile. "Heil Hitler!"

"Your father still alive?"

"No, no. He died years ago. Heart attack. My mother lives alone…alone with her saints and my father's army souvenirs." Jacob pushed the paper across the table to Carter. "I knew I could count on you." The paper lay on the table between them. Carter leaned forward, squinting at the address.

He flexed his fingers under the table. Two years after the accident, sharp twinges reminded him that his little finger and ring finger were gone. Whenever he felt the pain, he would flex his remaining fingers. It helped.

"If I do this…after I get the money, where will I find you?"

"Right here."

"The sign on the door says the White Spot closes at ten. It's nine already."

"Then bring it to the place I'm hiding."

"Where's that?"

"Five or six blocks from here. It's an abandoned garage in the alley that runs through the block between Odessa Street and Raglan Road."

"Is it safe?"

"Nobody ever goes there. Not in winter."

"Maybe I can't find it. I don't know this part of town."

Jacob frowned. "You can find it. Go two blocks east along Main—"

"I'll walk there with you now. I need to be sure." Carter tried to keep his voice steady, steeling himself. Using his left hand, he picked up the receipt bearing Mrs. Vogel's address. As he shoved the scrap of paper into his coat pocket, his fingers brushed the knife. At the counter, Carter paid for his coffee. He had just enough cash for that. Tomorrow he'd be eating steak.

On the sidewalk, Jacob walked bent over, hugging himself for warmth. Wind-driven grains of snow lashed both their faces. The temperature was minus twenty Celsius. It must be freezing in that garage, Carter thought.

It had been cold like this the night it happened. Jacob driving drunk. The car rolling. Carter pinned by his hand. Sandi, Carter's girl, crushed under the car. All Carter could see of her were her boots with the three-inch heels, and her crimson blood staining the white snow.

"We saved your hand," the doctor told him. "You're lucky you lost only two fingers."

"I lost my girlfriend," Carter said.

The doctor looked embarrassed to have been so clumsy. "I'm sorry," he said.

Every time Carter felt the phantom pain where his missing fingers had been, he felt the pain of his greater loss. Sometimes he deliberately made a hard fist so he could feel that pain. It helped him to remember Sandi—the clean smell of her shiny hair and the silky softness of her skin.

Jacob had escaped with a few bruises and one year in jail. Drunk driving. Motor manslaughter.

"I don't blame you," Carter had told Jacob on his first visit to the jail. "It could happen to anybody."

Jacob had wiped his eyes with the back of his hand. "I

wouldn't blame you if you hated me."

Carter had hidden the truth.

In the first weeks, he had felt nothing but pain and grief. But pain turned to anger and grief to rage. How do you kill a guy who's behind bars? You don't. You have to wait. So Carter had waited. Every time he had visited Jacob, he had thought how it would be. An eye for an eye, like the Bible said. That would put things right.

Then, this afternoon, one week out of jail, Jacob had done it again. Drunk. Stolen car. Young kid trudging home from school through the snow. Probably with one of those twenty-pound backpacks they all wear. You can't jump out of the way with something that heavy weighing you down.

Jacob didn't want to be sent back to prison. Well, he wasn't going to be. Carter had the knife in his pocket, a clasp knife with a guard to hold open the blade. He'd bought it just for Jacob that very afternoon.

In the garage, out of the wind, it felt warmer. The window —four panes of dirty glass—gave Carter just enough light to see what he was doing.

Since losing the two fingers, his right hand did not have the grip it once had. He knew that. But he was clumsy with his left. Pulling the knife from his pocket, he switched it to his right hand, ended up using both hands to strengthen his grip. Okay, he said to himself. This one's for Sandi.

The knife entered Jacob's back horizontally. It was a good, sharp knife with a narrow blade. It encountered no bone. There was not a great deal of blood. Carter pulled out the blade. After wiping it on Jacob's pant leg, he closed the knife and shoved it into his coat pocket.

Jacob had not screamed. A gurgling sound came from him as he collapsed. Then there was quiet. The only movement was the jerking of his limbs. It lasted only a minute. Jacob lay still, his cheek on the garage floor, one arm under his body and the other reaching forward as if he had been grasping for something when he died.

Carter pulled Jacob's wallet from his pants pocket. No bills. Just a few coins. Better take the wallet, though. It would give Carter some needed extra time if the cops required a few days to establish Jacob's ID. Even in winter, somebody might find the body.

* * *

Ten minutes later, Carter was walking east on Mill Street. Under a streetlight, he stopped and reached into his pocket for the scrap of paper with Mrs. Vogel's address. Holding the paper close to his glasses, he compared it with the number under the light by the front door. He took the five steps up to the front porch, stomped on the sisal mat to knock the snow off his boots and rang the bell.

The hall light came on. Through the frosted glass panel beside the door, he saw a shape shuffling toward him. He thrust the paper back into his pocket. Mrs. Vogel did not open the door at once.

"Yes?" she demanded through the glass.

"I'm Carter."

"Jacob's friend? Yes."

She opened the door. Carter stepped inside. Instantly his glasses misted. He could see nothing.

"Take off your coat."

"No. I'm not staying." But he removed his gloves.

With his left hand, he pulled off his glasses and shoved them into his coat pocket. He could see well enough without them, at least well enough to see the broad cheeks and snub nose of the woman who stood in front of him. She was in her sixties, a dumpy woman in a shapeless black dress, with thin, greying hair pulled into a tight knot at the back of her head. At the wide part in her hair, her scalp was yellow. Carter was not tall, just five-foot-nine. Yet the woman facing him came barely to his shoulder

"Come in, anyway," she said. "It's drafty in the front hall." Her English was clear, despite her German accent.

As Carter followed her down the narrow hallway, she asked over her shoulder if Jacob would soon be home.

"That's not something I can tell you, Mrs. Vogel. Jake's in trouble."

"So what's new?"

She led him into a small sitting room dominated by a white marble fireplace that must have been the homeowner's pride when the house was built…maybe a hundred years ago. A crack ran diagonally from the right side just under the mantel to the firebox opening.

Carter waited for the woman to take a seat before saying more. She settled into a deep armchair. He did not sit down.

"There's been an accident," he said. "Jake was driving."

"Is he all right?"

"Yeah, but he hit a kid, a boy about ten. The kid was walking along the side of the road."

"At night?"

"No. Four this afternoon."

"Where did this happen?"

"Right outside Kilbride, maybe a quarter mile from the village. Jake told me he wanted to stop. He would have stopped." Carter shrugged. "Look. He knew he'd fail the breathalyzer test. So he kept going." Carter shifted his gaze away from the woman's face.

"Is the boy hurt bad?"

"He's dead. It was on the six o'clock news. His father went looking for him when he wasn't home in time for supper. He found his son in the ditch, still alive. He died on the way to hospital. The report said he might have survived if he'd got medical attention right away."

Mrs. Vogel pressed her lips into a straight line. She inhaled sharply, then let out her breath. "Jacob must turn himself in."

"Look. Jake is hiding. He can't turn himself in. This isn't a first offence, you know." Carter felt the twinges again. This time he pulled his hand out of his pocket, flexed his index and middle fingers.

Mrs. Vogel saw his hand. She looked away.

"Jake told me he'd never go back inside," Carter said. "Not one more night in the cells. If the police arrest him, they'll charge him with motor manslaughter, plus leaving the scene of an accident. Jake has to get away. He needs cash."

She shook her head. "Tell him no. I can't turn him in. I'm his mother. But he gets no help from me."

"He's counting on you," Carter said. "He told me you'd give him money." Carter's left hand reached into his coat pocket, closed around the clasp knife. When she saw the knife, saw the blade snap open, Mrs. Vogel's face went pale.

"Oh!" she said. "Did Jacob tell you to threaten me?"

"He said to do whatever it took."

Both hands grasping the arms of her chair, she hauled herself to her feet. "I'll get my purse."

He followed her upstairs to a bedroom that was stuffed with dark furniture. Her black leather handbag lay on the heavy quilt that covered the bed. She opened her purse and pulled out a wallet. "Here," she said as she handed him a few bills. "That's all I have in the house."

"There's more. Jacob told me."

Carter raised the hand that held the knife, bringing it level with Mrs. Vogel's jugular. She stared at the narrow blade.

"Gott im Himmel." Her breath caught. *"Es gibt Blut."*

"Shut up with your Kraut gibberish," Carter said. "Hurry up and get me the money."

Carter looked around the room. Hanging on a nail beside a framed print of the Bleeding Heart of Mary was a silver crucifix. Worth something. But it might be hard to fence.

Mrs. Vogel was shaking so hard, Carter thought she might collapse right there in front of him. Her eyes were fixed on the knife. When he flicked a glance at the blade, he saw the stain of blood. Damn! Had she noticed? Would he have to kill her too?

"Get me the money," he repeated. "Jake's waiting."

"It's here. In a space under…"

She tottered unsteadily to the cast-metal heat register set into the baseboard. Peering at it, Carter saw that the screw that should have secured the grating to the frame was missing. With a grunt, Mrs. Vogel lowered herself to her knees. She lifted off the grating and laid it on the floor beside her. Bending her head, she reached her hand inside the open register. Her breathing was noisy, a wheezing sound. Her head turned toward him.

The last thing Carter saw was the flash from the Luger's muzzle.

When English teacher Jean Rae Baxter turned to full-time writing, she planned to concentrate on young adult fiction. Then she discovered that she also had a knack for crime. Her noir short story collection, A Twist of Malice *was published in 2005, and her mystery novel,* Looking for Cardenio, *in the spring of 2008. Between the two, her Y/A historical novel* The Way Lies North, *was released in 2007. She enjoys writing in both genres.*

The Silencer

Joy Hewitt Mann

There was a hit man who sang a bit
When he wasn't employed on a hit
So he muffled the bang
With the songs that he sang
And all for the poor victim's benefit.

A Three-Splash Day

Barbara Fradkin

Not a single promising-looking death among the bunch, I thought as I tossed the paper aside in disgust. I splashed another dollop of Bailey's Irish Cream into my morning coffee. I don't want you to get the wrong idea. I don't usually pour my first drink until well past noon, and even then it's a crisp, tingly Pinot Grigio with a very modest kick. But some mornings need more help than others, and this was shaping up to be a two-splash morning.

But then again, who was to stop me? Who was even to know? My dyspeptic, teetotalling father—he of the pursed lips and muttered prayers—had gone on to kinder, gentler pastures and my mother, even if I knew what beach she was on, would probably just wave her cigarette and crow, "Hell, let's call it a three-splash day!"

When you're sixty-seven years old and live alone—if you don't count the skunk living under my porch—you can do whatever the hell you please. If I wanted to spend my entire Saturday in my lace negligée guzzling Bailey's and poring over the obituaries, that's what I would damn well do. The lace negligée was to put me in the mood for husband hunting, and as long as I didn't pass any mirrors, it did the job just fine. I could remember the nights when Andreas would slide his fingers under the flimsy fabric, run them over my skin up my belly…

It made my body tingle just to think of Andreas. He was the best, for a while I thought the only, but when he left, there was Robert and Juan then… Who? Ah, Fred.

It was Fred who gave me hope now. He was living proof there could be life, a lot of life, in the old body yet. He was sixty-nine years old when I met him, bald as a bowling ball, with spindly legs, coke-bottle glasses, and hair growing out of his ears. But with the lights off and sexy leather briefs, what difference did it make? My skin was doing its own imitation of lizard by then, and my breasts were heading somewhere south of my navel. If he hadn't keeled over into the fish pond one day, I'd be with him still.

So it was really Fred's fault that I was reduced to sitting in my kitchen that morning, taking extra shots of Bailey's to get myself through the dismal selection of fresh meat on the marriage market. I hadn't thought I needed another husband. I'd been through five, none of whom had a decent life insurance policy between them. But Fred had been a retired lawyer with a portfolio bigger than the GNP of most Third World countries. How was I to know his four scheming children by his first wife had conspired to make sure I didn't see a penny? How was I to know my Panamanian divorce from Juan hadn't been entirely legal either? I'd managed to duck criminal prosecution—I guess my mature cleavage was still good enough for the myopic geezer behind the bench—but I walked away without a dime.

Even so, I hadn't really been in the mood for snagging a new man. To be brutally honest, the lace negligée is a fight to get on these days and an even greater fight to get off. And most mornings, I'd much rather sit in my lounge chair catching the morning sun, reading the paper, listening to fifties rock 'n roll and not having to talk to a damn soul. Not having to listen to anyone suck his teeth or fart up the stairs or whine about his Metamucil.

Peace. Freedom.

But who knew the Canada Pension would be so damn small! I thought with my modest settlements over the years, I'd be able to make ends meet once I turned sixty-five. I don't live big. My house is only fifteen hundred square feet, miniscule by my neighbours' standards. I like my Bailey's and my Pinot Grigio, but otherwise my food requirements are modest. Every ounce I eat settles around my waist and lasts for days anyway.

So I tried toughing it out for a year, but last year, on my sixty-sixth birthday, I got a letter from the Canada Revenue Agency. They want money from me! Four thousand dollars plus interest. I know I hadn't filed for a few years, but I mean—really!

So what's an old girl supposed to do? The marketplace isn't exactly littered with husband prospects in my age bracket. Time was, I used to be able to go down an age bracket—people always said I looked ten years younger anyway—but gravity gets you in the end. All those years under a sun lamp don't help either.

I signed up for yoga. All women, all complaining about their creaky knees. I signed up for a bowling league. I even— God help me—joined a church and tried the choir. All the remotely interesting men were either gay or had wives who never seemed to let them out of their sight. What is it about men over sixty that they'd sit at home asleep in front of the TV all day if their wives didn't organize them?

Those pesky wives. That's where I first got the idea of the obituaries. At church and bowling, I'd noticed that the best men all had wives. Maybe the wives kept them properly fed, clothed and groomed, so they showed well. Or maybe only the nicest men managed to hang onto their wives. Divorce takes a lot out of a guy, making him self-absorbed and resentful, but it can also be the mark of a man who doesn't know how to treat a woman. I know, because I tried out several in the church and bowling circuit, and I could sure see why their wives had tossed them out.

Bachelors are even worse. By middle age, they're a species totally apart, collecting rooms full of spare car parts and forgetting the dinner part of a dinner invitation.

No, the man you really want—the guy who knows how to treat a woman and who's still nicely fed and cared for—is the widower. He likes women, he's used to accommodating women, and he really misses a woman in his life. But you have to move fast. In every grieving widower's life, there are half a dozen women waiting to pounce. All offering a shoulder to cry on and a claw to sink deep into an unsuspecting back.

A widower is on the market for a maximum of a year, but usually you have to set the hook within the first month or two. The trick is to find out about them early enough to beat out the competition. And it's war out there. Available women over sixty-five outnumber men at least ten to one, and they've all drawn the same conclusions I have. A widower, as long as he's breathing, is a hot prospect.

That's how I came to the obituaries. I admit, it took me a while to stoop that low. At first I tried to ferret out the widowers in discreet ways. Peeks at their ring finger, which tells you nothing because these guys can wear the rings of their much beloved but very departed for years afterwards. Observation, questioning, word of mouth… I found you can never trust another woman to tell you about an available man. They horde those secrets better than CSIS. You can't even trust an unavailable woman to give you the tip. They save those valuable, vulnerable widowers for their own single friends.

After six months of trying to finagle encounters with new

widowers, only to discover the church secretary or the gardening club president had beaten me to it, I started reading the paper. At first it was almost by accident. "Peacefully after a courageous battle with cancer, Nancy, 62, beloved wife of Roger..." Poor Roger, I thought. You still have a few good years on you. How long before you're snapped up? I started counting. Almost every day there was some poor Roger or Jeff or Bill whose wives had been plucked from their lives in their prime retirement years, when they should have been planning cruises and holidays in Tuscany, not a wake.

"You can still do that," I'd shout at the paper, "with me." I'd love Tuscany, cruises, even that once-in-a-lifetime slog up a mountain in Tibet.

The first time I attended a visitation, I felt an utter fraud. Contrary to the claims of my ex-husbands' families, I do have a moral compass of sorts—just set a little further off true north. I looked into the grieving widower's damp eyes—it was Stephen that time, if I recall—and I extended my hand.

"My condolences," I murmured. "I used to work with Edith. She was such a lovely person."

And a look of puzzlement passed over his face. "Edith? Work?"

That was when I realized the value of research. From then on, I'd arrive at the visitations early and drift through the crowd, listening to the other mourners and joining in their reminiscences. To her work colleagues, I'd be a distant relative. To her friends, I'd be a former co-worker. I'd spend at least an hour collecting information so that by the time I approached the widower, I'd have a tamper-proof identity all worked out. It also gave me a chance to scope out the mark and decide whether he was worth the effort. By the end of my sixth visitation, I had developed a prioritized check list. At the top was a healthy, attractive appearance. Call me selfish, but I did not relish spending my last ten good years babysitting diapers and drool.

Second, evidence of a healthy bank account. No need to explain that, surely. Third, no signs of grasping, suspicious offspring. I don't mind offspring, but I wanted the "after all he's been through, just let him be happy" variety. This kind of offspring could even be useful in encouraging him to put away the dead flowers and the candle by his wife's picture, and to get out and live a little. Just deliver him into my hands, kids. I'd do the rest.

I found the perfect catch at my seventh funeral. Philip. Warm brown eyes, square shoulders, tapered waist, elegantly packaged in a charcoal Armani suit. And a smile that had zinged right through my groin as I introduced myself. "One of Lillian's choirmates." I'd even played my ace in the hole, a recent bereavement of my own (hey, technically it was true), so I knew how hard it was to keep up appearances. Gently I suggested coffee if ever he felt the need to let his hair down. A glimmer of gratitude lit his red-rimmed eyes, and I was just jotting my phone number on a scrap of paper (a business card being all wrong for this kind of thing) when a fifty-something fake blonde with enough nip and tuck to hold up the Lion's Gate Bridge appeared at his side. She smiled at me, hooked her arm through his and leaned into his ear.

"Philip, you must be exhausted. Come sit, and I'll bring you some tea."

Philip returned her smile dazedly. "Excuse me," he said to me as he allowed himself to be led away. "Ruth's been a godsend all through Lillian's illness. Lives across the street, spent half the day with us towards the end."

I'll just bet. What's that *Hamlet* quote about the funeral meats being barely cold? These hadn't even been served yet! This might be trickier than I thought. If the vultures knew a death was in the offing, even months away, they'd already be circling.

I admit, that's when the idea of murder first drifted across my mind. Harmlessly. I've done a lot of things in my life that have skirted the line, but I've never hurt anyone intentionally as an end in itself. So when the idea of dispatching Ruth came to me, I savoured it, laughed at it, and returned to my obituary columns. But the idea, stubbornly set, refused to die entirely. As I continued to browse the columns ("peacefully after a long battle…" "surrounded by loved ones…") I imagined the legions of Ruths hovering in the background. I began to toy with scenarios. Go to the funeral, extend a comforting hand with just a touch of excitement—let's not forget these guys are men first, who've gone without for months, maybe years—identify the Ruths at their side and plan a convincing accident.

Another funeral, another chance to offer comfort…

Who would ever connect me with the victim? I use my own name at the visitations, but I never sign the guestbook, and my name—Ann Czyryanitski—is a dyslexic's nightmare.

Thus, by the time I reached my sixty-seventh birthday, I was well on my way to convincing myself that a little murder, while not my first choice, was at least on the list. But then suddenly there was a dearth of new widowers in the acceptable age bracket. Day after day, I read the obituaries. Women were living into their nineties or dying in their forties, leaving husbands who were not only twenty years younger than me but saddled with a house full of teenagers. No thanks.

In a desperate moment, I did think about murdering a perfectly healthy wife, but the truth was, those women had paid their dues. They'd put in thirty, forty years with a guy, so they were entitled to their golden years and a hefty inheritance at the end of the line.

So here I was in the middle of my two-splash morning,

wondering who I could bump off to free up a man, when my thoughts strayed back to Philip. To his guileless brown eyes and his perfectly tailored suit. It had been three months, long enough for him to be over the shock of his wife's death and for his own yearnings to stir again. Had Ruth solidified her grip? Was she still bringing him casseroles, or had he begun to reciprocate? "You've been so kind. At least let me take you out for dinner."

Maybe she'd been the one to force the next step. "Philip, you have to start getting out of the house. Lillian would want you to go on."

As I poured my third cup, with just a smidgen of Bailey's this time, I decided some subtle snooping was in order. Purely for research purposes. Did the hovering Ruths of this world really get their man? How long did it take?

Along with my unpronounceable name, I have a car that would be the envy of private eyes everywhere. A six-year-old silver Honda Civic that looks like half the other cars on the road. It had been Fred's, my own yellow Miata having been repossessed without mercy in the Great Income Tax fiasco. As an added precaution, I streaked a little mud on the license plate. I picked a blustery Saturday evening in October for my first reconnaissance mission. If Philip was alone at home on Saturday night, Ruth had been a bust.

He lived in a gabled, three-storey stone house in the upscale Civic Hospital area. The good news was that it was quite close to my own much more humble Hampton Park home, thus justifying my presence in the neighbourhood should I attract attention. The bad news was that it was on a quiet side street which had almost no through traffic but a veritable army of alert dog walkers. A parked car might be noticed, particularly if it showed up several times.

I parked on the next block and walked towards his place.

Trees bent in the wind, and dead leaves scuttled along the sidewalk. I burrowed my face into the faux fur of my coat as I passed by a man walking his dog. He lifted his head for a cursory glance before scurrying on, probably eager to get home. I slowed as I neared Philip's house. A black Audi sat in the drive, and lights glowed in the windows on the first floor. Shadows moved back and forth behind the gauzy curtains. One shadow. Two shadows. Someone was with him! Was that person the owner of the Audi, or did it belong to Philip?

I couldn't make out any features from this distance, particularly through the curtains, but I had brought along a dainty pair of opera glasses. No private eye should be without them. I was just trying to focus the blurry mess when another dog walker rounded the corner and headed towards me. Damn! I strolled on as if looking for an address. The dog stopped to poop. The owner waited, unwrapped a bag, picked up then spent at least five minutes tying the bag in a thousand, impenetrable knots.

I reached the end of the block, hesitated, and then ducked out of sight behind a large spruce in the corner yard. My stilettos were sinking into the soggy ground, and the damp was freezing my toes by the time the dog and owner ambled by, not ten feet from me. The dog—one of those nasty-tempered little mopheads—gave a low growl and started around the tree, but thank god the owner yanked him back, muttering about skunks and vicious cats.

Hugging my coat around me, I scurried across the street. I had to make sure it was Ruth before my murderous musings went any further. By the miracle of Canada411.com, I had determined that an R. Strickman lived diagonally across the street at #16. Ruth would be making a definite step up if she snagged Philip. Her own house was a sagging, clapboard two-storey with a purple Neon parked in the single-car drive. The porch light was the only one on. I sneaked up the drive and around the back. No lights on there either. I checked my watch, which read eight thirty. Ruth didn't strike me as the eight thirty-to-bed type. At least, not in her own bed.

But I wasn't about to leave room for error. I returned to my car, gratefully turned the heater on full blast, drove around the block and tucked my pint-sized Honda behind a behemoth of a SUV just down the street. By slouching in the passenger seat, I was nearly invisible but had a perfect view of Philip's front walk. His mystery dinner guest would be illuminated for a full five seconds by the brass coach lamp in his front yard.

By eleven o'clock, my enthusiasm for sleuthing had worn very thin. My legs were stiff and cramped, and my bones ached with cold. Plus I was bored silly. After a pack of noisy teenagers trooped by around ten, not a soul had come down the street except two dog walkers, hustling their charges impatiently from bush to bush.

She's staying the night, I realized, kicking myself for being so stupid. What were the candles and the formal dinner for, if not a prelude to dessert in bed? I was just manoeuvering myself over the gear shift into the driver's seat when the porch light went on up the street, and a figure stepped out into the beam. I whipped out my opera glasses. Ruth, all right, turning on tippy toes to press her lips to his. They lingered until I thought they'd both asphyxiate, then she pranced down the stone steps, purse twirling and fingers waggling over her shoulder. For a moment I pictured her tripping and pitching head first onto the flagstone walk. No such luck. Blowing one final kiss, she disappeared into the shadows of the street.

I looked back at Philip, who hovered in the doorway as if he couldn't stand to have her out of his sight. He was barefoot, tousled and delicious. She's primed the pump nicely, I thought. Reawakened his primal needs and his hunger for life. I felt my own body hum at the thought.

Ruth had to go.

It would have to look like an accident, of course. A good, old-fashioned hit and run seemed easiest, especially on a dark, rainy night on that poorly lit backstreet. But I'd watched enough *CSI* to know about paint chips and tire marks and databases of auto repair shops. I'd have to steal a car to do the job, and that just sounded too complicated. I'd had a sheltered childhood, what with the teetotalling bible-thumper for a father, and I'd missed the part about hotwiring a car. Besides, nowadays cars beeped and flashed loudly enough to be heard across the Atlantic.

I thought about a house fire—an electrical short seemed like the best idea, given that ancient house of hers—but death was far from a sure thing. Besides, I'm not a monster. She had to die, but I didn't want her to suffer. I thought of shoving her off something high, like a rooftop or a cliff. That would be quick and merciful, but I couldn't think how to lure her up there.

Meanwhile I started to watch her, tailed her to the grocery store, to yoga, to the spa and the nail salon. The woman was the definition of self-absorbed, but there was something mischievous, almost endearing, about her shameless vanity.

I soon realized why people hired a professional for these jobs. I didn't think I was up to staring at her eyeball to eyeball while I bumped her off. It would have to be something arm's length. I could break into her kitchen, slip some poison into her orange juice, and wait. In my cabinet, I still had a supply of Fred's heart medicine that should do the trick.

I picked a cold, sleety evening when I knew she was over at Philip's. Not even the dog walkers were out. Soggy, wet leaves cushioned my steps as I sneaked into her backyard and through the kitchen door, which I'd discovered she never locked when she was across the street. A dog barked in the neighbouring yard, but otherwise nothing stirred. A dim light was on in her hallway, enough to light my way.

I stood in the kitchen, messy like my own with dishes piled in the sink, coffee cups and wine glasses all over the table and a large, half empty bottle of Bailey's on the counter. I hesitated. Should I put the drugs in there? It seemed a waste of excellent booze, and perhaps she was only an occasional one-splash person.

CSI had taught me well. I was wearing gloves, a dark plastic raincoat and socks over my sneakers. I peered at the meagre contents of the cupboards and fridge. A loaf of bread, some milk and cheese, and some cans that had collected dust. No juice. The woman wasn't much for cooking, and her appliances looked like garage sale rejects. The toaster in particular caught my eye. One metal side panel was falling off, and the cord was frayed at the base. I'd had one of similar vintage once, and it had blown me across the room when my hands were wet.

Perhaps a little water on the counter underneath, barely noticeable when she staggered down to make breakfast…

I was back outside in less than fifteen minutes. The plan wasn't foolproof, but at least it would look like an accident without the complication of drugs showing up in her tox screen. If it didn't work, the drugs were a good fallback for the next try.

I had a bad moment in the middle of the night when I pictured Philip in her kitchen making her breakfast in bed— she was just the type to love that—and blowing himself to kingdom come. I almost aborted the whole mission, but when I rushed over there the next morning, her house looked the same as ever. The news reported no accidents. Days passed, until I was sure the water had dried up. Was it worth another try? How often did she go near that toaster anyway? Or even near her kitchen, for that matter.

A week later, I was back in her kitchen, giving electrocution one last chance. I doubted the two lovers ever spent the night at her place. Why would they, with that palace across the road, probably outfitted with the latest in dream kitchens? This time I was in and out in less than five minutes, leaving a fair-sized puddle in my wake. The dog didn't even bark.

The next day I stifled my impatience till noon before driving over. I spotted the cop cars from a block away. Four of them, plus a firetruck and an ambulance.

And most telling, a coroner's van.

I admit, I was a bit surprised by my reaction. I couldn't drive away, couldn't even move a muscle. Afterwards, I couldn't eat for a day. It took some getting used to that I had killed that woman with the prance in her step, the twirling purse and the Bailey's on her counter.

I drove by the house the next day, thinking maybe I'd been wrong about her death. The crowds and excitement were all gone, but yellow police tape flapped in the cold, and a lone police cruiser sat in the street outside Philip's house.

It was almost a week before her death notice appeared in the paper. "Suddenly at home..." Just the barest minimum, no fanfare or celebration of life. I had to force myself out of my house to attend the visitation. I took extra care with my dress, hoping to put myself in the mood. A demure, dusty rose suit over a plum camisole with just a peek of cleavage. At my age, a peek is all you want. A modest gold chain, pearl earrings and a light hint of make-up. I put a dab of sparkle on each eyelid. Men never notice it, but it gives just a glint of mischief.

The funeral parlour was fuller than I expected. Who'd have thought that such a vain, shallow woman could collect so many friends? They breezed around exclaiming at the photo display and peering into the coffin. I headed the other way, scanning the room for Philip. He wasn't there. I had a bad moment before I convinced myself it was early yet. I kept one eye glued to the door while I worked the room, catching the bits of gossip her friends seemed eager to share.

"Stark naked at three in the morning…" "Bailey's all over the floor." "And him right upstairs. So like Ruth, to go out with a bang!"

I closed my ears and turned away. That's when I saw him, sitting alone on a sofa at the far end of the room. Same Armani suit, same forlorn look.

I hefted my cleavage, sucked in my stomach and headed towards him, words of condolence already forming on my lips. "So sorry for your loss. I knew her from yoga class, we shared so many laughs…"

I was ten feet away when a police officer appeared in my path. Five foot ten, chestnut hair swept into a ponytail, not a hint of sparkly make-up on her liquid brown eyes nor an inch of cleavage beneath her tailored uniform. In an age bracket at least three decades down from mine. She sat at his side on the couch, laid a hand on his arm, and held out a cup of tea.

"Here, Philip, drink this. It'll help you feel better."

His eyes were dazed as he took the cup from her, but the smile he offered was grateful. Even warm.

Barbara Fradkin is the author of the gritty, psychological mystery series featuring quixotic Ottawa Police Inspector Michael Green, which has won back-to-back Arthur Ellis awards for Best Novel. Her short stories appear in numerous magazines and anthologies, including all the Ladies Killing Circle books. As a child psychologist with a fascination with how we turn bad, most of her work is dark and haunting. In "A Three-Splash Day", she takes a refreshing break.

When the Whistle Blows

Coleen Steele

I knew it as soon as I saw the kid. Those wide green eyes, the pug-like nose, and the shock of poker-straight fair hair that would eventually dim to a mousy brown. When he gave his name, it clinched it. He was Hal Watterson's kid.

And I was a dead man.

Our school car had been unhooked the night before, and left on the siding by a little cluster of shacks about twenty miles north of Cartier, a tiny dot on an Ontario map and a forty-minute rail ride beyond Sudbury. About twenty years earlier, before the Depression hit, the provincial government got the notion to use railway cars to bring education to the northernmost outposts. The scheme survived the hard times and actually flourished, so much so that the number of routes increased, and there was a job for me when I completed my certificate after the War. For the past two years, I've been following the CP line between Cartier and White River, and back again, stopping for four or five days in tiny settlements along the way, opening my school car to the children of the north.

It suits me fine, this posting so far removed from Toronto. I never worried about bumping into old acquaintances and believed I'd left my old life behind. That's why it came as such a shock.

I hadn't even noticed the boy at first. I had ushered the children into their first day of the 1949 school term and directed each of them to one of the dozen desks the car contained. When I'd glanced over them to take stock, I'd seen a typical northern class: kids of British, Mediterranean, Eastern European and Native origin, ranging in age from six to sixteen. It wasn't until I had them stand one at a time and give their names that I saw the demon in their midst. An eleven-year-old boy with a timid demeanour whose apparent apprehension of his new schoolmaster was nothing compared to the terror he struck in me. His name was Charlie. Charlie Watterson.

So dumbfounded was I by seeing him there in front of me, that I scarcely heard the remaining children. My attention and my gaze continuously flicked to the Watterson boy, as if my mind could not comprehend what my eyes were seeing and must keep checking for an error. But there he was, looking innocent and innocuous sitting there with his hands folded neatly on his desk.

I felt ill at the sight of him.

"Yes, well," I stumbled after the remaining students had provided their names, "um, let's get started."

I don't know how I got through the day. Somehow I forged ahead, trying not to dwell on what the Watterson kid's presence meant to my life. I remember my heart convulsing and pounding frighteningly against my ribs every time the boy stirred. I hadn't tasted fear like that since my battalion advanced through the Italian mountains with Jerry snipers taking pot shots at us.

"Are you not feeling well, Wilf?" my wife, Katie, asked when the last of the students had departed for the day. "You haven't seemed yourself." Katie was in and out of the classroom during the school day, helping whenever her tasks as wife and mother didn't keep her busy in our family quarters in the other half of the school car.

"No. No, I'm not feeling very well." I wasn't lying either, but I couldn't meet her concerned gaze. I began pushing the desks to the side of the cabin to make room for the people we were expecting. Our day didn't end when the school day did.

"Why don't you lie down? I can look after the visitors this evening. And the stew's already simmering on the stove."

"What about Janie?"

Katie laughed. "You know you don't have to worry about her. She's never short of people to fuss over her."

She was right. It was remarkable how a two-year-old coquette could tease the tender side out of even the roughest of men. And some of the people drawn to the school car were pretty rough. By trade they were miners, or trappers, or loggers, or section men that worked the railroads—tough physical labour for tough physical men. I've never had a bit of trouble with any of them; they doff their caps when they enter the car and give us their Sunday school best.

During the day, they send their children to me, and in the evenings they come with their wives, eager for a taste of the outside world. For my part I generally enjoy their company and find this aspect of my job gratifying. And it was considered part of my job, to bring "King and Country" to these northern denizens.

But that evening I left it to Katie to see to their cultural and social needs. Retreating to our bedroom in the private section of the car, I declined Katie's suggestion that I lie down, knowing there was no way I was going to get any rest, not with my nerves on edge. Instead, I paced.

I just couldn't believe that Hal Watterson was here.

And in this tiny community, it was only a matter of time

before he found me. My name wouldn't mean anything to him; I'd taken care of that, adopting a new one when I signed up in thirty-nine. Hopefully that would buy me some time. But sooner or later, our paths would cross.

What was I going to do? He knew me. He knew the man I was before the War. The life I'd led. There was no way he'd stay quiet about it. It was personal with him.

I know I should have cleared matters up when I was discharged from the army. I'd meant to. I really had. But when I got back, things kept happening.

Immediately following the war, the government had offered all of us decoms free college and university programs. I couldn't pass that up; I'd always wanted to be a teacher, but in the thirties there was just no way I could afford the schooling. So I decided to grab the chance and get my teaching certificate, then go back and face the music. That only made sense. The opportunity wouldn't last forever. But then, well, once I got my certificate, a teaching position came up, and being a vet, I went straight to the top of the list. How could I say no?

Even then, I still intended on going back and owning up, as soon as I got my feet on the ground. Really.

But then I met Katie.

* * *

"There was quite a crowd tonight," my wife reported after having put an already sleeping Janie to bed.

"Oh," I said. "Any new people?" This was our second year on this route, and most of the residents were familiar to us.

"Yes. Mr. DaSilva brought his young bride over from Italy. Such a sweet girl, but doesn't speak a word of English. And a

Mrs. Greenfield. She's the mother of that new first former, Lizzie. She has arthritis in her hands and was so grateful when I offered to help her write a letter to her sister in Kingston."

"No men?" I asked. A low rumble registered in my mind, and for a moment I thought it came from my stomach, it was clenching so tightly.

"Well, there was Mr. McCurdy, Mr. DaSilva, Mr. Tulliver, and…"

Four short blasts of a train whistle cut through the night air as the accompanying rumble grew louder.

"…oh yes, there was a new gentleman tonight: a Mr. Watterson." Katie brushed out her soft chestnut curls as she sat before her vanity mirror. "He seemed very nice. No wife. He's raising a boy on his own. The poor boy's mother and sisters died in a car accident. Mr. Watterson's a section man," she added, referring to his job for the railway, her voiced raised to be heard over the approaching train.

I don't know if it was a gasp or a gurgle that escaped me as I struggled for breath, but I remember being saved any explanation by the roar that drowned out everything else.

"I hope it doesn't wake Janie," Katie said as the sound subsided and the car's shaking lessened to a tremble.

"No. No, I'm sure it won't." Watterson. Oh, God, it really was him.

"Well, if the Monday Night Special won't do it, nothing will," Katie laughed.

I'd forgotten about that train. It roared past every Monday night like clockwork, its time dependent on our location. Here, just above Cartier, it passed between nine-nineteen and nine-twenty-three. At our next school stop, it would go by closer to nine-forty-five. And unlike some of the other trains that eased up past our sided car, the Monday Night Special flew by at full-throttle, bouncing us around in its wake.

Watterson. What was I going to do about him?

"Hmmm. Pardon?" I said. Katie had resumed her review of the evening, but I hadn't heard any of it.

"Oh, I'm sorry," she said, her voice full of concern. "You're still not feeling well, are you? You go to sleep. Hopefully you'll feel better in the morning."

But in the morning, she could see that I was still not myself.

"I just need a few minutes to let my breakfast settle. Perhaps you could go let the children in, and I'll join you shortly." If Hal had walked his boy to school, I wanted him gone before I made an appearance.

"Certainly, darling. Are you sure you don't want to go back to bed? I could hand out the assignments."

It was tempting. I knew Katie could handle being a teacher for the day. She'd been halfway to getting her own teaching certificate when I met her. She only gave it up to marry me, and as it was, with the nature of my job, her studies didn't go to waste. She had already proved a great helpmate and substitute teacher. But I couldn't allow her to take on all my duties. Besides, the idea of staying holed up in our quarters all day, dwelling on my problem, was not very appealing.

So I assured Katie I'd be fine and watched from behind one of her gingham curtains as the children arrived and the few adults that accompanied them went on their way. Hal Watterson was not among them. Young Charlie had walked to school by himself.

The relief I felt at being given a reprieve from bumping into Hal should have allowed me to concentrate on my class and the day's lessons, but it didn't. It was another day like the last, where I struggled to concentrate on the children's poetry recitations and their multiplication tables. I have no idea how many of the latter were bungled without correction, and I only just saved Toronto from moving east of Montreal on the map we were labelling.

And through it all sat Charlie Watterson. His eyes, so big and round and innocent, held no knowledge of the pending doom he represented. They fixed on me unwaveringly, putting me off my stride. They were so reminiscent of Hal's and…of Marge's. I tried to ignore the boy, but still for all their innocence, those green depths taunted me, accused me.

When at last I was able to ring the bell to release the children for the day, I did it hastily then fled to my own compartment. Katie, bless her, jumped in and saw the students off, then opened the door to adult visitors.

"Perhaps we should send for a doctor or ask the next freight to carry us down to Sudbury," Katie suggested later that evening when she was finally free to join me.

I must admit I toyed with the idea of fleeing south to Sudbury, or anywhere for that matter. But too many questions would be asked. A good doctor would know there was nothing physically wrong with me. And I didn't like the idea of being tarred with the brush of emotional or mental strain; a teacher couldn't afford that indictment.

"No," I told my wife. "I'm just fighting off a cold. A little extra rest this week, and I'll be right as rain."

Katie gave in and agreed to leave the doctor for the time being. She graciously insisted on shouldering my evening duties for the remainder of the week as well as her own, all while keeping a watchful eye on me. I struggled through the lessons with the children, trying to focus on all of them except Charlie; I had come to loathe the boy.

On Friday I gladly said goodbye to Charlie Watterson and his father's spectre. And Katie was thrilled to see me bounce back to my usual self by the time we hoisted the Union Jack in the next settlement, thirty miles to the north, announcing the school was open for business. She watched with relief as I welcomed my new class and cheerfully greeted the men and women who straggled in once the children's lessons were over for the day. I'm glad to say I saw nothing threatening in their weatherworn faces.

Those days were a relief to me, but I knew it was only a respite, not a reprieve. That really began to sink in as I lowered the flag and battened down our belongings for the rumbling journey to our next stopping point. Oh, we were still headed north, further from Hal Watterson, but in a few weeks time we would hit the end of the line and work our way back south again to that little settlement just north of Cartier.

*   *   *

I spent hours turning the problem over in my mind, struggling to find a solution. And the more I thought about it, the less fearful and the more angry I became. Who was Hal to threaten me? What had I done that so many other men hadn't done, or wanted to do, during those years of hardship? They had been desperate times, and I'm sure many had done things they weren't proud of, or would rather forget. Why should I be held accountable now?

And I would be, if Hal had his way; I had no doubt about that. Hal would be relentless in pursuing the harshest punishment possible. My family life and my job would vanish in an instant.

With my mind running in that direction, it's not surprising that it came to the conclusion that it did: get rid of Hal.

I didn't accept that solution easily, of course. I did suffer some twinges of conscience. I mean, it wasn't exactly the same as killing enemy soldiers in the War. But by the time we reached the settlement north of Hal's, I was resolute in my decision; I merely needed to work out the means. A couple of ideas did present themselves, but there was always one fault I didn't know how to work around, and that was keeping my wife and daughter out of the picture. But the day before we were to strike out for Hal's settlement, Katie came to me with a request that offered its own solution.

"I was wondering if you could do without me for a few days?"

"What? Why?"

"Well, that young Mrs. Henderson is expecting to give birth any day, and I know she'd feel much better if I was near when it happened. She hasn't really made any friends here yet, and we've kind of taken to each other, us both being from west-end Toronto."

"I see. But what about Janie?"

"Oh, she can stay with me. It's a small place the Hendersons have, but the two of us can squeeze into it for a few days. Janie'll think it an adventure. And she's really looking forward to seeing a brand new baby. You wouldn't mind too much, would you, dear?"

"I guess not," I said, trying to force some reluctance into my voice. But inside I was thinking, *yes, yes!* "All right. You stay and see to Mrs. Henderson. But then you take the next train down," I insisted, knowing it would all be over by then.

My wife kissed me for being so sweet.

*   *   *

I sent the sealed note home with little Charlie Watterson that

Monday afternoon, the first day of school. I addressed it to "Mr. Watterson, Private and Confidential" and requested he meet with me that evening to discuss his son. I wrote that it was of the utmost importance and that he was best not to mention it to anyone due to the sensitive nature of what I had to say. Now, how could a father fail to respond to that?

I set the meeting for nine fifteen, when any visitors to the school car should have gone and asked that he come to the door at the south end of the car, the door to our private quarters. He was to wait there to be admitted, and I warned I might be a little late if stragglers held me up in the classroom.

That evening, the schoolroom was crowded. A group of women, disappointed Katie wasn't there, flicked through the Simpson's and Eaton's catalogues, marvelling at the electric washers and dryers, and the latest in fall fashions, all of which seemed worlds away from life in northern Ontario. One young woman, not yet a mother but eager for the role, gathered the children who'd accompanied their parents, and regaled them with tales from *The House at Pooh Corner*. The male contingent congregated separately, with two or three content to peruse old newspapers, another pair engaged in a game of checkers, and a larger group struck up a poker game.

Like a good host, I did my part and spared a moment and a word with everyone. A couple of the ladies helped me pass around coffee and the Toll House cookies Katie had baked two days before. Around eight o'clock, when each of the groups was immersed in their chosen activity, I slipped out.

I was gone about fifteen minutes in total. When I returned, I slid into the chair next to Mr. McCurdy.

"Katie tells me you're eager for another crokinole tournament," I said, not giving anyone a chance to comment upon my absence and hoping to deflect any thoughts that may have wandered in that direction.

McCurdy grinned. "Who, me? What's the prize going to be this time? A book? A box of chocolate bars? Cigarettes? I won't let Tulliver cheat me out of it this time, whatever it is."

"Cheat? I beat ya fair and square." The maligned Tulliver, and one of McCurdy's fellow card players, spoke up. And the argument was on, with good-natured barbs and insults flung back and forth, to the amusement of the others around the card table.

I sat back and relaxed.

By eight thirty, most of the visitors had packed up and left, leaving only a trio of stragglers behind. This wouldn't have worried me unduly, except that the three were embroiled in a debate over who was likely to claim the Stanley Cup that season: Ted "Teeder" Kennedy's Maple Leafs or "Tough Ted" Lindsay's Red Wings. Such a discussion, especially with the men involved, could last days, if not all hockey season.

And the classroom clock continued to tick along, edging closer to nine o'clock.

"…with Lumley between the pipes, the Wings are a cinch."

"Are you joking? He's no match for the Turk."

"Oh, yeah? Remember that brawl two years ago? Lumley was more than a match for Broda then."

I could feel my heart begin to beat louder in my chest. I needed to get these people out of here.

"Yeah, well, who won the Vezina last year? Broda, that's who."

"Only because they felt sorry for him, having to carry the rest of those bums."

The clock struck nine. Panic began to set in. I fought to control it. I couldn't show any nervousness or unusual behaviour that might be remarked upon later.

"Bums? Well, those 'bums' won the cup last year, didn't they?"

I had to appear calm. Like I hadn't a care in the world.

"Pure luck. Where did they finish for the year, tell me that?"

I yawned.

Thank God for small miracles: McCurdy saw it and took the hint. "Aw, we're keeping Mr. Clark from his bed. We'd best be off, Mr. Bertolli. Besides, Tulliver here's so thick, he'll never get it through his head that the Production Line can skate rings 'round the Kid Line."

"Ah, you're full of beans," Tulliver replied, but all three men got to their feet and shrugged into their coats.

I said goodnight and saw them off, remembering to warn them to "watch for bears," as was my usual leave-taking. I watched as they passed out of the light cast by the open schoolroom door and into the night, their voices carrying back to me their on-going debate.

I doused the lights in the classroom, waited about two minutes, grabbed my coat, then cautiously reopened the door and slipped out. I cut across the main track and made my way through the sumach bushes that flanked it on the opposite side, stealing southward to where I would have an unobstructed view of the school car's private entrance. The tangled branches of the sumachs were leafless now, allowing me to see through them but still offering adequate cover in the darkness of a northern November night.

I crouched down to wait.

By my calculations, it would be about eight minutes after nine. Hal was always pretty careful with his times, so I expected he'd be by presently. It'd been twelve years since I'd seen him, of course, so he could have changed. But surely not Hal. He'd always been one of those dogged, down-to-earth types who never change and who see everything in black and white. That's why I knew he'd never forgive me, nor understand my point of view. He wouldn't know what it had been like for me. He hadn't been married, not back then. Not during the Depression. Like I was.

I thought I caught the faint sound of a train whistle in the distance, and I began to worry that perhaps Hal had become tardy with age after all; or maybe the letter had not been enough to entice him. Under my heavy duffle coat, I began to sweat, though the night air was frosty enough for my breath to catch in cloudy puffs. Mentally I felt the minutes tick by.

Then the crunch of gravel allayed my fears.

I peered through the blackness and was soon able to pick out the figure I'd been waiting for. I smiled smugly to myself. Hal had come.

My relief turned to disbelief, though, as I made out a smaller form trudging along beside him. The fool had brought the boy with him!

Watching the pair follow the siding, their heads bent as they picked their way along the tracks in the dark, I considered calling the whole thing off; stepping out from my refuge and flagging them down. But it was too late for that. Hal would recognize me, and my life would be over.

Charlie's young face pushed into my thoughts. The way his eyes had fixed on me in class, their innocence mocking me, haunting me.

I hardened my resolve and stayed where I was.

Hal looked huskier to me; bigger than when last I'd seen him. Working the rails could do that to a man, adding brawn where there had been none. But the swagger was as I remembered.

When he was only about twenty paces from the school car, my ears picked up the low rumble of the approaching freight car; the Monday Night Special.

Hal swung himself up on the little platform that serviced the rear entrance of the school car and knocked on the door. I watched as he waited, his ear cocked for the sound of movement from within. There was none. He knocked again. Charlie climbed up beside him and plunked himself down, throwing his legs between the railings.

The train's rumble was growing closer, but neither Hal nor the boy paid it any heed. They heard that sound every day, and both probably knew that a train passed through at this time every Monday night.

I edged as close to the pair as I could without surrendering the cover of the sumachs. I almost regretted having broken the back light earlier in the evening; I would have liked to have got a better look at Hal to see if he still had some of his sister in him after all these years. And I found myself wondering what she looked like now, my wife—I mean, my other wife. And our three children; I didn't even know if the youngest was a boy or a girl.

I jumped as Hal swung down from the platform. I wondered if he'd heard me, or sensed I was there. But then he leaned against the platform railing and lit a cigarette, and I relaxed. He wasn't going anywhere.

I knew Hal would never forgive me for deserting his sister. But men did that then, during the Depression. Just walked out and didn't look back. Well, at least some did. You've got to understand, I had no money, no job, and no hope. And every night when I came home from looking for work, there was Marge. She never reproached, never showed any disappointment. But she was there, with her ever-growing belly, reminding me of my failure. I couldn't take it. One night I just didn't go home. And I admit, it was a relief. From then on, I only had to worry about scraping together enough to feed myself. It was still tough, but the pressure was gone, and I made do. Then the War came and offered jobs to so many of us.

The freight train rounded the bend south of the settlement, and its headlight cut through the night like a beacon, just as it whistled its usual approach warning. I'd always thought the sound of a train whistle at night sounded melancholy, but not tonight.

Hal nonchalantly glanced in the direction of the train, probably reminding himself to wave to the engineer when the locomotive passed.

But it wasn't going to pass.

I'd pulled the switch. The Monday Night Special was going to take the siding at full speed.

The gleaming eye of the freight train hit the back of the school car, illuminating Hal's face. It still looked so much like Marge's! I stepped from my cover to distract him from the thousands of pounds of locomotive bearing down on him. I also wanted him to see me, to know it was me.

The crack of the branches as I ploughed through the bushes brought Hal's head around sharply. He peered at me then opened his mouth to call out but faltered. Recognition slowly dawned. Just as I'd thought: all these years later he still knew me.

"How's Marge?" I threw it out there as a taunt. So there would be no doubt.

"Marge?" His glare was full of hate. "She's dead. Been gone ten years. Her and the girls."

Now I was the one caught off guard. Marge dead? Since before the War; before I met Katie.

"The children too?" This didn't seem possible.

Hal stared at me. Slowly he said, "The girls."

The train's whistle shrieked in short urgent blasts.

Both Hal and I spun toward the approaching train. Then our gazes jumped back together. Terror and bewilderment blazed in Hal's twisted expression.

My mind scrambled to make some sense out of what I'd just learned. Marge and the girls gone. Then my marriage to Katie was valid. Then there was no need to…but there was. My past still held a dark blot, one the school board would not appreciate of a man in my position. And Katie. Sweet Katie. What would she think of me?

I heard the screech of metal upon metal as the brakes were thrown. But I knew with grim satisfaction the engineer's efforts would be in vain.

Hal took a step towards me, his arms flailing.

For the sake of the engineer's eyes, I waved at Hal as if I were waving him out of danger. And as Hal took another step in my direction, I wondered if I had miscalculated, counting too heavily on his confused state holding him hostage to his fate.

"Dad!"

Hal froze. My brother-in-law reminded me then of a deer I'd once killed; its eyes glassy in the headlights as it stood there waiting for my car to hit it.

"Dad!"

Ah, Charlie! Hal might have made it if it weren't for him. For Hal wasn't a deer, and his immobilized state was only temporary. But instead of saving himself, the fool retraced his steps, backing towards where the boy sat with his legs caught between the platform's railing.

The whistle shrieked louder, the noise deafening.

Hal's gaze was locked with mine. His horror was still evident, but there was also something else now. Perhaps acquiescence, as he accepted the fate rushing towards him. Or…triumph?

Something nagged at me. What had Hal said?

I heard the screeching of the brakes. Saw the sparks they threw up. I felt the fiery breath of the engine.

And in an instant, I knew why Hal had been late. What had delayed him. This section man who would know about switches and train schedules.

The girls.

And then I saw the iron muzzle of the Monday Night Special.

It wasn't on the siding. It was on the main track.

As was I.

Not "the children". The girls. My head jerked towards Charlie. The boy with the haunting eyes so much like…oh, god…Marge's!

I heard my own scream.

Coleen Steele writes crime and suspense fiction from her home in Bowmanville, Ontario. Her stories have twice been short-listed for Arthur Ellis Awards, and she has won the Bloody Words Conference's Bony Pete Award as well as Imagination Theater's inaugural Phil Harper Award for Best Radio Script. This is her second venture into a Ladies Killing Circle anthology.